SMILE NOW, DIE LATER

Vivien Armstrong titles available from Severn House Large Print

Beyond the Pale
Fly in Amber
Fool's Gold
Rewind

SMILE NOW, DIE LATER

Vivien Armstrong

Severn House Large Print
London & New York

This first large print edition published in Great Britain 2003 by
SEVERN HOUSE LARGE PRINT BOOKS LTD of
9-15, High Street, Sutton, Surrey, SM1 1DF.
First world regular print edition published 2002 by
Severn House Publishers, London and New York.
This first large print edition published in the USA 2003 by
SEVERN HOUSE PUBLISHERS INC., of
595 Madison Avenue, New York, NY 10022

British Library Cataloguing in Publication Data

Armstrong, Vivien
    Smile now, die later. - Large print ed.
    1. Antique dealers - England - London - Fiction
    2. Detective and mystery stories
    3. Large type books
    I. Title
    823.9'14 [F]

ISBN 0-7278-7301-6

Printed and bound in Great Britain by
MPG Books Ltd, Bodmin, Cornwall.

For Doctor Heather Binney,
my technical advisor.

One

At the time I thought discovering Max's body hanging from the high rafter in his studio the most terrifying moment of my life. It wasn't. Later it became all too clear that finding Max was merely the beginning of my troubles.

My name is Zoe Templeman and I work for antique dealers like Max Loudon-Fryer between stints with museums, churches and even, on occasion, specialists – mostly foreign collectors who need valuable textiles conserved. A weird job to choose, I admit: working alone in a dingy workshop, repairing shreds of fabric so no one can spot the joins. At thirty-two years old I should be having fun, mixing with people of my own age, for Pete's sake.

I do have a boyfriend – hardly a boy and rather more than a friend: an illustrious cosmetic surgeon, no less; a man of substance with a list of patients straight off the Social Register and an income to match. So what? Doctor Haydon Masure is, rock bottom, just another stitcher like myself, wouldn't you say?

Two

Zoe stood in the dawn half-light of the unlit studio, staring up at the body twisting rhythmically in the draught from the open door. The rain drumming on the skylight seemed to reverberate through her head as if to accompany the dancing corpse at the end of the rope.

Cauterized by shock, her voice box inexplicably failed; only her legs remained unparalysed, backing her out of the door of their own volition, only buckling as she stood trembling under the October downpour in Max's shrubbery.

Summoning every ounce of strength she bolted round to the front door and beat on the glass panelling, screaming. 'Saba! Saba! For God's sake let me in.'

A light went on upstairs and a figure in a long gown wielding a heavy-duty torch finally slid into view, silhouetted on the staircase, immobile, her eyes wide with fear.

Zoe attacked the doorbell, shrieking at the black-haired houri in a red djellaba, Max's latest acquisition, the new housekeeper. Bolts were noisily drawn back and Zoe fell inside, gripping Saba in a fierce embrace, sobbing on to her shoulder as the door silently closed behind her.

They stumbled inside and Zoe collapsed on to the lower step and, gasping for breath, leaned against the newel post, burying her head in her hands. With an effort she pulled herself together and attempted to rise, but Saba shoved her back and crouched down, her hands pressed against Zoe's shaking knees.

'I must get the police! Now, Saba, now!' She struggled up. 'It's Max. I think he's dead. In the studio!'

She focused at last, and ran to use the telephone in Max's office, the frantic girl at her heels trailed now by a small boy in pyjamas who had soundlessly joined them. Saba snatched up the child and, breaking the connection as Zoe lifted the receiver, yelled, 'No! Zoe, please. No. Not yet. Give me a chance to get out of here.'

Zoe spun round, anger sparking like a lit fuse.

'For Christ's sake, Saba! Max may still be alive. There might still be a chance. We've got to get help straight away.'

Weeping, Saba fought for the phone, and the boy clutching at her robe started to sob.

Exasperated, Zoe suddenly let go. 'Why? Why are you frightened of the police? Are you an illegal or something? If you clear out I shall have to tell them you were here, that you let me in. Look, I can't stand here arguing. Do as you like, but running away will only make things worse. How long has Max had you here?'

'Three weeks.'

'Well then, the neighbours will have seen you and the boy – isn't he at school?'

'He's only four! Zoe, it's not trouble with the police, I promise you – but all this will get in the papers. Was it a robbery? Was Max attacked?'

'He hanged himself. But we're wasting time. I shall get an ambulance and the police will come knocking at the door and I won't lie for you, Saba. Why should I? I hardly know you.'

'I thought we were friends.'

Zoe pushed her away and called 999, finally in control. The girl stood rock-like, the skinny kid in her arms, saying nothing.

After a moment Zoe pulled her aside and eyed her coldly.

'See here, Saba. Be sensible. Go back up-stairs with Ali and stay in your room. I'll deal with the police. Listen carefully: I let myself into the studio with my own key. I found Max. I ran round the front to get into the house and you opened the door. You've been temporarily employed as Max's house-keeper since the end of September, right? I'll tell the police you're moving in with me at my place in Battersea, OK? Here's the address.'

Zoe scrabbled in her pocket and passed over her card just as the bell jangled in the hall. She grasped Saba's arm.

'I don't know what you're afraid of, but if you keep your cool no one's going to take any notice of you. I doubt whether an elderly man's suicide will even get a half-column on the back pages and listing his employees is hardly relevant – it's not as if you even found the body.'

'Suicide? You sure, Zoe?'

'Absolutely. Now, just stick to the facts, don't elaborate and when the police say you can go, take a taxi to my workshop and tell my assistant that I said you could wait there. His name's Nick. Now scoot. Get dressed and wait upstairs till they need to talk to you.'

The doorbell pealed again, a man starting to bang impatiently on the stained-glass panels.

Saba flew upstairs and Zoe let the police officers in, leading them through the house, surprised to find the connecting door to the studio unlocked.

Yellow leaves had blown into the room through the gaping garden door, swirling against the chair that lay on its side under Max's feet, his velvet slippers still in place, the fabric scuffed thin, his silk dressing gown billowing in the breeze as the younger officer of the two hurried to close the door with her gloved hand. She put on all the lights, the place now cruelly illuminated like a stage set.

'Was this garden door open when you discovered the body, miss?' the sergeant asked, quite kindly Zoe thought, her mind taking in the details of the room at last.

'No. I have a key to the back door. I came to collect an urgent parcel Max asked me to deliver.'

'And your name?'

'Zoe Templeman.'

'You work for this gentleman?'

'On and off. I conserve antique textiles and Max gives me jobs from time to time.'

'He expected you this early in the morning?'

'Not exactly. He must have thought I'd collected it last night, which was the original arrangement, but something cropped up. He knew I was catching the ferry from Dover today but I come and go as I please. He trusted me to pick up stuff we'd agreed on and I dropped in when I'd got the time. With me having a key it didn't tie him down if he had an appointment elsewhere. Generally he kept the door through to the house

12

locked – I just didn't think straight this morning ... the shock ... I just instinctively flew out the way I'd come in.'

He gave her a hard look but let it go at that.

While they were talking, the WPC was peering at the body and making emergency calls on her mobile.

'Shouldn't you be calling an ambulance?' Zoe urged, darting a glance at poor Max, who had now ceased rotating, his face a mask.

'Bit late for that, Mrs Templeman,' she dryly retorted.

'Miss.'

'Right you are. Now, to get back to your part in all this. Your key doesn't give you access to the main part of the house?'

'No. I can't go through. I just use the back door. Max—'

'Hang about. Max who?'

'Max Loudon-Fryer. He's a dealer. Specializes in antiques for the more tasteful interior decorators. Used to have a showroom in the Fulham Road, but the lease expired some months ago.'

'DI Kennedy's on his way, Sarge,' the constable quietly interjected.

'Great.' The response was bleak and the WPC gave a wry smile.

'Anyone else at home?' the sergeant continued.

Zoe shrugged. 'Max lived alone. There's a housekeeper, Mrs Raz. But she's only been here a couple of weeks, so not much good at answering questions I'd say.'

'Live in?'

'Yes.'

'Did he have a business partner?'

'None.'

'Been living here long, this Mr Loudon-Fryer?'

'I couldn't say. Ever since I've been doing work for him anyway.'

'Which is?'

'Just over four years.'

'Good payer?'

Zoe nodded, not quite so confidently this time, the sergeant noted. 'Did you touch anything, Miss Templeman?'

Zoe shook her head, forcing herself to take in the whole spectacle for the first time: the broken angle of poor Max's stringy neck, the lolling tongue and bulging eyes, his grey hair falling about his ears in thin strands. Hardly the Max she knew, the pomaded old rogue she was used to.

The dank mist had risen, the rain diminished to no more than a drizzle, but Max's studio now blazed under the halogen orbs he used only for the closer inspection of his valuable goods, its macabre occupant now spotlit, clearly the star of the show.

Zoe slumped on to a bench, her face

ashen. The sergeant looked up from his notebook, startled by her sudden collapse, and asked the constable to take her out.

'Flush out this housekeeper, Barney. Get her to make some tea. Kennedy'll be here any minute; we don't want the scene compromised. You know what he's like.'

The WPC took her arm, but as they reached the door the sergeant called out, 'Any suicide note, Barney? Spotted an envelope? Anything?'

She shrugged and propelled Zoe outside. 'Which way's the kitchen, miss?'

'Down the hall, through here. I'll make the tea – no need to call Saba; she's terribly upset and there's her little boy to look after.'

'Just as you like. But the inspector will want a word with her when he gets here. Nasty business, but we'll soon get the place tidied up, don't you worry. Nice man this Mr Fryer?'

Zoe smiled. 'Loudon-Fryer. Poor Max always insisted on the whole mouthful. Yes, he was a decent enough old bloke. Tight wad, like the rest of them, but fair. And Max could appreciate a piece of craftmanship like nobody else in London. Could spot a fake a mile off.'

They went down to Saba's kitchen and made a big pot of tea, Zoe suddenly feeling famished, wishing now she'd had breakfast before jetting over to Max's place to collect the de Maurnay tapestry. What would happen to it now? Would all his things be put in quarantine till after the inquest? And, would she, once the dust settled, ever get paid?

Three

Zoe sat in the kitchen with the policewoman for over an hour, the cold mugs of tea leaving wet rings on Max's beautiful refectory table. She guessed 'Barney' had been instructed to keep an eye on her, refusing to allow her to take tea up to Saba in her attic rooms or to fetch cigarettes from her bag in the study.

Heavy feet spasmodically tramped through the marble-tiled hallway, the inspector's hectoring tones all too audible through the wall to Zoe, their hostage kept on ice till the preliminaries had been dealt with.

Eventually, the sergeant popped his head round the door and beckoned Barney for a quiet word in the hall. Zoe glanced at her watch, wishing now she hadn't left her mobile phone in the car. It would have been useful, if only to warn Nick of the impending arrival of a petrified stranger plus child at the workshop. Whatever next? There was hardly room for a camp bed in the corner, let alone lodgers. Why on earth had she got herself involved with Saba, who clearly had a dodgy history of some sort? A drug supplier on the run? Owing money to her pimp?

Max had picked Saba off the street when he was kerb crawling one night in King's Cross, he had boasted. Zoe had pretended to be unimpressed by this little confidence, but snatching a prostitute off the pavement and offering to share one's home was not the Good Samaritan role Zoe associated with her erstwhile employer. Still, it was a factor that his previous housekeeper had disappeared in a cloud of smoke the week poor Max had had to close his showroom. Never rains but it pours and, lately, rumours in the tight circle of international dealers to which Max belonged had floated around the salerooms like the first whiff of smoke. Word passed to Zoe, a tip-off from an auctioneer that she had better watch it: Loudon-Fryer had a cash-flow problem that could bring his empire tottering about his ears and the debris might shower all over the place.

Later, the policewoman returned and seemed determined to be chummy. 'I'm Barney Parsons,' she said. A thickset girl in her mid twenties, at a guess, whose trunk-like form bulked out by the uniform invited no messing. She grinned and said she had to make coffee 'for the A team', as she put it.

Zoe rose from her seat and collected up the mugs and teapot, indicating a row of canisters on the worktop to which the WPC swiftly applied herself, filling the kettle to the brim and dealing with the Aga like a veteran.

'I'm a country girl myself,' she said. 'Lovely kitchen, this; reminds me of home.'

Zoe rinsed the mugs and they chatted away all-girls-together-like, moaning about the rain, giggling about the no-nonsense lace-ups women in the Force were obliged to wear. Zoe, hiding her own barely contained hysteria at the pass to which this apparently normal day's work had brought her, went with the flow, sensing that a rapport with this girl might be useful.

'Any chance of me getting out of here soon?' she ventured.

'Not a hope. Not till the inspector gives the all-clear, anyhow. He's still talking to the housekeeper. A right smasher that one. Our Inspector Kennedy'll take his time, you bet.'

'Got an eye for the girls?'

'Usual middle-aged stuff – nothing objectionable. Still, it's not often he gets a Miss India type on the books.'

'Saba's Pakistani.'

'Oh, really? I suppose you're right. Any good as a housekeeper?'

18

'Don't ask me. I'm only the messenger girl. Called in to pick up a parcel and been stuck here ever since. My bag's in the study. Any hope of me retrieving it? I could do with a smoke.'

The constable fussed with the tray of coffee like a pro, assembling milk and sugar, proper cups, even a packet of biscuits she found in the pantry.

'I'll ask,' she said, hefting the tray and moving to the door. 'Wait here. I won't be a tick. What sort of bag is it?'

'A satchel, backpack type of thing. I left it on Max's desk when I phoned 999.'

Zoe held the door for her, catching an unwelcome glimpse of men bundling the body through the hall into a mortuary van backed up to the front door. Max making his final exit. She shivered, slamming the door on the chill wind sifting through the house, wishing the day would end.

Before the WPC got back to her wardress duties, Zoe was summoned to the studio to be greeted by one she took to be the man in charge.

He rose briefly then reseated himself at Max's table, an Anglepoise lamp focused on several sheets of paper before him, introducing himself with scant ceremony.

'My name's Kennedy. Please pull up a chair – hey, not that one!' he snapped, brushing her away from the chair under the

19

rafter, now righted, that Zoe realized was the one on which poor old Max had clambered before testing the rope. Bloody hell!

She located a canvas director's chair folded against the wall and pulled it across.

'Sorry to have kept you so long, Miss Templeman, but Mr Loudon-Fryer left us in the dark, so to speak. Perhaps you can help us?'

'Inspector?'

He nodded. Zoe perched rigidly at his elbow, her patience barely controlled, and leaned over the table eyeing him coldly.

'Listen, Inspector Kennedy. You seem to have got the wrong idea about me. I'm supposed, right now, to be on my way to France with a valuable tapestry Mr Loudon-Fryer had already sold to a very important Paris dealer, just in case you're thinking of jamming a stop order on all the stuff in this studio. I'm just a pawn in this game, Inspector. I just work for these guys and their professional approval is vital to me. May I at least call my contacts and tell them what has happened?'

'What *has* happened? You tell me.'

The inspector's tone was equally frigid and Zoe paused, confused by his manner. She had had no previous run-ins with the police and this one was hardly the 'thicko' variety dramatized on TV cop soaps. His suit was crumpled but the shirt starched within an inch of its life, the tie unspotted and his closely shaven head boasting a full grey stubble like a prickly cactus.

'What do you mean?' she muttered.

'There's no suicide note, no obvious woman trouble and, according to the few contacts I have so far made, Mr Loudon-Fryer enjoyed an unblemished reputation in the museum world. An expert on Jacobean furniture, agreed? Now why the sudden death wish?'

Zoe rephrased her prepared statement. 'I'm just the Girl Friday in all this, honestly. I liked Max. We had a good working arrangement, but that was as far as it went. His private life was private. I believe there's an ex-wife tucked up in Kensington somewhere, but I've never met her. His colleagues held him in good repute and as far as I know he never cheated anyone, had no enemies and seemed perfectly chirpy last time we met. Are you suggesting he was murdered?'

'That's for the forensic people to pronounce on. Naturally, there must be an inquest and as a matter of course I must ask you to submit your fingerprints. For elimination purposes,' he smoothly added. He sipped his coffee, watching her closely, her eyes suddenly shadowed by anxiety. A pretty girl but skinny. No make-up. Thick black hair cut close like a cap, long legs in opaque tights, a mini-skirt and black leather jacket. He glanced at his notes. Thirty-two years old, according to the sergeant. Sharp-tongued, he guessed, but warmhearted, it would seem. Why else would she offer a bed to the housekeeper woman, a person she hardly knew, by all accounts? A conspiracy cooked up between them?

'Why would you want my fingerprints?' she stuttered.

'A mere formality – prints are destroyed immediately our enquiries are complete, Miss Templeman. The housekeeper, Saba Raz, has already co-operated with us. But talking of formalities, may I confirm your address? My sergeant seemed somewhat unsure of the details.'

Zoe took a deep breath and rattled off a mini-CV.

'I have a workshop in Battersea with a bed-sit upstairs that I sometimes use if I'm working late. Here,' she said, passing over a business card, which he clipped to his notes, fixing her in a tight gaze as she stumbled through the complicated business of her relationship with Haydon.

'But mostly I live with my boyfriend, Doctor Haydon Masure, at 6 Claydon Gardens, SW1.'

'Belgravia?'

'Er, yes.'

'And very nice too. As a matter of fact I've heard of Doctor Masure. An extremely successful plastic surgeon.'

'Y-yes, that's right,' she squeaked, startled by the inspector's range of information.

'Not that I know anyone who could afford Doctor Masure's expertise, and certainly you, Miss Templeman, have no need to consult him professionally.' He grinned, the cold manner dissolving in his pleasure at catching his victim on the back foot. He glanced down at his notes.

'Mrs Raz tells me you've offered a bed to her and her boy at your place of work. Why would you do that?'

'She's terrified. Superstitious about staying here alone, in a house where someone has died, I suppose. She has no family ... It's only a temporary squat, just until she can find a new job.'

'Housekeeping? Or was her relationship with the deceased less formal?'

Zoe bridled. 'How the hell should I know? Why don't you ask her?'

He shrugged. 'Well, let's get back to business. Would you kindly go over your movements this morning once again? Let's "take it from the top", as they say. In your own time, Miss Templeman.'

Four

Once the inspector let me go, I dodged into the empty study to pick up my bag from Max's desk. His papers had been thoroughly sifted – by the police presumably – the discards piled loosely to one side, his bank statements and private correspondence tethered under a brass paper-weight. Born nosy, I surreptitiously browsed through the more interesting items with a gloved hand: receipts from clients, accounts from auction houses, even a bill from yours truly, listing additional expenses involved in the work on the de Maurnay tapestry.

A letter from his solicitor caught my eye and before good taste got a chance to kick in, I whipped it into my bag and let myself out of the front door. Barney stood guard, giving me a cheery salute as I breathlessly settled into my car at the kerb. Stealing a dead man's correspondence is not my natural style, you understand and, cripes! – how fear ratchets up a thumping heartbeat.

Zoe parked round the corner and made a

couple of phone calls, firstly to Nick to explain about Saba and secondly to Max's solicitor. The latter took a while, lawyers' receptionists being programmed to deflect unknown callers, especially unknown callers demanding to see the boss urgently, right now, this very minute. Zoe refused to go into details with the gorgon at the other end of the line, relenting only to rustle up some co-operation by insisting she represented one of Mr Gilbert's most valued clients, Mr Loudon-Fryer. That did the trick. After a consultation she agreed to fit her in at twelve o'clock.

Her call to Nick enjoyed a much smoother passage, her part-time helper being all too delighted to entertain Saba, the dark-eyed beauty, until Zoe could get back to the workshop.

'Probably be some time late this afternoon, Nick. Can you cope till then? Saba's pretty shaken up. I expect she told you – Max hanged himself. I said she and the boy could use the flat for a couple of days. Grab some money from the petty cash and take them out for a bite to eat round the corner. Would you mind?'

'Sure. No problem. By the way, that Japanese kimono survived its sponge bath. Looks great.'

'Really? Just pin it out on the rack, Nick. It's awfully threadbare in places – won't survive hanging up till I've netted the bad bits. And keep Ali away from the sink – you know what little boys are, though from what I've seen of him he's pretty timid. Saba can keep him amused at the big table; give her the run of the stationery cupboard, scissors and glue and stuff. Play it by ear; I'll tell you the full story when I get back.'

'I take it the Paris trip's off?'

'Yeah. Pity that. Can't talk now; I've got more calls to make.'

She got through to Haydon at the surgery without any fuss and outlined her change of plan.

'The poor old soul hanged himself you say?' Haydon whistled softly, his air of disbelief bringing home to her the really bizarre situation she had landed herself in.

'It gets worse. I've got Saba, Max's beautiful hooker, plus her child, bedded down at the workshop.'

'Eh? You must be joking!'

'Wish I was, dreamboat. I said they could use the upstairs flat for now. Can we meet for lunch? Can't rabbit on now, I've got to dash, Max's solicitor's agreed to see me at noon. Sounds callous, I know, but I want to get myself to the front of the queue when Max's estate's wound up. Off the top of my head I guess he left me over three thousand short, and for an encore I'm obliged to fulfil this jaunt to Paris at my own expense just to keep in with de Vries. Which reminds me: I must put him in the picture before he sends out a search party for his bloody tapestry.'

Haydon was hardly listening; Zoe could hear him muttering to his secretary in the background, chuckling over some private joke, his amiability charming patients and office cleaners alike. No wonder he was one of the most sought-after surgeons in the depressing world of cosmetic reconstruction, the man's unsinkable optimism giving the most ravaged face cause to smile. Zoe often wondered what he saw in her, but then few relationships were made in heaven, were they?

'Venetia tells me I've got a slot at two fifteen if we shuffle the ladies about a bit. That do you? Quick nosh at the Café? Anyway, what's the rush? I thought we'd have an evening free now you've cancelled the Paris jaunt.'

'Oh, do shut up, Haydon. Just accept that I need a shoulder to cry on right now. Finding a man swinging from the rafters before breakfast's not the best way to start the day.'

She rang off, the note of hysteria in her retort echoing in her brain like a warning bell.

Leaving a brusque message at de Vries's gallery in Paris and promising to ring him at home that evening, she sat in the car, weighing up her chances of success with

Max's solicitor. There was the dubious advantage of bringing bad news, but Mr Gilbert was, she hoped, not the sort to shoot the messenger.

His firm occupied a sprawling office in North London. Zoe managed to find a supermarket car park nearby and spent ten minutes in the ladies' room making herself look saner. She gazed in the spotted mirror over a grotty hand basin, all too aware that her normal healthy glow had, in the course of the interminable morning, taken on a prison pallor, her eyes still bloodshot from the emotional switchback of coping with finding Max, rescuing Saba and shadow-boxing with the police.

Zoe climbed the stairs, sourly considering the list of partners' names etched on the firm's brass plate, hoping her lifeline, Mr Gilbert, was an accommodating lawyer with a soft spot for arty types.

The gorgon turned out to be quite young, in fact, her defensive telephone manner all part of the job description, presumably. She wore a cerise jacket and stilettos and smiled, though the smile did not quite reach her eyes. Zoe was shown in straight away, the solicitor rising from his desk to shake hands, his curiosity overcoming a perfectly natural anxiety about the girl's demand for an immediate audience.

She sat down, dumping her bag on the

floor, and attempted to stretch her mini skirt over her wobbling knees. Without more preamble she explained her working relationship with Max Loudon-Fryer, pausing for full dramatic effect before lobbing the grenade.

'Max is dead, Mr Gilbert. Hanged himself. I found the body this morning and thought, as his solicitor, you should be one of the first to know. The police are still at his house.'

Gilbert's jaw dropped, his professional manner shot to pieces. 'Dead? You discovered the body, you say?'

Zoe patiently outlined events, drawing ultimate satisfaction from describing her rescue of Max's live-in lovely who, at best, would not survive investigation.

'You say Mr Loudon-Fryer employed this person as a *housekeeper*?'

Zoe shrugged. 'The house looked clean enough – certainly no worse than when Mrs Baker, his previous housekeeper, was in charge. Also, she has a little boy.'

'And you have them at your flat?'

'A bed-sit over my workshop.' She passed over her business card. 'It's not much of a place, but I was anxious Saba didn't make a run for it and draw attention to herself. Make the police think there was more to it...' she lamely concluded.

Gilbert ran a nervous finger under his

collar, his gaze clouding over in contemplation of the embarrassments in which seemingly respectable clients such as Loudon-Fryer could involve themselves.

'Your speedy response is very commendable, Miss Templeman. We would not wish the newspapers to get the idea that there was any sort of sex scandal in this tragic event. What are you proposing?'

'I thought it might be possible for you to advance an emergency payment to Saba Raz in lieu of wages, perhaps? I've no idea if she's been paid – the arrangement has been in place less than a month. But I'm sure there must be some way of recompensing this poor woman for lack of notice not only of her employment but of the sudden loss of accommodation. I can't afford to subsidize Mrs Raz myself, Mr Gilbert, and we wouldn't like her to be tempted to go to the press with goodness knows what background music about your client, would we? Max did, after all, pick her up on a kerb-crawling expedition, and when he spoke of it to me seemed proud of the fact that she was a reformed streetwalker.'

Gilbert visibly paled. 'Ah yes. I see your point. Do the police know all this?'

'Certainly not. And at present Saba only wishes to lie low – she has her son to think about. She's actually a very nice woman, Mr Gilbert. Perhaps you would like me to bring

30

her here so you can meet her yourself?'

'Oh no! That won't be necessary. Could you tell me the name of the person in charge of the ... er ... investigation?'

'Detective Inspector Kennedy. If you're quick, you'll catch him at the house. They're still searching for a suicide note. Your advice would be enormously helpful to them, I'm sure – any information about Mr Loudon-Fryer's circumstances, problems with his ex-wife, perhaps?'

'Has anyone told her?'

'I doubt it.'

'They never divorced, as it happens, merely separated. His death will throw everything into even more of a muddle than before.'

'Sorry?'

Gilbert pulled himself up short. 'Thinking aloud, Miss Templeman, just thinking aloud. Was that all?' he asked hopefully.

'Well, now you come to mention it, there's my own business account to worry about. When you recover Max's papers you will find he owes me a considerable sum for professional services and I am still under some obligation to deliver a valuable item, the de Maurnay tapestry, to its owner, a dealer in Paris. Max sold the tapestry to Monsieur de Vries; I was contracted to undertake certain repairs and, after Max's approval of the work, to take it to France

31

myself. He trusted me to take proper care of it, you see, and I need to retrieve it from the studio. Could you negotiate with the police? At present the house is under a sort of ban and Inspector Kennedy needs to be reminded that not all the items in Max's custody were his own property. Some were with him for valuation and some sold but, like the tapestry, awaiting consignment. Since his showroom closed down Max kept all the stock in the house and goodness knows what the insurance cover includes. Once the police leave, the place will be empty and the contents a massive security risk. I left my key with the inspector but I'm sure someone representing poor Max should safeguard the house. All those treasures...' she said, opening her hands in a gesture of despair.

Gilbert now looked thoroughly rattled, rising to escort her from the office, anxious to consult his partners about this young woman's perfectly valid demands: (i) Hush money to pay off the so-called housekeeper; (ii) debts to reimburse not only this Miss Templeman but presumably a host of other claimants; and (iii) there was that pesky wife of his to deal with, Desiree Loudon-Fryer – all of them under the delusion that his old friend Max had been a rich and respectable London dealer, a member of the Association, no less. Good God, if this latest rumour about Max taking a girl off the

32

streets to live in his house was true, the financial storm clouds stacking up were the least of it. No wonder the poor devil had decided to walk out on it all.

He hastened to reassure Zoe that he would take immediate steps to safeguard her interests, led her to the door and barked at the gorgon to make another appointment for Miss Templeman the following week, by which time she would, she assured him, have a final invoice including her own services and a list of Saba's expenses.

She found herself shunted out pretty damn quick and couldn't resist a smile as she put her car into gear and sped off to lunch with Haydon at their favourite eaterie, the Love Café.

Five

If Max's solicitor thought he could pre-empt the police in beating a path to the widow's door, he had sorely underestimated Detective Inspector Kennedy. As soon as Zoe had retreated, Gilbert put through a call to Desiree Loudon-Fryer, staring miserably at the heavy rain, hearing it gushing noisily down the drainpipes outside the window as he waited for her to answer.

'Ah, Francis. This is a surprise. A legal problem?' she fluted in that maddening trill that had gone out of fashion even for television announcers.

'I need to see you urgently, Desiree. There's been an accident and—'

'The inspector's here now, Francis. He told me what happened. Pop round later, would you? We'll have tea,' she said, cutting him off short. Gilbert sighed. He was all too familiar with Desiree, a lady of a certain type common in the rarefied purlieu of Brompton.

She put down the receiver, replaced her earring and moved back to the chair opposite the inspector. Her flat occupied a considerable footage of a mansion block opposite the Royal Albert Hall, the heavy furniture and plum-coloured drapes giving the room a Victorian air, not helped by dark skies looming over the park emitting spasmodic rumbles of thunder. Kennedy was more of an Ikea man himself and this formal drawing room made him squirm. Bringing bad news was, unfortunately, often his lot, but he had to admit that the reaction of Mrs Loudon-Fryer was something new.

He had arrived unannounced, finding the lady engrossed in a black-and-white movie, the worsening weather, he guessed, keeping her away from the shops. Although clearly nearer fifty than forty, Desiree Loudon-Fryer was somehow ageless, her shoulder-length blonde bob smooth as a bird's wing, her pretty hands fluttering from the pearls at her neck to the hem of her tweed skirt. Her response to the tragic news was muted and, in Kennedy's experience, hardly the normal reaction to bereavement. Her china-blue eyes briefly closed then flew open again in a moment, tearless and blank, her self-control – if that was what it was – a miracle.

He decided to pull no punches and described in detail the situation Zoe Templeman had stumbled upon so early that morning.

'You mean that stitchery girl found him? And you think he had been dead for hours?'

'The initial examination would indicate that Mr Loudon Fryer took his life last night. The housekeeper heard nothing.'

'What housekeeper?' she shrilled, careful accents that the more distressing news seemed not to affect suddenly taking on an astonished tone. 'Mrs Baker left weeks ago.'

'A temporary help, so I'm told. She's gone, not wishing to upset her little boy by the situation in the house.'

'Max employed a person with a *child?*' – the word 'child' infused with horror, as if the man had introduced an orangutan into his home.

Kennedy nodded, swiftly moving on,

wishing now he had more to go on.

'Without wishing to distress you further, Mrs Loudon-Fryer, I must gather more information for the Coroner about your ex-husband's state of mind. Perhaps there is something you could share regarding—'

'We were never divorced,' she interrupted, her voice now steady.

'Separated?'

'For a year or two. The arrangement suited us both: no one else was involved and, when my mother died and left me this flat, Max and I decided I would be more comfortable here.'

'Did your husband express any unhappiness about this decision? A wish for a reconciliation?'

She laughed softly, bringing her handkerchief to her lips as if to stifle the response. 'Oh no. We were each used to our own little ways. People become quite selfish living alone, Inspector, and Max's business was terrifically social. I prefer a quiet life myself. May I offer you a drink?'

'No, thank you, I've got several calls to make. My main problem is, there's no clue as to why he suddenly did it. The people I have spoken to – other dealers and Miss Templeman – seem to think he was his usual self. Had you any reason to expect this calamity?'

She busied herself pouring gin and tonic,

36

fiddling with ice and slicing a lemon, seemingly unfazed. Kennedy waited, biding his time.

She smiled, seating herself once again. 'Feminine intuition, Inspector? Absolutely not. Max and I bickered, as estranged couples do – about money, mostly; but I have a private income and my demands were rather more for the sake of principle than for any practical purpose. I was, of course, dismayed to hear that Mrs Baker had left, but then she worked for me for years. Perhaps she preferred to be employed by the lady of the house.'

'Mrs Baker, the previous housekeeper, didn't telephone you? Complain of her circumstances after you moved out?'

'I am not in the habit of being familiar with the staff, Inspector. It never pays.'

'Have you her new address?'

'No. I have no reason to squirrel away old connections of that sort.'

'Not even for a Christmas card?'

She glanced at him with a glint of contempt. Kennedy felt himself rebuked and rattled out his next questions in the hope that the bloody woman would crack, giving him some clue about the wretched soul who had decided to end it all with a length of rope.

'His financial situation was always fluid, of course,' she drawled. 'Buying and selling involves an inevitable time lag and recently I got the impression things had gone badly wrong. The shop lease was not renewed for a start and my monthly cheques were often in arrears. I mentioned it to the solicitor once or twice – that was the gentleman who telephoned just now – but these people are very close, and even an old friend like Francis Gilbert works under a pall of client confidentiality, of course, especially when a marriage fails. People tend to take sides, don't you find that?' She smiled, sipping her gin and eyeing him keenly.

Kennedy sighed. 'Perhaps *I* should speak to Mr Gilbert myself. The firm's name is listed among your late husband's papers but the correspondence he left was not much help. I suspect much was destroyed.'

Her attention shifted back to the window and, as if only now realizing how dark the afternoon had grown, she rose and switched on several pink-shaded lamps, which, even Kennedy had to admit, gave the place a bit of a glow without greatly illuminating it. He wondered what Mrs Loudon-Fryer looked like in full daylight; her skin, pale as alabaster, appeared as if the lucidity of summer brightness never penetrated these rooms. In subdued lighting the woman certainly passed as an English rose, if that sort of thing appealed. An English rose with thorns, Kennedy decided, closing the interview. Reaching for his sodden raincoat, he backed into the hallway, his hostess smiling in that vague, lifeless manner which was both intriguing and bloody irritating.

He activated the ancient lift, which clanked and hissed its way to the ground floor, feeling himself thoroughly out of sorts, knowing that he'd probably wasted the best part of the afternoon. He steamed softly inside the car, the dampness permeating the interior like bad vibes, and shot off back to the police station. He phoned his sergeant, only to be told that a solicitor, a Mr Gilbert, accompanied by a burly security man, was waiting at the house.

'You'd better get back over here, sir. This Gilbert bloke wants to pull up the draw-bridge and get a security team in here to keep an eye on the antiques and stuff.'

Kennedy swore softly, privately acknow-ledging a personal abhorrence of hanging with its link in his mind with official retribu-tion. A bad way for an innocent man to go. He abruptly pulled himself together, banishing these unprofessional musings. A case like this should have been wrapped up hours ago. No evidence of anyone else involved. No break-in. No robbery. No sus-picion of accidental death during the throes of sexual deviance like some of those silly buggers you heard about who got their rocks off by playing dangerous games. Old man Loudon-Fryer liked girls, for God's sake, or why employ a looker like that Raz female? Living the bachelor life, free of that harpy of a wife of his, he could have employed a bloke to look after the house, a gentleman's gentleman, if that was the way the wind blew.

Judging from the girly magazines Barney had found in the bedside drawer, there were no weird angles to the guy. If suicide was the answer – and how else could you explain it? – it wasn't sex, drugs or rock and roll that had driven him to the edge.

Kennedy forced himself back out into the rain and headed for the scene of the crime, if crime it was.

'Pity about there being no note, though,' he mused, watching his windscreen wipers skim wide arcs in the wet as he waited at traffic lights. 'These bloody suicides got no consideration.'

Six

Zoe stopped off at a general store and stocked up with supplies for Saba and the boy. It was still tipping down, but lunch with Haydon had lifted her gloom; the man commanded a sunny mini-climate all of his own.

The workshop occupied a corner site on a run-down arcade of disused shops, the entire area under threat of compulsory purchase prior to redevelopment. Zoe had got it cheap, but time was running out and the building itself was showing signs of decay, its rotting woodwork and loose tiles reminding her of one of her frayed tapestries. Finding another place in London would be expensive, but most of her contacts were in the city and abandoning the centre would be a gamble.

Also, there was Nick to consider. Nick worked part-time, paid by the hour while he finished a post-degree stint at the Royal College. He needed the cash and she needed an assistant who was flexible, enthusiastic and not too fussy about menial tasks:

like entertaining Saba, for instance. How many snotty textile conservators she knew would pitch in to welcome an outsider in a workshop where space was at a premium to begin with? The so-called upper-floor flat comprised a room under the eaves choked up with a double bed and a massive armoire, its shelves stuffed with spare fabric and box files; but there was a shower and lavatory squeezed on to the landing and a kitchen, of sorts, downstairs.

She let herself in, calling out to Nick, who crouched over a vacuum hot table at the end of the long narrow room, the solvent fumes catching her breath.

Saba and the child were seated at the big table, their heads close as they pored over Zoe's compartmentalized box of embroidery threads, the strong overhead illumination enveloping them in a bright pool of light. Ali was excitedly rearranging the skeins of silk in bands of colour, his small fingers skimming the tiny bundles like humming birds.

'Hey, look at you, Ali! I've been meaning to tidy up that box for weeks.'

Saba looked up anxiously, the boy grinning from ear to ear.

'Nick said it would be all right,' she murmured.

He came over, ruffling the kid's dark hair. 'Course I did. Saba's cleaned up the loo too.'

Zoe grimaced. 'Not before time, I bet. I've brought some food,' she said, dropping the shopping bags on a chair. 'Do you think you can manage here till something turns up, Saba? There's only a microwave and a toaster, but it's warm down here and there's spare blankets in a trunk upstairs.'

Saba had changed into jeans and a yellow sweatshirt, her long black hair tied back in a ribbon. Her remark in rebuke to Zoe that morning – 'I thought we were friends' – had caught Zoe where it hurt. They *had* been friends of a sort, hitting it off straight away, Saba's placid disposition a change from the disapproving manner of Mrs Baker. Having, as far as she knew, never before encountered a professional in the 'love for sale' market, Zoe had found herself instantly charmed by Max's new housekeeper and the atmosphere in the house was, since Saba's arrival less than a month before, so much more relaxed. All of this made Max's suicide the more shocking. Apart from the pain of losing his shop in Fulham Road, Max had seemed calmer of late, philosophical in hard times that even Zoe herself had encountered in the turbulent atmosphere of the salerooms, where tales of bankruptcies, established businesses taken over by foreign buyers and the increasing miasma of clever art fraud fooling even experts like Max had wreaked havoc.

Nick finished up and donned a big yellow cycling cape before launching himself out into the downpour.

Saba made a pot of tea and suddenly switched on the radio to catch the news. There was no mention of Max, but when they resettled round the table the talk inevitably hinged on the tragedy. Saba sent her son upstairs to fetch his colouring books as Zoe shared the latest developments.

'I'm trying to get a pay-off for you. The solicitor's sympathetic. Have you *no* money to tide you over?'

Saba winced, admitting that Max's terms of employment had been sketchy.

'Bed and board, a housekeeping allowance, of course, and cash in hand when I needed it.'

'No insurance stamps? No regular salary?' Zoe incredulously retorted.

'I wasn't sleeping with him, if that's what you mean,' Saba snapped.

Zoe squeezed her hand, feeling a bit of a nag, realizing all too clearly that tiptoeing round Saba's sensitivities must be a first consideration if they were to survive being thrown together like this.

'Here,' she said, taking fifty pounds from her purse; 'something to see you through until—'

'I can't take money from you!'

'Look on it as a loan, Saba. Listen: don't even consider making a quick buck out on the streets. If the police pick you up, Inspector Kennedy will drop on you like a ton of bricks. *He* thinks you're just an innocent domestic caught up in Max's troubles – the police don't know how you got the job and frankly, while you stay quietly in the background, Kennedy doesn't care. If he asks, say Max put up a card at the newsagent's round the corner, the place where he used to buy his sandwiches. People advertise there for cleaners all the time, I've seen loads of ads there myself. At nine-fifty an hour it struck me I'd be better off charring than going blind doing this thankless job of mine,' she added bitterly.

Saba sighed, slipping the tenners into the pocket of her jeans. 'Max told you where he picked me up?'

'Yes. Silly old sod thought he was being saintly. Getting a housekeeper for bed, board and expenses was fucking miserly, if you ask me.'

'Oh no. Max was a real kind man,' Saba insisted, sniffing into a sodden tissue and smiling at Ali as he bounced back down the stairs clutching a bag of toys. He settled beside his mother at the table and the two women drew closer, whispering like kids in bed after lights out.

'I was desperate that week he picked me

up,' Saba said. 'I had no money at all and I wasn't much good at it,' she admitted. 'And the other girls were suspicious. I got beaten up once. Being a loner on the streets is very dangerous, Zoe,' she added earnestly.

'I bet. But you're an intelligent girl; surely you could find something else? Shop work? Modelling even – you've got the looks for it.'

'There were reasons,' she said darkly, stroking the nape of Ali's scrawny neck. 'Anyhow, I'd only been on the game a fortnight when Max drove up and took me to his house. He had a sixth sense, you know – could spot a baddie from instinct. I told him about my son and he said I could move in till I found something better. Couldn't pay much, he said, but I would be safe.'

'Safe?'

'I'd taken this room behind King's Cross station, see. But the landlord said I owed more rent. A huge amount. Crazy money. Max rescued me, but they never give up, those people.'

'That was why you were so scared? In case Max's death hit the headlines? Photographs of you and Ali, even?'

Saba nodded, collecting up the mugs and rinsing them at the kitchenette Zoe had rigged up in the corner of the workshop.

'I think I'll try and get work away from London. I've got O Levels you know. I can use a computer.'

'I'll see what I can do. I've friends in the country. Just lie low here for a bit till I've shaken down Max's solicitor. You deserve some sort of redundancy pay-off.'

The phone rang and Ali started to wheeze, a painful breathless heaving that Saba hastened to relieve with a 'puffer'. Zoe spoke sharply to her caller, eyeing the child with serious concern. She put down the receiver.

'Is he all right?'

'Asthma,' Saba murmured, cradling the boy as his breathing slowly recovered.

'It's the chemicals in here. Let me open the window, Saba – the rain's stopped now.' They fussed over the boy, his watery smile reassuring them at last.

'That was the inspector. He wants me back at the house immediately. They've found something in Max's car: a hammer covered in bloodstains. They assume I would know something about it, God knows why. And that's not all: together with a lot of auction catalogues there's an envelope stuffed with money – five thousand pounds. I've told them Max often carried huge amounts of cash to pay for goods so he could make a quick getaway, but the police don't understand the way the system works. They seem to think I'm their captive insider in the antiques lark. But why the hammer? They think it's human blood and want me to look at it before it's sent off to be tested. Surely they don't think he mugged someone at a petrol station and robbed the till?' Zoe's feeble joke fell like a lead balloon.

'Anyway I've got to go back straight away. You be all right here on your own? Here, take my keys – I'll telephone if I'm coming back. You'd better keep the door double-locked, but the bars on the windows are strong; I have to keep this place secure because of the valuable textiles.'

Saba's eyes were wide with fear, a thread of violence seemingly unravelling from Max's rope to entrap them all.

Seven

I grew more apprehensive the nearer I got to Max's house. My day had started too early, too violently and far, far too confusingly for a simple girl. I had known Max Loudon-Fryer for years and regarded him as one of the few dealers with an unblemished reputation. But rumours insidiously clouded my certainty, whispers about bad debts fanned into reluctant credibility. Then there was the mystery of why Max had failed to renew the lease on his shop, a mecca for all the top dealers from Europe and America. He could hardly expect these men to trail across London to view his wares in a converted studio at his home.

Cash in Max's world changed hands at minor auctions, porters being generously cultivated for tip-offs, but at his level transactions were often conducted merely on a handshake, trust, strangely enough, being the linchpin between men trading on the greed and acquisitiveness of both specialists and ignorant collectors alike.

And where did I fit into all this? Me with my now-you-see-it-now-you-don't repairs and out-right make-overs of valuable textiles? A specialist market with few experts, Max being the foremost British connoisseur plus a handful of foreign dealers scattered between New York and Monaco.

I would have to try to explain all this to Kennedy, but the hammer...? The hammer was something else. A handgun I could, at a pinch, have understood: Max moved in a dark world sometimes infiltrated by ugly customers; but a hammer? *Give me a break!*

The front door stood ajar, a constable standing under the porch sheltering from the rain, which seemed to have been falling since dawn, the battering from leaden skies malevolent as an Old Testament act of attrition.

Zoe slid inside on the nod, shaking out her umbrella and dumping it on the hallstand before tracking down the loud voice issuing from Max's study. The inspector was sounding off at his unfortunate sergeant, his face flushed with temper. The desk was littered with paper, clearly having been subjected to a thorough going-over since Zoe's filching of Gilbert's letter that morning.

She stood on the threshold trying to look composed, her eyes shadowed by fatigue. Kennedy continued to lambaste the sergeant, and when he did finally pause, she spoke up.

'OK. What now?' she said coldly.

Caught in mid-flow, Kennedy spun round, eyeing her with suppressed irritation. He extended an arm indicating a chair, with a curt nod dismissed his disgruntled sidekick and moderated his tone.

'Ah, Miss Templeman. Good of you to hurry over. We need your advice.'

Zoe perched on the sofa, wary as an alley cat. 'I thought I'd said enough already.'

'Well, things have moved on since then. All this paper,' he said, waving at the littered desk; 'I get the impression the deceased relied on you for more than specialist repair work. You undertook little errands for Mr Loudon-Fryer.'

'Occasionally,' she admitted. 'Since he gave up the shop he had no assistant to call on. I helped out when I could.'

'Travelling to Paris, for instance?'

'It is necessary for me to keep in with the foreign buyers and Max paid my fare and expenses, which suited me.'

'Two birds with one stone?'

She nodded. 'But the Paris job is special. I have repaired a valuable art work for Monsieur de Vries and I am the only one who can show him what is new and what was original. It affects the value and—'

'Is it that good? Your conservation, I mean. It's undetectable even by an expert?'

'I like to think so, Inspector. And on that subject, when can I return the tapestry to the client?'

'Well now, that's a ticklish question. The solicitor's been here, stamping round making demands, but I would be grateful for your opinion of the stuff stored here. He reckons some of it may be subject to claims and my sergeant has been attempting to unravel the receipts in Mr Loudon-Fryer's desk. Without much success. He knows bugger-all – please excuse me, nothing – about such things and I wondered if you could walk round the studio with him and point out any items that might not belong here? Also, I need to piece together Mr Loudon-Fryer's movements over the past few days. These catalogues,' he said, passing over a sheaf of booklets, 'were in his briefcase and had been heavily annotated. One auction took place in Chester six days ago and another in Bath a couple of days ago. Did he mention any of this to you? Some of the items underlined were tapestries and antique bed hangings.' He continued speaking as Zoe flicked through the lists.

'I've spoken to the auctioneers,' he went on. 'None of the numbered lots marked here was sold to Mr Loudon-Fryer, although he was definitely present, which would make it seem that he either made two useless journeys or, as I believe sometimes happens, made subsequent arrangements with the buyers the goods were knocked down to. Can I ask you to cast your eye over the stuff here and see if any marry up to those listed in his proposed bids?'

Zoe bridled. 'A dealers' ring, you mean? That's unprofessional. Max was too decent to indulge in that sort of back-street trading. His reputation would have been ruined if a rumour like that had got about.'

The inspector looked sceptical but let it pass. 'Did he usually drive himself or travel by train?'

'Depends. If the weather was foul, or if the auction was far away, he took the train; but mostly he drove himself.'

'Alone?'

'I suppose so. I was not in his confidence about travelling companions, Inspector. You seem to think I was some sort of partner, but I wasn't. No such luck. I was more of a gofer, to be honest. I needed the cash and if it fitted in with my current commissions, I was happy to play along.'

'Prompt payer?'

She hesitated. 'It generally worked out in the end.'

'I only ask because there were several final demands among the correspondence and from my enquiries in the trade the inference remains that the dead man had hit a very rough patch. His cheque stubs indicated regular large withdrawals but his bank balance shows little coming in.'

'It's been a bad year in the antiques business. East Europeans have started muscling in and the American stock market has a fluctuating influence on exports.'

'I'm sure you're right. Even so, even you, Miss Templeman, a most trusted colleague, have already approached his solicitor about your outstanding account, I understand.'

Zoe looked uncomfortable, feeling like one of the first vultures to be observed alighting on the carrion. Poor Max.

Kennedy offered her a cigarette and she gladly lit up, her hands shaking as he held a match for her before lighting his own.

'Mr Gilbert was only doing his job, Miss Templeman, answering police questions that may well indicate the reason why the victim chose to hang himself. The Coroner needs to have some indication of the man's state of mind and any financial troubles are particularly important in the absence of any suicide letter. There's evidence of a stack of paper having been incinerated in the hearth in the studio.'

He waited for a response but Zoe merely looked blank. He briskly continued.

'However, Mr Gilbert wants the police out of here as soon as possible, which is understandable, and your expert assistance would facilitate this to everyone's advantage.'

'But it *is* suicide, isn't it?'

'A suspicious death, as we say. Complicated by the dis covery of the hammer in the boot of Mr Loudon-Fryer's car.'

Zoe flinched, dropping ash on her skirt. Here goes, she thought, the million-dollar question.

Kennedy drew a transparent bag from his briefcase and passed it over. It was a perfectly ordinary hammer, the sort any builder would use.

'Hardly a delicate instrument for testing for woodworm, is it?' he said.

Zoe shook her head, hastily placing the thing on the desk, fascinated despite herself by the brownish stains encrusting what she took to be a small clump of hairs to the claw head.

'Any ideas?'

'Absolutely none,' she stammered.

'A handyman, was he, your friend Max? A DIY enthusiast?' he said with a grin.

She stiffened. 'Hardly, Inspector.'

'Ah well. We'll have to see what the forensic boys have to say. But, to get back to these provincial auctions: would he have stayed overnight?'

'Definitely not. Max always came straight home if he possibly could. As you know, he carried wads of cash and often small sale items. Colombian art was one of his little sidelines. Have you looked in the safe?'

'Empty. Sergeant Cooling's taken the study, the bedroom and the studio storeroom apart. Nothing,' he said with finality, stubbing out his cigarette in one of Max's filigree bonbon dishes. The front door crashed shut, sending vibrations through the house. Kennedy hurried into the hall shouting at WPC Parsons, who was attempting to bar the two who had burst in. Zoe sidled out, hoping to slip away.

Kennedy pushed forward as if to break up a fight. 'Ah, it's you, Mr Gilbert. I didn't expect to see you again today,' he said, glaring at the lady at his side. 'And Mrs Loudon-Fryer.'

The widow was appropriately attired in a black-silk mackintosh, raindrops shimmering on her cheeks like crocodile tears. Gilbert held a small suitcase, presumably hers, and tried to guide his client to the door of the studio.

'Mrs Loudon-Fryer wishes to visit the scene of the tragedy.'

'Impossible at present, I'm afraid.' Kennedy stood firm and Barney stepped smartly across the hall to guard the studio door. 'We have yet to complete our investigation of the scene. Miss Templeman here has agreed to help my sergeant with his stock-taking.'

'I'm moving back home,' the widow said, her voice ringing clear as a death knell. Both policemen were taken aback and Gilbert drew Kennedy aside, insisting on his client's rights, fast-talking with enough legal jargon to support a dozen writs. Zoe emerged from the shadows.

'Can I go now?' she asked, retrieving her brolly and edging to the door. Kennedy broke away from Gilbert, wagging a warning finger at her.

'I'll ring you at home then, Miss Templeman. Remember what I said: co-operation with the police is your civil duty, you realize.' There was a note of desperation in his voice that made her smile.

Nodding a polite goodbye, Zoe quietly opened the door and made off towards the car, leaving Kennedy, Gilbert and the steely-eyed woman grouped together like an operetta trio left on stage when the curtain fails to come down.

Eight

Zoe rushed back to Haydon's flat and made herself a pot of tea to calm her nerves. It was as if she had been caught up in a mudslide, her feet snatched from under her, finding herself fighting for breath in a sea of filth. Max. Max of all people. Why? And all those insinuations from the police about his cash-flow problems. Everyone hit a bad patch from time to time, didn't they? And that wife of his was probably an expensive item even if he had cut his own outgoings to the bone by not only giving up the shop but dismissing the housekeeper and employing instead an amateur hooker on a dubious freelance basis.

Zoe sipped her tea, swallowing a couple of aspirins in an effort to knock her raging headache on the head. Being bundled up with Saba at the workshop was a complication she could have done without, and if it hadn't been for the boy, Zoe admitted she would have been less sympathetic. What did anyone really know about the girl? For all she knew, Saba had been conning Max all along and was now in the process of bundling Zoe's valuable antique textiles into a removal van. She shuddered and took her teacup to Haydon's drinks cupboard to top it up with a shot of brandy.

That hit the spot.

When Haydon got home just after seven, she was still asleep on the sofa, her black hair tousled like that of a Japanese doll, her skinny legs curled beneath her. He grinned to himself as he quietly stacked up the tea things and dumped them in the kitchen. She woke as he switched on the lamps and jerked up, blinking in the light like a rabbit caught in the gleam of a poacher's torch.

He gently budged up beside her and stroked her hair. Zoe relaxed, vaguely aware of a sniff of antiseptic or something horribly medicinal lurking beneath the aftershave. She swiftly removed his jacket and tugged at the striped tie and the buttons of his starched shirt. Making love on Haydon's cream tweed sofa really was the only antidote to a poisonous day.

After a shower and feeling quite her old self again, they decided to eat out; but it was only when they were into their third glass of wine that Zoe had unwound sufficiently to give Haydon a résumé of her second run-in with Inspector Kennedy.

'A hammer?' he gasped.

'Shush, not so loud!' She leaned across the

table. 'It gets worse. A bloodstained hammer. Found in the boot of Max's car.'

'Jesus!'

Zoe nodded, forking into her antipasto with awful gusto. It was quite an achievement to shock Haydon, the fabled shock-proof sawbones.

'And naturally this insufferable policeman thinks the worst. You knew Max, Haydon. Wasn't he just the gentlest man alive?'

He was baffled. 'Max might have been defending himself, of course. A man who flashes wads of money around at auctions gets a name for himself as a big spender. Even people like Max aren't always what they seem, sweetheart. Believe me, I treat ladies who you'd think wouldn't say boo to a goose and later, when they've got their facelifts and new bums, quite a few turn into real cows, apparently.'

'Not *mad* cows, though? Not going around bashing people on the head with hammers.'

'What makes you think I only treat women? Some of my patients are real villains.'

'Really? Crooks you mean? Who?'

Haydon laughed. 'Politicians mostly. Actors on the skids, all sorts of—'

'But who?' she persisted. It occurred to her that Haydon rarely talked about his work, his forte being to beguile the other person to give secrets away. He tapped the side of his nose. 'Did your mother never tell you that curiosity killed the cat? No one you would know, anyhow. Tell me about your inspector. What's he like?'

'Balding. Tall, thickset and with the squashed ears of a boxer.'

Haydon laughed. 'Perhaps you should give him my card. Cauliflower ears are a doddle.'

'He couldn't afford your fee and, anyway, probably finds thuggish looks an advantage in his line of business.'

'Thuggish?'

'No, that's unfair. Short-tempered and a bit too macho for me, but intelligent. And intuitive, I'd guess. Wants me to pick over Max's stuff to see if he's got anything he hasn't paid the salerooms for.'

'He thinks Max was a fence? Peddling stolen goods?'

Zoe grimaced. 'I'm not sure what he thinks. He's got this bee in his bonnet about Max driving all the way to Bath and Chester to attend auctions and then, on the face of it, not buying anything. But Max needed to keep in the swim, be seen around, if you get me.'

'Networking?'

'Sort of. These dealers feel the vibes, need to know which way the wind's blowing, what's sexy and what's going out of fashion. Driving round and not coming away with something isn't a total dead loss. Anyway,

Max travelled all over – flew to the States at least three times a year and was over to France every other week. Not having the shop to worry about left him more free time to swan around. He wasn't getting any younger. Maybe he was thinking of chucking it in.'

'But not at the end of a rope, surely?'

Zoe paused, her fork in mid-air, suddenly losing her appetite. She laid down her knife and took a gulp of water.

'Well, no. That's my problem. I saw Max only a few days ago and he seemed just the same as usual. We arranged for me to pick up the tapestry yesterday; he said I could let myself in and he'd leave it in the studio ready boxed up and addressed to de Vries. The paperwork – Customs forms etc. – were sent round to the workshop special delivery.'

'But you didn't go over to his place yesterday.'

'No. Nick was working on a piece of Jacobean lace I was worried about. I stayed late making sure the stains had come out and decided to call in at Max's early this morning instead.'

'On your way to Paris?'

'Bloody hell! I've just remembered. I promised to ring de Vries this evening and tell him the latest.'

'He can wait.'

'I'll call when we get home. Don't let me forget.'

'But really, apart from the mysterious hammer jamming up the works, the inspector's not seriously putting forward anything against a suicide verdict? I would have thought hanging was impossible to construe as anything *but* suicide.'

'Who knows? He's not confiding in me, Haydon. Kennedy says quantities of paper have been burnt in the fireplace in the studio. Thinks Max was torching information, I suppose. Can these boffins reconstruct burnt fragments?'

'Possibly. Depends ... Fact remains, Max was apparently short on sales lately. Probably depressed. But instead of focusing on the financial shortfall, has this master detective considered the obvious? Looked into Max's medical history? His doctor may have given him bad news. Not everyone can face up to a long illness and, for some, suicide might seem to provide a nice quick exit.'

Zoe brightened. 'Now why didn't *I* think of that? Surely that would be the first thing the Coroner would want to know?'

Haydon persisted, worrying at the poor corpse like a terrier with a dead rat. 'And there's this new housekeeper of his ... Funny business.'

'Saba. Which reminds me: I've got Saba and the kid safely tucked up at the workshop for now. Only a short-term measure, but I don't really trust her to stay off the streets until the investigation's over. She's penniless, Haydon. Max owed her wages and until I can persuade Mr Gilbert to—'

'Max's lawyer?'

'Mm. I'm hoping Mr Gilbert's going to give Saba some sort of redundancy cheque, the excuse given to keep her version out of the papers. He hasn't guessed that would be the last thing Saba would want – publicity in the press dragging out all the skeletons in her cupboard. Wait till you see this girl, Haydon; Max sure picked a stunner to replace Mrs Baker.'

He signalled the waiter to bring a fresh bottle and, while the table was being cleared, thoughtfully regarded the girl beside him on the banquette, his mind clicking away like a metronome.

When they were alone once more, he squeezed her knee and spoke in that low tone which Zoe laughingly called his bedside manner.

'Look here, darling,' he said, 'you've had enough. This inspector bloke's got no right to demand that you spend days sifting through Max's tat to satisfy his cock-eyed notion of iffy goods, possibly stolen. Why don't you drive down to Stonecrest first thing in the morning? Friday I can get away early and be with you by six.'

'What about Kennedy?'

'Leave him to me. As your doctor I'll say you're in shock – in no state to answer any more questions at present.'

'You'll speak to him yourself?'

'Why not?'

'What about Saba?'

'Kennedy knows where to find her, doesn't he? Can't think what else the girl can add to her statement, but if you're worried, I'll get my own solicitor to be with her if the police want another interview. How's that?'

'Oh, would you, Haydon? Saba's terrified of getting involved with the police. Here,' she said, jotting down Max's address and home number. 'But don't let your lawyer know we're trying to shake down Mr Gilbert for a leaving present for Saba; he might think she's hiding something, had some fix on Max and is holding out for a pay-off. Incidentally, the widow's moved back in.'

'Into Max's house?'

'Yes. Probably bringing a "heavy" in with her on the face of it to secure Max's property.'

'Bad news?'

'Well, on first impression this lady's no shrinking violet, for sure. Tell me, if Max's estate is really bankrupt, how would she stand?'

'Listen, baby, I'm only a poor medic. Why

don't you ask your new mate Mr Gilbert? Zoe, don't change the subject. What do you think about shooting down to Stonecrest till the smoke clears?'

She turned it over in her mind. It wasn't such a bad idea. Stonecrest was Haydon's country house on the edge of Romney Marsh. She could be down there in less than an hour if she left London at daybreak. It would take her out of Kennedy's target area, she could leave Saba and the boy under Haydon's wing for a while and, best of all, would have at least a weekend to herself, a couple of days to think things out.

She grinned. 'Anyone told you you're a genius, Doctor Masure?'

'Since you ask, not since my last patient looked in my mirror this afternoon.'

She cuffed his shoulder. 'Bighead!'

Nine

Stonecrest is a turreted mock-Tudor house set in several acres of scrubby garden, most of the land being leased to Roddy Meirs, a former City trader turned pig breeder.

I often badger Haydon to discover what on earth made him choose such an ugly place, but he always laughs it off, never gives me a straight answer and agrees that it's only the proximity to London that offers any sort of attraction. Haydon does not even like the country and takes little pride in Stonecrest. He even bought the place fully furnished and has never bothered to change so much as a curtain rail.

I blame his sister, a psychiatrist called Meriel, a snobby bitch who turned on me after I'd aired my doubts with, 'Of course Haydon needs a rural retreat. No one in their right mind stays in town at the weekend, and if they do, they make quite sure none of the neighbours knows about it. One of my patients admitted she drew her curtains on a Friday evening and lived in gloom until Sunday night, having lied to all her friends about owning a cottage in Wiltshire.'

Zoe arrived later than planned, diverted by floods outside Heathfield. The house stood empty all week, though a surly old codger called Bert Styles kept an eye on the place aided by his pair of Rottweilers and a burglar-alarm system that could be set off by as little as a marauding cat.

Haydon had inherited Bert along with all this high-tech security from the previous owner, a nervous type, one would have imagined, as the horrible furniture and repro chandeliers were certainly not worth going to gaol for. Haydon had taken the easy line, as usual, accepting the place as it stood, seemingly indifferent to its clumsy gentrification.

Stonecrest had only two, maybe three, advantages, as far as Zoe could see. It was only ten miles off the M20 and within easy striking distance of the Channel ports and the Channel Tunnel connection at Ashford, making it ideal as a staging post for Continental forays.

The third advantage was pure serendipity: their neighbour, forty-one-year-old Roddy Meirs. Roddy was not your average pig farmer: his smallholding abutting Stonecrest had been carved from the estate and he had been raising his Gloucester Old Spots for five years, ever since having been made redundant from one of the blue-chip trading firms in the City. Roddy was a whole bundle of fun and had, despite the dire fore-bodings of the locals, made the farm pay by funnelling his organic produce into his own farm shop and persuading other farmers in the district to diversify with him. Roddy's wife had pushed off with half his redundancy money as soon as she realized he was serious about chucking in his dealer's lifestyle for mud and pigswill. He lived alone, 'happy', as Zoe delighted in telling him, 'as a pig in shit.'

She stopped off at Bert's cottage and he deactivated the alarm system to let her into the house. Bert was no country yokel either and his taciturnity, grey stubbled head and tattooed forearms placed him squarely in the aging football hooligan slot. Haydon reckoned Bert was a bit deaf and had, on one occasion, winkled out the fact that their caretaker had once held a middleweight boxing title. If Bert was deaf, he was lucky: at least he couldn't hear the guard dogs snarling at every intruder, baring their teeth and breaking into full throttle as Zoe edged her car up the overgrown drive, Bert following on foot. At night Bert often let them loose in the grounds. At night Haydon and Zoe had given up stepping outside to look at the moonlight.

Once Bert had satisfied himself that the whole place was unfettered, he marched off down the drive, his powerful arms swinging like a gorilla's, his steel-capped boots striking loudly on the tarmac.

Zoe shut the front door behind her, glad to be alone, thankful that Meriel's suggestion that they keep on the live-in housekeeper at Stonecrest had been adjusted to employing the woman on a daily basis. Haydon liked to have the place to themselves too, and rarely invited friends to stay, although eating out was never a problem, Roddy Meirs and any one of his passing girlfriends sometimes joining them for a run into Folkestone, where they had discovered a pub with a terrific line in fish and chips.

Zoe switched on all the lights, always a first move, the dark panelling and mock-oak beams giving the rooms the semblance of a megabuck tourist hotel. The hall was enormous, the grate in its baronial fireplace laid with false logs and ashes which, to Haydon's glee, not only glowed when the gas was lit, but staged sound effects of hissing flames and crackling timbers. The whole house had been dealt with in a similar money-no-object style, the walls clustered with antlers, stuffed animal heads and massive hunting scenes in gilt frames, the horses snorting and rearing up like a cavalry charge. The entire house was so wonderfully 'naff' that Zoe almost forgave it, the heating system tipping the balance in its favour, since Haydon insisted that the place be ready for occupancy at any time, despite the electricity alone's practically requiring a power station all of its own.

She wandered into the kitchen and rooted round for fresh coffee beans and sliced bread from the freezer. She settled in the window seat in the dining room with a breakfast tray on her lap, watching a flight of mallards circle Haydon's lake, a rare shaft of sunlight catching their bright plumage as they wheeled over the water. The sky was dappled like a grey mare, a band of conifers on the boundary disguising the proximity of the motorway.

After unpacking her bags she tried to phone Haydon at the surgery but drew a blank, his receptionist being irritatingly vague about his whereabouts. Nick, presumably doing his study period at the museum conservation lab, had switched off his mobile and the phone at the workshop seemed to be permanently engaged. Now, feeling unaccountably anxious, she rang the consulting rooms again, this time on Haydon's private line, and left a message on his answerphone.

'I'm worried about Saba; the phone at the workshop seems to be off the hook – probably only Ali larking about, but I can't get hold of Nick at present. I'll try him again later and ask him to check it out. Listen, Haydon: I'm switching off my mobile; I don't want Kennedy to chase me down here, so don't give him this number if he asks. I'm too traumatized to answer any more questions, remember? I'll pop over to Roddy's farm shop now and get some food for tonight, so don't bother about booking a table at Vinny's – we'll eat in, shall we?'

Feeling in need of cheering up, she changed into a Barbour and wellies and trudged over to Roddy's farm. Roddy was a mate, a decent bloke who, from sheer good nature, had won over the dispirited farming types who were clinging to livelihoods even more precarious than making a living in the futures market. Roddy's pig farm was a piddling venture in comparison with his neighbours' wide acres and his lack of agricultural experience gave them all temporary respite from their own struggles, as they waited for his inevitable fall.

However, Roddy's enthusiasm was hard to resist, his battles with the form-filling and squabbles with the bureaucrats grudgingly earning the admiration of the locals as they watched and waited for Stonecrest Farm Shop to belly-up. After a year or two, a couple of farmers were persuaded to supply him and then, as if in chorus, they were all suddenly begging to join in, Roddy's optimism seemingly as virulent as swine fever.

The farm shop began to supply outlets in London, Roddy's business connections bearing fruit; his gambler's instinct, honed by years playing the markets, and his ability to charm bank managers with a credible business plan paid off. 'Beginners' luck, cushioned by City bonuses,' the doom forecasters muttered. A fool and his money etc. etc.

So far, his luck had held, and Zoe knew that a sandwich and beer in Roddy's chaotic kitchen was just the pick-up she needed.

In fact – sods' law – he wasn't home. It really wasn't her day, she miserably decided. He wasn't at the farm shop either.

'Off to London, love. On one of his jaunts – some sort of food fair or sommat. Back tonight. Shall I tell him to give you a call?'

Mary Malone was one of the farmers' wives glad of a shift at the shop, glad of a bit of pin money to put by for the kids at Christmas.

Zoe bought some supplies for the weekend and trailed back to the house, feeling oddly bereft, which was ironic, since one of the big attractions that had brought her down here in the first place was some time alone, a few hours in which to get her head round poor old Max's suicide.

She did some work on a frayed altar cloth in the afternoon, a piece of Victoriana she had put aside for weeks, some long-dead lady's embroidery, an example of devotion that had, by any rational consideration, had its day; but Zoe had reluctantly agreed to repair it for the church in the village, the vicar, a fervent soul intent on her own notions of the Lord's work, being an impossible woman to refuse.

At seven o'clock, when she had almost given up, Haydon finally put through a message via his receptionist.

'Hi. It's Venetia here. Haydon asked me to tell you something's cropped up and—'

'What?'

'He didn't say. An emergency. Anyway, he said to tell you he can't get down to Stonecrest till late, probably after midnight; and would you please get the guest room ready, he's bringing a friend?'

'Shit!' Zoe muttered as she pottered about the kitchen turning off the oven, transferring the daube of beef to the Tyrolean-style pine breakfast bar.

'The whole bloody point of coming down here, Doctor Masure, was to give me a chance to draw breath. Why invite people *this* weekend of all times?'

Perhaps, she conceded, as her temper cooled, the stupid man had let himself in for a long-overdue invitation to one of his dreary colleagues. Please God, she prayed, his sister Meriel hadn't invited herself down for a first-hand version of Max's suicide, an account straight from the horse's mouth of the reactions of a neurotic female who

73

discovers an old man swinging from the end of a rope. Meriel was a practising psychiatrist – and Meriel *loved* her work.

Zoe waited up. When she heard wheels on the drive, accompanied by the inevitable racket from Bert's dogs, she made the best of it and opened the door with a hostessy smile even Meriel would have been bowled over by.

Haydon emerged from the Range Rover looking suitably shamefaced, and shrugged helplessly in unspoken apology as he opened the passenger door and helped his guest to alight.

Zoe's smile froze. 'Saba! What on earth are *you* doing here?'

Ten

Having Saba join us in the country hit me where it hurt. My initial recoil was basic instinct – totally illogical, of course, because (a) Saba was not Haydon's type, or so I thought at the time, and (b) she was only yet another of life's victims caught up in the no-holds-barred scrap to keep a roof over their heads.

The fact that she was so pretty was not an issue, believe it or not. I had become so familiar

74

with Saba's huge dark eyes that her looks barely registered. But human nature being what it is, I regarded Stonecrest as a place for Haydon and me alone. Dog-in-the-manger, admittedly; but it was somewhere where we could forget the rackety life in London, a place for laughing and loving, an ugly, rambling excrescence blighting the landscape but, in the last resort, home.

Zoe led Saba straight to the guest suite on the first floor, the flashy opulence of it all seemingly making no impression on her, and Haydon laid Ali on the bed. Saba looked all in, her face pale as a bruised peach, her eyes bloodshot. There had been no explanation, Haydon's warning glance as he carried the little boy up the stairs forestalling any questions. Saba refused tea or anything to eat, swiftly undressing the child and slipping him between the sheets in the huge four-poster, his dark head instantly buried in the frilled pillowcase. Haydon slipped away.

Saba, unspeaking, vacantly accepted Zoe's perfunctory tour of the rooms and stood gazing out at the dull glow of the motorway lights in the distance like a prisoner under house arrest.

Zoe shrugged and murmured 'goodnight' before hurrying down to join Haydon in the library. This was Haydon's favourite bolt-hole, the walls lined with volumes she suspected had been bought in bulk, by the yard. Unread and probably unreadable, the books merely formed a backdrop, Persian rugs absorbing every footfall, leather chairs and sofas inviting non-readers to huddle round the fake log fire, cosy as maggots in a pile of pashminas.

'Here, darling, I've poured a whisky and soda for you,' he said, hugging her briefly before steering her to the sofa. Haydon was jumpy, which was unlike him, and Zoe sipped her Scotch, eyeing him with unspoken reproach. He wore a thick blue sweater smelling vaguely musty and crumpled corduroys snagged with an L-shaped tear at the knee. His mood was guarded: not smooth old Haydon Masure at all.

'No good looking at me like that, Zoe. You're lucky I was still in town. If I'd jerked off here first thing, like you, God knows what would have happened to her.'

'Saba?' Her voice rattled, brittle as the ice cubes in her glass.

'She's *your* millstone, remember. I'm only the poor bloody bystander in all this.'

Zoe felt a trigger of alarm, her bad humour evaporating in a shiver. 'What are you talking about? Saba's in trouble with the police?'

Haydon looked up, startled. 'No, of course not! Why should you think that?'

'Look, Haydon, start at the beginning.

76

You've lost me completely. Why bring her here at all? Saba was perfectly happy at the workroom; Nick was keeping an eye on her.'

He rubbed his chin, a tic flickering at his lower lip, then looked her straight in the eye at last. 'Do you want the good news or the bad news?' he said with a ragged laugh.

'Just get on with it, Haydon,' she snapped. 'I'm no good at mind games.'

'OK. The bad news is, your workroom's had it. I've brought most of the stuff here with me. Nick helped sort out the necessities.'

'What?' Zoe grabbed his arm. 'A fire? Saba set fire to my workshop?'

Haydon pulled away, laughing. 'For Christ's sake, Zoe, stop blaming Saba for everything. It wasn't her fault. I knew you wouldn't want her down here, but I couldn't think of anywhere else once it got so late. It was raining.'

'What's the weather got to do with it? Saba's used to roughing it, believe me.'

'The place was flooded. Haven't you seen the news? The drainage systems all overloaded even in London.'

'A flood? You sure? What about the textiles? Nick helped, you say.'

'All three of us have been working our balls off, Zoe. Poor bloody Saba was up most of last night trying to swab out; she's been a fucking marvel. If that girl hadn't been on the spot, you would have lost every-thing. She phoned Nick first thing and when he got there he found buckets all over the place and the floor swimming. A drain outside must have backed up or something ... the stink!'

'Good God! Why didn't anyone contact me?'

'Nick *tried* to reach you, but your mobile was switched off, remember? He got on to me instead. I told him to keep baling out till I could get there. Between appointments I took the Range Rover over and left it with him to evacuate the textiles, and I caught a taxi back to the clinic. I told him to handle it, to leave you right out of it till we'd got the place cleared.'

Zoe's breath came in shallow bursts, her heart thumping. 'It's been raining for weeks ... but I thought the place was OK.'

'Saba told Nick water started dripping through the ceiling that night – loose tiles, I guess. She managed to move the bed and tried to mop up, but then something burst in the street and water started seeping in under the door.'

'Poor thing,' she muttered. 'She would have been better off staying at Max's.'

'Nick was the hero of the hour, of course. Did his best, but by the time I got back there tonight it was clearly a lost cause.'

'Why didn't you ring me here?'

'What was the point? There was nothing you could do. Nick and Saba were working like beavers for hours; dragging you back to join in would only have complicated things. I borrowed some dry clothes for Saba from Venetia and Nick bundled as much as could be saved into the car. I gave him a hundred quid to carry on with, though frankly the poor guy deserves a medal. With your work-room washed out I imagine he'll be looking for another job.'

'It's that bad? Really?'

'Even if it's cleared up and the roof repaired, the place won't be fit to use for months – if ever. Damp would ruin the fabrics, wouldn't it?'

Her eyes widened, the full consequences of the disaster finally dawning on her.

Haydon ploughed on defensively. 'Bringing Saba down here was the only thing I could think of. And the kid's not well – been coughing his heart out all day. Hope to God he's not shaping up for a bout of pneumonia; he looks pretty frail.'

'Perhaps you could get that private doctor in Ashford to look Ali over in the morning. An emergency call-out?'

Haydon agreed, prising the tumbler from her hands as he took her in his arms. 'It'll all work out, you see. You needed a new workshop and apart from your technical equipment the rest is saved. You insured?'

Zoe nodded. 'But I expect the equipment can be salvaged. I'll get on to Nick in the morning – prostrate myself in gratitude, find out the score on the electrics.'

They snuggled close on the sofa, Haydon exploring the softer contours of her bony frame, teasing her about her cold bottom, promising a thorough toasting if she could be persuaded to disentangle herself from under his damp sweater and come to bed.

Later, clasped under the feather duvet in Stonecrest's master bedroom, Zoe ventured to touch on that other disaster in her Slough of Despond.

'Inspector Kennedy, Haydon. You did speak to him about me doing a runner?'

He opened one eye. 'Yes, sure. No problem. But he insists on seeing you first thing Monday morning about the hammer. At the cop shop, nine sharp.'

'I'm to be *interrogated?*'

'More a case of preferring to get his feet under his own desk, I'd say. He mentioned that the widow had moved back in and, without actually spelling it out, my guess is she's making Kennedy's life a misery. Feels safer in his office, poor sod.'

'No suicide note surfaced yet?'

'Kennedy wasn't sharing any gossip with me, darling. Got quite miffed when I asked – out of purely professional interest, mind – whether he had considered old Max's medical record being a factor. I went on to describe various avenues he might investigate, but he cut me off at the knees damn quick. Doesn't realize what free advice from me's worth.'

Zoe giggled, picturing Kennedy's response to unsolicited advice from a know-all like Haydon. Haydon touting medical tips would merely add to Kennedy's list of unwelcome commentators including Mr Gilbert, the solicitor, and his client, the formidable Desiree Loudon-Fryer.

She sobered, wondering why the inspector was so keen to question her again about Max's hammer and turned to quiz Haydon about this odd conversation of his; but Haydon had crashed out, snoring gently, his breath warm on her cheek.

'By the way,' she whispered in his ear, 'what was the good news?'

Eleven

Ali was sick, worryingly feverish, the thin rattle of his cough painful to hear. Saba was beside herself, smoothing his damp hair and murmuring some dark unknowable mantra.

Haydon got his chum Doctor Hall over to the house first thing and, after a thorough examination and an injection, even Saba relaxed.

'Not too serious, Mrs Raz; children's temperatures rocket and subside just as quickly. Best place for him here. Just keep Ali in the warm – not too hot, mind – and give the little chap an extra pillow and plenty to drink. Keep up the antibiotics and let him up as soon as he's able. Unless you're worried, I'll not see him again until Monday. OK?'

Ali produced a polite smile and Saba beamed. Zoe, hovering in the doorway, gave a sigh of relief, hardly bearing to consider the consequences if Saba had not been snatched from the flooded workshop. Her own unwelcome response to Saba's arrival at Stonecrest skewered her with guilt and, after showing the doctor down to the library to join Haydon for coffee, she ran back upstairs and hugged Saba with genuine affection, and persuaded her to have the scrambled eggs she had left warming in the kitchen.

After Doctor Hall had left, Haydon bullied Zoe to join him for a stroll. The weather had cooled, the air was frosty, the sunshine bouncing off Stonecrest's turrets as if to prove a point about the perfidy of meteorologists as a breed.

They togged up and walked over the fields to Roddy's place, always a happy stamping ground when shaking off the stress of a week in the city. Roddy Meirs lived in one of a pair of former farm cottages next to the barn now converted into the shop. In its heyday Stonecrest must have employed scads of gardeners and farmworkers, but the remaining fields were now merely occupied with Roddy's pigs, who lived the life of Riley, free to roam about, and sleeping in individual huts set in rows like a village high street. Zoe loved watching the piglets scattering about, the sows eyeing them indulgently like mums chatting outside the school gates.

Haydon had regained his cool, his smooth manner sunny as the bright morning itself. Zoe remained anxious, a brief conversation with Nick doing nothing to allay her fears. They arranged to meet at the workshop as soon as she got away from her interview with Inspector Kennedy on Monday morning, but even Nick was despondent about the equipment, the hot table being the most doubtful item for repair.

Roddy had a fire glowing in the kitchen range, the sunshine slanting through the windows leaving pools of brightness on the terracotta floor tiles. The cottage had been roughly redecorated, the adjoining semi kept habitable and warm for Roddy's numerous City friends who came down for weekends. The pigs were raised half a mile away, their noisy lovemaking and summer pong out of range of the farm shop and its environmentally choosy customers.

'Hey, look at you with your long face,' Roddy jeered as he held Zoe at arm's length after giving the customary bear hug. Her eyes filled with tears, two sleepless nights and an uncheering conversation with Nick having stripped away all defences. Roddy's joshing instantly broke up and Haydon burst in with an edited version of the whole saga.

'And the bloody workshop flooded the night after you found poor old Max had snuffed it? Whew!' Roddy said, wiping his brow in a farcical gesture of commiseration. 'It wasn't your day, was it?' he added, and they all three burst into laughter despite themselves, the sheer malevolence of some ancient deities pouring every sort of misery on one poor girl's head ludicrous in its sheer brutality.

'We need a drink,' he said when their outburst subsided. 'A serious slug of alcohol is called for, folks.'

He reappeared from the shed with a bottle of Bollinger and rummaged in the larder for crystal flutes and a jumbo-size bag of crisps. Roddy's home was peppered with remants of his former jet-set lifestyle, a snazzy espresso machine jostling with chipped mugs, and designer toys lurking behind piles of farming manuals. His career as a futures dealer had left an indelible mark: in times of stress champagne was the only cure.

They settled round the kitchen table, chewing over the details of Zoe's ghastly couple of days, Haydon grabbing the limelight, hamming up a glorious mental picture of Saba in beach shorts wading barefoot through the floodwater, hopelessly failing to sweep the stinking effluent out of the door.

'Trouble is, that's not the end of it,' Zoe chipped in, her smile evaporating as she reviewed the situation. 'The little boy's too ill to go anywhere else and Saba urgently needs to find another job, something with accommodation, presumably, so she can keep Ali with her.'

'And we don't really want someone at Stonecrest, do we, darling?' Haydon said. 'We've already got a housekeeper.'

'How's she with figures?' asked Roddy.

Zoe shrugged. 'No idea. But she can use a computer, so she's clearly not dim.'

'I only ask because I need some back-up with the bookkeeping, if she'd like to give it a try. And the cottage next door's free. She could move in and use my office behind the shop. What do you think?'

Zoe looked stunned and glanced at Haydon, who nodded enthusiastically. 'Really, Roddy? You're not just being a good neighbour?'

He refilled their glasses and proposed a toast. 'If that girl's as gorgeous as Haydon says, I don't care if she can't add two and two. She'll soon get bored with being in the backwoods here anyway. I bet she'll give me the old heave-ho within a month.'

Zoe patted his arm. 'Listen, Roddy: it's wonderfully kind of you, but why don't you wait till you've seen her, had a chance to try her out in the office? We're in no hurry to throw her out; it's just not practical to keep her mooching about Stonecrest with nothing to do – we couldn't give Brenda her cards; she's been cleaning the place for donkeys' years, knows every nasty knick-knack.'

'Brenda came with the house. Like Bert,' Haydon said.

Roddy grinned. 'Haydon, I can't *believe* you bought that monstrous mansion lock, stock and barrel including an ex-con and a nosy old busybody like Brenda Clack. Wonderful name for the world's champion gossip, isn't it? Mrs Clack! I couldn't have invented it myself.'

'Changing the subject, Roddy, where's that dog of yours?'

'Teabag? Out rabbiting or cadging from Mary in the shop, I suppose. Do you know, that lying sod of a breeder who sold him to me said, "A Spinoni's a one-man dog." Straight up. Teabag's a lovely dog but offer him a bit of toast and he's anybody's. Mind you, he always turns up at dinner time, knows it's the best billet for miles. The pigs hate his guts, of course.'

Haydon laughed, wishing his own life was that simple. Roddy's hairy hound was just the sort of animal he had always wanted from when he was a kid; but Haydon's life had been mapped out since the cradle, a career in medicine inevitable in the Masure tribe, a clinic amid the exclusive surgeries of Marylebone the ultimate goal.

Haydon swigged the dregs of his champagne and pulled Zoe to her feet.

'Lucky you're not driving,' she said, giving him a push.

'Too damn right. Only driving I'm doing this afternoon is driving my you-know-what where it's nice and warm.'

'Whoa! Hold on, chums. There's poor chaps here who have to work today. Dirty talk like that'll have me touching up Mary Malone behind the counter.'

'Watch it,' Zoe warned. 'Bert's already got the hots for your Mary, so gabby Brenda tells me – threatened to break her bloke's legs if she turned up for work with a black eye again. Incidentally, is it true Bert's been in prison?'

'Our Bert?' Roddy grimaced. 'Local rumour. Probably nothing in it. Didn't the previous owner fill you in, Haydon?'

'Nope. Just said Bert came with the house, no argument. But he's a brilliant security man, teetotal, believe it or not, and originally employed as a bouncer at the Bermuda Club in Clacton. Sounded OK to me.'

'No mention of doing time?'

'Zilch. Anyway, being a decent sort myself, as long as Bert does the job and keeps his dogs off my backside, who am I to baulk at employing felons? Plenty of them employ me,' he added with a bitter laugh.

Zoe pulled him outside, feeling Haydon needed to sleep it off. Poor bloke hadn't had such a brilliant time of it himself, sorting out the workshop fiasco and rescuing the victims. She squeezed his hand, burying her own inside his pocket.

They tramped home via the woods, breathing in the drifting scent of smoke as they passed a garden with its bonfire of autumn leaves. Stonecrest was not a real country house. Most of the estate had been sold off years before and developers had snatched up valuable plots as soon as building permission had been granted. It was secluded enough to give the impression of a rural bolt-hole, yet set bang in the middle of the southern counties' busiest junctions and a stone's throw from the coast. It even had its own helipad, a ludicrous facility as far as Haydon was concerned, a man who hated flying; but a helicopter had clearly been a luxury that Stonecrest's former owner felt he could never do without.

Zoe had occasionally questioned Haydon about this vendor, but he claimed ignorance and the estate agent involved, a man called Freddie McPherson, whom they had bumped into at a New Year's Ball at the Grosvenor, also claimed amnesia about the details of the deal when she pressed him. 'Fair enough,' Haydon had assured her as he had steered her back to the crowded bar; 'McPherson brokers hundreds of deals every year, probably sells his own house so often he can barely remember his current address. Skims the financial tide, like they all do.'

'Walks on water, you mean,' she had said, deciding that Haydon's professional confidentiality was so ingrained it even coloured his private life. The eminent plastic surgeon kept his records so secret that naming names was a painful affliction best avoided.

When they got back to Stonecrest after their walk, Haydon's head had cleared and Zoe had finally relaxed, knowing there was nothing to be gained by agonizing over the possible ruin of her livelihood. She determined to avoid Haydon's invitation to share his bed for the afternoon and, instead, do what she had put off thinking about since Saba's unscheduled arrival: she would unpack the textiles from the Range Rover and assess the extent of the damage. Nick being on hand had been a godsend; he was just the person to treat the fragile fabrics with delicacy, to save what he could and pack the rest with the care of an undertaker laying out a ravaged beauty in her winding sheet.

These comforting thoughts were swiftly poleaxed when she crossed the threshold to encounter none other than Fay Betteridge, their local vicar, presumably making a duty call on the sinners of the parish. Saba hovered in the background, obviously agitated, supposedly having little experience of the female species of priest. Fay Betteridge stood four square in the baronial hall, her bouffant hairstyle stiff as a busby, her smile wide – as Haydon rudely commented – as a coalhole.

'I called in about the altar frontal, Zoe,' she said, 'and this lovely girl told me about your dreadful flood. My dear, what a tragedy! Is our cloth saved?'

Zoe swallowed a sharp riposte, the village altar cloth being on a par with a dishcloth compared with the valuable textiles she was hoping to unpack.

'Oh yes, absolutely, Fay. I kept your cloth here. It's quite safe, almost fully restored, in fact – only needs a refresher in my special sink. I would have taken it back to London with me on Monday to finish off if that ghastly accident hadn't intervened. I'll dab it over here and return it to you next weekend, if that's all right?'

'Shall I make some tea?' Saba suggested.

'Excuse me, folks,' Haydon put in, throwing a kiss at the visitor; 'lovely to see you, Fay. You should come more often – we've got a darling small guest staying just now, but he's feeling groggy, so perhaps another time?'

'Saba's boy?' she replied, turning to halt Saba's escape to the kitchen. 'Getting better I hope?'

'On the mend,' Zoe said, steering Fay towards the sitting room and giving Saba a signal to put on the kettle.

'Perhaps I could pop in again, Saba? Later this week? When he's fully recovered. He's got a birthday on Thursday, you said – I'm sure he'd love to see the dear little school we have in the village. Wonderful headmistress we have. So fortunate.'

Saba nodded, backing off, leaving Zoe to cope with this unexpected visitation.

'Come through, Fay. The altar cloth's in here. I'll show you how far I've got. It's a beautiful piece of work, Victorian needlework at its best.'

Saba brought a tray of tea through to them, pleaded nursing duties upstairs and scuttled out, leaving Zoe to wonder what malign presence had her in its sights, that troubles came not singly but in whole battalions?

Twelve

Roddy came out with a funny remark the other weekend. Haydon had stepped over to the farm shop to choose some steaks, leaving the two of us sitting at Roddy's kitchen table finishing off a bottle of Beaujolais. Now, don't jump to any conclusions: Roddy and I are pals and he has never voiced so much as a jealous word, so this sideswipe at Haydon came right out of the blue.

'I can never make out what it is with you two,' he said; 'you're so utterly unsuited.' When I looked up, all surprised, he went on, 'Well, we all know the guy's a hot-shot surgeon and not short of a bob or two but, Zoe, you're not an ingénue to be taken in by that urbane manner of his, and you're certainly no gold-digger. Yet you're dazzled by the bloke. Does his seamless charm never bother you? Haven't you noticed that Haydon very rarely looks you in the eye?'

I blurted out a jokey response, refusing to take him seriously, but afterwards, knowing Roddy to be on my side, it worried me. What was he trying to say?

On Monday morning Zoe drove back to

London before breakfast, arriving at the police station at nine sharp. The sergeant on the desk looked nonplussed at her insistence on having an appointment with Kennedy.

'The inspector's off on a new investigation, miss. Hang on. I'll see what's what.'

Zoe fumed, cursing Haydon, who had clearly got his wires crossed when he told her to present herself for more questions about the bloody hammer.

The sergeant, a stalwart with grey cropped hair and a friendly face, returned from the back office closely followed by another middle-aged officer Zoe assumed to be part of Kennedy's team. He held out his hand, introducing himself as Trevor Simpson, the Coroner's Officer, explaining as he led Zoe into an interview room that he was finalizing his report prior to the inquest. His manner was affable and, fending off Zoe's contention her appointment was with Kennedy, said, 'No, no. He told me to expect you. The inspector has pretty well tied up all the loose ends, Miss Templeman. He's passed over the file to me now.' He patiently explained his role as Coroner's Officer: 'The nearest thing to a nine-to-five job in the Force,' he cheerfully admitted.

Zoe relaxed, glad to be assured that Max's death was now in the 'Out' tray as far as Kennedy was concerned.

'There isn't much I can add to my

statement,' she said, warming to this soft-spoken copper who seemed to be the tail-end Charlie in Kennedy's investigation.

Simpson went over the sequence of events on the morning Zoe had discovered the body, recrossing the ground Kennedy had established with her.

'You say you were a day late, the deceased having expected you before?'

'Yes. To collect the tapestry. I was taking it to Paris.'

'Yes, I understand that. In fact, I have examined the tapestry myself, Miss Templeman – a wonderful piece of work.'

'You unpacked it?'

'I'm afraid so. The inspector seemed to think it might have a bearing on the case. There was nothing wrong, of course; the paperwork was in order and our nasty suspicious minds regarding the smuggling of illegal items was—'

'Drugs? You suspected Max was using export art works to conceal a traffic in drugs!'

'Not necessarily. But when a death occurs, every avenue must be explored and antique dealers have been known to smuggle out stolen pictures and so on wrapped in carpets. Naturally, I need hardly comment on such nefarious goings-on to a professional person like yourself.'

Zoe tensed, suddenly aware that this

nicely spoken officer was sharp as a tack and no mere rubber stamp for the Coroner.

'What concerned me,' he continued, 'pure curiosity on my part; was how a slight young lady as described by my colleague would actually carry that very heavy item to your car, which was, I understand, parked at the front of Mr Loudon-Fryer's house.'

Zoe relaxed. 'Oh, that's easy. There's a trolley – a converted golf trolley Max keeps in the studio for what he called "light removals". I use it when the need arises and actually it's a terrific help – transports Max's Colombian art works, small sculptures, you name it. Even Max could trundle it about if he had to.'

Simpson jotted a note in his file and went on to question her about Max's finances. Zoe was circumspect, claiming only a vague understanding of her late employer's alleged money troubles. Simpson smiled, agreeing that the intricacies of cash flow in the fine-arts trade were hard to unravel.

'As it happens, Mr Loudon-Fryer's business accounts were in serious disarray, Miss Templeman, and the Coroner will, I've no doubt, regard this problem as a major factor in his suicide.'

'It *was* suicide, of course. What else?'

'The absence of a letter or any warning signs apparent to his wife or colleagues is a consideration, but for a separated couple the relationship of the man and his wife seemed to be amicable and causing no undue stress. In fact, the widow has generously agreed to instruct her solicitor to cover her late husband's debts from her own resources.'

Zoe took a breath, wondering why on earth Max had not asked Desiree to bale him out before taking that final jump to his death. Or perhaps he had. Perhaps the weeping widow's generosity only flowed from remorse. On reflection, Zoe thought not, the woman's frigid personality impressing her after only a fleeting meeting. Even so, if what the Coroner's Officer had let slip was true, Saba's pay-off looked secure, not to mention Zoe's own outstanding account. She tried to concentrate on Simpson's continuing commentary on the case, but she seemed to have lost the thread. Abruptly she interrupted, Haydon's own insistence on a health angle suddenly seeming terribly important.

'Perhaps it wasn't Max's business worries that tipped the balance, Mr Simpson. Perhaps he was terminally sick – had only weeks to live and kept his illness to himself? People do.'

'Of course they do. I come across such secrets all the time in my work. But I can assure you, Miss Templeman, that your anxieties on that score are entirely

97

unfounded. His GP assures me that Mr Loudon-Fryer went to a private clinic for a full check-up only three weeks before his death. The man was, for his age, in perfect health – was assured, after the most exhaustive tests, that he could live to be a hunded.'

'So much for medical prognoses then!'

'I'm afraid we cannot ascribe the poor man's state of depression to health reasons. Was there anything else you wished to add, Miss Templeman? It was very good of you to help me with these small details – gives me a more rounded picture to put to the Coroner. I shall be in touch as soon as a date for the inquest has been fixed.'

Zoe rose, anxious to be free of the seemingly unending investigation of what, to anyone's view, was a straightforward suicide.

As he held the door open for her, she realized he had never mentioned the hammer, the very thing Haydon had said Kennedy wanted to question her about.

'Just one thing, Mr Simpson. The blood on the hammer?'

Simpson laughed, his eyes crinkling in genuine amusement. 'A terrible red herring, Miss Templeman. We pulled the inspector's leg about it this morning when the results came in. The blood on the hammer proved to be from an animal. The lab went through extensive and expensive tests, only to find that the supposed victim of the hammer blow was not human after all. The blood was that of a dog.'

'A dog?'

'Some sort of Italian breed, I'm told. Fairly rare, but hardly worth calling on the expertise of a team of forensic scientists to examine dogs' hairs.' He sobered. 'It remains a mystery; no one seems to know how the blood got there. Probably nothing to do with Mr Loudon-Fryer at all; but we shall never know now, shall we?'

Zoe drove straight to the workshop and found Nick outside stacking sopping cardboard boxes for the refuse collectors. She locked the car and pulled a long face in greeting.

'Nick, you're a saint. Leave all that rubbish and let's go inside and have some coffee – if the electrics are still working?'

'Yeah. It's safe enough now, though brace yourself, Zoe: the place is a shambles.' He grinned, squeezing her arm in sympathy.

He was right. It was a terrible mess, probably aggravated by the frantic attempts by everyone to stem the flow that night. Buckets still littered the floor and an evil-smelling mop was propped against the door.

Zoe leaned against the bench wide-eyed, appalled at the extent of damage brought about in just a few hours. But the coffee helped.

'Did Haydon tell you he lobbed a hundred quid at me before he left, Zoe?'

'Yes, sure. You deserve it. You saved most of the stock, you and Saba.'

'Well, I really appreciate it. He's a bloody decent bloke, that man of yours.'

'Mm.' Zoe thoughtfully sipped her coffee. 'Haydon's been tremendously generous all round. When Saba arrived, Ali was in poor shape. Haydon's paying for a private doctor to put him right, and while Saba's staying at Stonecrest on her own, he's opened an account for her with a local taxi firm so she's able to get out of the house.'

'What about this bung he put my way? Is it a fancy retainer or something?'

'Of course not! Just a big thank-you for baling me out. I'll pay you myself for today's work and any other hours you put in till I get resettled, but if you get another offer in the meantime, you take it, Nick. Goodness knows how long it will be before I'm back on line, and top-class conservators like you are soon snapped up.'

'Well, I'm not skint and I can always do temporary fill-ins at the museum. If you're on the lookout for a new set-up I'd rather wait and work with you, if that's OK?' he said, going on to outline his suggestions for some improvements on their former methods and describing a brand new extractor fan that was in line with new legislation on ventilation in the workplace.

By this time they had both warmed through and Zoe's initial shock had abated. Cheered by Nick's enthusiastic anticipation of a new studio, they set to.

Zoe was privately less sanguine about new premises and Nick's assumption that they would still be together in this new location worried her. Could she afford to rent a new place in the centre? And if she *did* find a suitable workroom and fitted it out, could she still afford to employ an assistant?

Thirteen

They worked all morning clearing the ground floor, putting the valuable fabrics to one side and salvaging what they could. Zoe put through several phone calls, cancelling orders, advising clients of her temporary closure, ordering a skip and speaking at length to the insurance company.

Nick went out to fetch some sandwiches from the corner shop and Zoe took the opportunity to ring Mr Gilbert, the solicitor.

'Ah yes, Miss Templeman. I wanted to speak with you. I have good news.'

'Great! Good news has been avoiding me lately.'

He coughed, Zoe suspected to enhance the dramatic effect of his offer. 'My client, Mrs Loudon-Fryer, has left two cheques with me, one for your own professional services to her late husband and another, a most generous settlement, if I may say so, for Mrs Raz.'

'How much?' Zoe barked, taken aback by Desiree's swift agreement, legal prevarication allegedly being the norm.

'Six hundred pounds for Mrs Raz, if she agrees to sign a letter of confidentiality.'

'Confidentiality about what?'

Gilbert coughed again, lowering his voice: 'Regarding the exact nature of her services, of course. I understand the police have finished questioning her and nothing untoward has surfaced so far, and therefore—'

Zoe stifled a giggle. 'Do you wish Mrs Raz to come to your office?'

'No, no, no. But where can I contact her? She left Bisley Road for your Battersea address, but the telephone at your workshop, which Inspector Kennedy suggested to me, seems to be out of order.'

'Actually, my workroom is no longer functioning, Mr Gilbert. Mrs Raz and her son are temporarily living at Doctor Masure's house in the country.' She explained about the flood damage and spelt out Saba's new address.

'Doctor Masure is a friend of hers?'

'I live with the doctor at Claydon Gardens,' she patiently repeated. 'I gave his London address to the inspector and when my bedsit above the workroom flooded out we offered Saba a place at Stonecrest.'

'Oh, yes. Very kind, I'm sure.' Gilbert sounded unconvinced but hurried on to give the rest of his 'good news'.

'There is a small condition attached to the final settlement of your own arrangement with the late Mr Loudon-Fryer, Miss Templeman. His wife has, as I said, most generously offered to pay off all his outstanding debts, but the poor lady is having problems sorting out the stock.'

'I thought the police had left?'

'Yes indeed. But they left considerable confusion.'

'You should see the confusion in my workshop!' she retorted, knowing full well what bloody Desiree was hanging out for.

'Please! It has been a distressing time for us all and the unfortunate widow doesn't know which way to turn. Can you not find it in your heart, Miss Templeman, to spare her some time?'

'There is the matter of a seventeenth-century tapestry that I am under a considerable obligation to place with the French owner without further delay. What does she say about that?'

'Ah yes. Mrs Loudon-Fryer is very worried about this valuable item in her care. It has been manhandled by the police, I understand. You will wish to check its condition before it is repacked and this is one of the matters on which my client needs to consult with you.'

Zoe could see the writing on the wall. Desiree needed her to help sort Max's stuff and the pay-off for being co-operative was the handing over of the de Maurnay.

'OK,' Zoe wearily agreed. 'I can't work here at present; my place is ruined. I'll give Desiree three days of my time and that's all. I shall expect my cheque up front, of course. Put it in the post today and I'll play the game on your terms. Will tomorrow do for a start? Say nine thirty? I shall have to fit in with the insurance assessor who has promised to come some time this week, but if you're willing to write to Saba at Stonecrest, on receipt of her written assurance that her lips are sealed, the best thing would be to open an account with a building society for her. She doesn't have a bank account and if you set her up with a local branch in Ashford or Maidstone, then we can call it quits, can't we, Mr Gilbert?'

The noise at the other end of the line sounded like a choking spasm, but finally Mr Gilbert framed a suitable reply and Zoe put down the receiver just as Nick arrived back with a six-pack and a couple of jumbo-size ham rolls.

The afternoon went like the wind, Zoe snatching a moment to speak to Haydon at his consulting rooms, who, having heard the news from Gilbert, promised to be home on time for a celebratory dinner.

'Celebrating what, exactly?' Zoe dryly enquired. 'Anyway, I seriously need a shower. This place is filthy, Haydon. You were right. I needed a disaster like this to lever me out of this grot-hole. Nick's going to ask around to see if anyone knows of a cheap place I can rent.'

Nick cycled off at five, the unrelenting rainy season having finally abated, the darkness of the afternoon black as midnight.

Zoe sat at the big table, stirring a mug of coffee and mulling over her options. The hoist could eventually be transferred to another workshop together with the tapestry frame and the big washing sink; but the vacuum hot table was a write-off and Nick was absolutely right in insisting on a decent extractor system, the toxicity of solvents being a hazard in any small working area. A new computer would be useful, but the existing filing cabinet could be recycled, only the contents of the bottom drawer having been irretrievably damaged. She made desultory efforts at clearing the contents, chucking out a bin liner full of sodden receipts and photographs already smelling of mould and incipient decay. She left the bedroom upstairs alone, the wet duvet and pillows heaped in a corner, the doors of the armoire hanging open to reveal shelves full of ruined fabrics.

It was all very dispiriting, the effect of Nick's enthusiasm seeping away as the piles of rubbish grew. She decided to call it a day. The skip was booked for the morning and once the detritus was off the premises the insurance people could get a better view of the expensive pieces of equipment for which her claims would hopefully be accepted.

After a lengthy shower in Haydon's marble bathroom, and having changed into a black silk jersey shift he had bought for her in an effort to see his best girl without the inevitable jeans, she mixed a jug of iced dry Martini and felt quite proud of her efforts to tally with poor Haydon's dream ticket.

She put on some music and lay on the sofa, gazing at her crossed ankles in their fishnet stockings propped on the arm of the couch. Roddy was right in a way. She and Haydon moved in such different circles that adjustments on both sides were inevitable. Zoe reckoned that most of the adjustments were on her side, but Haydon must have been attracted to her gamine style in the first place, so why try to change it?

Roddy didn't see the whole picture, of course. Haydon was so different from any other men in her life that the 'incompatibility' Roddy found incomprehensible was the exciting part. He *was* mysterious, though not in the evasive way Roddy inferred; but Zoe had to admit Haydon's life beyond the hothouse of their relationship was hidden from her. They rarely associated with his medical colleagues, he seemed to have no buddies, and Zoe never tried to drag him along to exhibitions or saleroom previews. Antiques bored him and her tapestries left him yawning, Haydon's flat being as impersonal as his consulting rooms. Perhaps, Zoe conceded, Haydon's total lack of interest in his surroundings here in London, not to mention that overstuffed joke of a house, Stonecrest, was one of his most endearing characteristics. He was focused on his work and the esteem of the medical establishment. In that way he was just like Max, whose standing in the world of antiques had been an obsession. Was it a man thing, Zoe wondered? Could she ever have such tunnel vision? Probably not.

The sound of his key in the lock broke off this pointless appraisal. 'Bugger Roddy,' she murmured. Weren't there enough troubles without questioning the bedrock of her happiness?

Next morning, after checking in Nick to

oversee the stacking of the skip and to alert her at Bisley Road should the insurance assessor turn up out of the blue, she clocked in to help Desiree clear up the muddle and confusion poor old Max had left behind.

Fourteen

Desiree was already at work in Max's study when Zoe arrived, receipts, annotated catalogues and correspondence neatly piled on a gate-legged table set up beside the desk. She had been let in by a fresh-faced young man, presumably the security element, an overdramatic touch Zoe thought, bearing in mind that Max had been trading at half-cock for months. But perhaps Desiree was the nervous type; or there again, perhaps having a nicely muscled chap in attendance gave her a lift.

Desiree rose as Zoe walked into the room, her smile bright as the diamond studs in her ears. She wore her blonde hair tied back in a headscarf, her plain navy jersey and opaque tights reinforcing the impression that she was all togged up for spring cleaning. To be fair, Desiree had a rotten job on her hands. Max had always kept his own files, self-assessment tax returns being a constant cloud on the horizon not helped by the cash transactions and unrecorded expenses that bedevilled his accounts.

They shook hands, wary as two cats on a wall, but Desiree sent Young Lochinvar off to make a pot of coffee, which only went to show that substituting a man for a sullen housekeeper like Mrs Baker had been a smart move. They got to grips with the mountain of paperwork straight away, working together cross-referencing the items thought to be Max's against the numberless objets d'art stacked in the studio. Max's latest foray into the Colombian art market was a complication, Zoe knowing even less than Desiree about these fashionable sculptures and urns.

'Awfully chic, don't you think? Sell like hot cakes in the States, I'm told. The trouble is, there are so few experts who can tell the good ones from the duds, and fakes abound.'

'Did Max actually know much about it?'

Desiree laughed. 'Probably not – relied on a few people he trusted to advise him and after that crossed his fingers for luck. Max was a true believer in Lady Luck. Look, Zoe, I'm a bit fed up with all this paperwork; I've been at it all weekend. Let's have a bite to eat in the kitchen and spend an hour or two this afternoon examining the rest of the stuff in the studio. I'm expecting some people to collect some pieces they left with Max for valuation, and a man from Sherborne's is due at three.'

'The estate agents?'

'Mm. I'm selling up here as soon as I can. Bad atmosphere.' She shuddered and Zoe felt a spasm of pity. Whatever Desiree's failings, Max's hanging himself in what had been their home would have been a traumatic experience for anyone; you couldn't blame the woman for wanting rid of it. She found herself warming to this fabled ice queen.

Later, they manoeuvred the de Maurnay tapestry on to the big table in the studio and unrolled it. The police had unpacked Max's carefully applied wrappings, leaving the hanging jumbled up like a dog's bed.

Zoe found herself hyperventilating, her pulse racing as, unheard, Desiree rattled on in the background. Zoe ran her fingers over the fine threadwork as she peered through Max's magnifying glass, checking for fresh damage. Finally, she straightened, smiling grimly.

'It's OK. No bones broken,' she said with a ragged laugh.

Desiree walked around the table taking in the full picture.

'It's beautiful,' she whispered. 'Quite, quite lovely.'

The tapestry glowed in muted golds and greens enlivened by pale flesh tones and the rare glimmer of bright, bright blue.

'It's Adam and Eve, of course,' Zoe said. 'The provenance proved beyond question it was commissioned by a Cardinal de Maurnay.'

The central figures stood on either side of the tree, Adam eager-eyed, his hand reaching out to take the apple. Eve was curvaceous and mightily appealing, her hair rippling across her shoulders like a cape, a smile playing about her parted lips; but it was the serpent that fascinated Zoe, its lascivious eye picked out in yellow silk, its smile broad as a crocodile's, its coils circling the tree trunk culminating in a smooth head tilted towards Eve in an elegant curve.

'I bet that old cardinal kept it in his bedroom,' Desiree chortled. 'Sexy baggage, isn't she?'

'Absolutely. Still, the wretched Adam's lame excuse has always got up my nose: the woman tempted me. What a cheek! Typical male trick, shifting all the blame.'

'I love it. Pity Max sold it really.'

'It was in a terrible state when he got it, all moth holes and rust marks. Took weeks of work, not to mention meticulous cleaning.'

The doorbell jangled through the house and both women paused, straining to hear. The security man knocked and put his head round the door.

'A Mr McPherson to see you, missus. He said you were expecting him at three but he's early.'

'Show him into the sitting room, would you, Jason? I'll come through shortly.' Desiree flew about tidying her hair and rattling out instruction to Zoe should the other callers come for their valuables while she was engaged with the estate agent. 'You don't mind, do you, sweetie? Everything's packed up and labelled for them, but make sure they sign a receipt before they go – stationery's on Max's desk.'

The door slammed behind her and Zoe was left alone with the tapestry. She examined her repairs through the lens and, finally satisfied, reassembled the discarded wrappings and went off to find Jason to help her to seal it up with bubble-wrap and hessian and heave it on to Max's trolley. Zoe was used to hefting such unwieldy items, but Jason wiped his brow in nervousness as the job was eventually completed. Muted voices floated from the hall, Desiree's fluting accents somehow alien in Max's solid old house. The door opened and they came in, the estate agent close on her heels, his pinstripe suit and college tie smooth as an oil slick.

'Some tea, Jason, for three. In the sitting room. Please?' Zoe smiled, Desiree's wicked grin bringing to mind the curve of Eve's lip as she offered the apple. Jason scuttled out and the man held out his hand to her.

'Hi. It's Freddie McPherson, isn't it? We've met before. Don't you remember? At that New Year's Eve dance. I was with Haydon Masure.'

Desiree looked on, her interest in Max's clever little stitcher growing.

'But of course,' he replied, rattling out generalized enquiries about Haydon, Haydon's country house, Haydon's glowing reputation amongst the smart set, of which, clearly, McPherson counted himself a founder member.

'Actually, Mrs Loudon-Fryer, I won't stay for tea, if you'll excuse me. I've another appointment at four thirty and I'd like, if I may, to come back on Thursday with my photographer and a secretary.'

'Of course. Shall we say after lunch? Zoe and I are hoping to have sorted out Max's things by then.'

He departed in a faint whiff of antiperspirant just as Jason struggled from the kitchen with the tea tray. Zoe was glad they were to have tea in the sitting room, the memory of finding poor Max hanging from the rafter only days before beginning to bear down on her like a migraine.

Desiree poured, passing a plate of biscuits, her own tea pale as amber, a sliver of lemon floating on the steaming surface in contrast to Zoe's two lumps of sugar; but Desiree's manner was all sweetness, the attendance of the personable McPherson and the presumably upbeat assessment of the value of Max's property blowing away any bad vibes.

'Tell me about this Doctor Masure of yours,' she said eagerly.

'We've been together for nearly three years. He's a surgeon, does marvellous work with burns victims.'

'A plastic surgeon?'

'Mm. Though he never talks about his patients. Freddie McPherson probably gave the wrong impression. Haydon hates the limelight.'

'Well, well. How fascinating. But he must be older than you surely?'

'Ten years. We met at a charity cross-country run on Hampstead Heath. I fell badly and twisted my ankle. He took me home.'

'How romantic!'

'Yes, I suppose it was. Anyway,' Zoe briskly concluded, 'that's enough about me. I haven't yet thanked you for coming up trumps with the money for Mrs Raz or for my cheque, which Mr Gilbert says he's putting in the post.'

Desiree seemed not to hear. 'Max was older than me, too. More mature men are so attentive, don't you think?' She blinked back a tear. 'Silly, isn't it, getting all sentimental about an old rogue like Max. But when one has been married for years, worn ragged by a man's shortcomings, one doesn't stop regretting. Hanging himself like that. Over money! Senseless.'

Zoe hesitated, unsure of her status in the shifting sands of this new and puzzling situation.

'You're sure it was his debts?'

'I suppose it must have been, though goodness knows Max's cavalier attitude to money was a source of terrible disillusionment and kept me in a state of anxiety for years. He was a gambler, you see – always was – and winnings are tax-free, which Max considered a terrific one in the eye for the government. Thought himself lucky and mostly came out on top, or so he said. Gambling clubs and casinos, that sort of place. He adored the glamour, the atmosphere. Never betted in a sordid way – betting shops, racecourses or such. I think it must have started on our honeymoon. Monte Carlo. Just a flutter at first, but he was hooked. Compulsive behaviour, my shrink calls it. Max kept it very secret always. His reputation as a dealer was the most important thing and no one guessed he was winning and losing thousands at the tables at the same time. Ultimately, I had to admit defeat. When my mother died, I inherited rather a lot of family money and Max's eyes really lit up. I knew it was time to break away, make a dash for it while my own little fortune was intact. Max was not a grasping man, believe me – a nicer fellow would be hard to find – but he became involved with a bad set and it was a constant fear for me, especially as I was committed to keeping his secret.'

'Have you mentioned all this to the Coroner's Officer? Perhaps he was being threatened by those casino people.'

'Oh no. I couldn't betray Max now. No, he paid his betting debts on the nail, made a clean break before he died. It was the first thing I checked. That's how Jason got to be here. I had had dealings with a detective agency years ago when I first suspected Max was spending recklessly. I thought it was another woman – silly old me. I found the agency in Yellow Pages and asked Mr Perry to make discreet inquiries. He gave me a full report: no lover on the side, just this passion for the tables. I never admitted to Max I had gone to such shabby lengths, but he could see how upset I was and confessed that he had a little hobby, which was the under-statement of the year. I promised never to mention it again – he could handle it, he said. So I banked down my fears and man-aged to cope but, as I said, once I inherited Mummy's estate and became quite comfortably off, it seemed the right time to break away. I still loved him, but I couldn't take any more of living on the edge, waiting for the bailiffs to knock on the door.'

She sighed, sipping her tea, her blue eyes soft with recollection. 'When poor Max ended it all I was terribly shocked – so unlike him: a man who for half a lifetime had lived dangerously with no apparent effect. Something must have tipped the balance. I immediately called my old chum Mr Perry at the detective agency and he suggested I have Jason living in for a bit, as a sort of bodyguard, just until Mr Perry had made certain there were no bad people dunning Max for gambling debts, people who might try to intimidate me. But there were no gambling debts; he assures me that everything had been settled in full just as if Max knew I must be protected, because gaming clubs would be less forgiving than his normal business creditors. I put up a hard front to defend myself, of course, but deep down I never stopped loving that wicked husband of mine.'

Zoe clasped her hands in her lap, dismayed by Desiree's extraordinary disclosures.

'It was only his business creditors who suffered. Poor man didn't want it to come out afterwards, you see, and I shouldn't have mentioned it to you, my dear. But sadly, because it was you who found his body – I'm told Max expected you to be well away from here before he did it – I feel I owe you an explanation. Our little secret.'

Zoe felt herself pinned to her seat, unable to move, knowing she should make some sort of gesture but far from certain whether this unique confidence obligated her to this stranger, made her some sort of accomplice.

Desiree pushed back her hair with a tired sweep of her heavily ringed fingers, the self-imposed responsibility of defending the dead man's reputation stripping away the cold facade she had been at pains to present to society.

Suddenly she darted to a side table and took out a packet from the drawer, turning to pass it to Zoe with an apologetic shrug. 'Sorry, I should have remembered this before – it went right out of my mind.' It was an unsealed envelope clearly addressed to Zoe in Max's bold hand. It lay in her lap like a time bomb, her instinctive recoil anticipating some sort of message from the dead.

'It's quite harmless, Zoe dear. Just a set of house keys Max obviously knew to be yours and put away perhaps a week or two ago. I expect you've been hunting high and low, couldn't think where you'd left them.'

Zoe extracted the heavy bunch of keys in bewilderment, her mind blank. There was no note, no indication when Max had set them aside for her and, as she was about to protest, Desiree stood up, stacking up the tea things, smiling over-brightly as she said, 'Let's get on, shall we? The light's fading. You can leave the tapestry here till you're free to go to Paris, if you like. It'll be perfectly safe now Jason's here.'

Fifteen

When I got back to the flat, Haydon had gone. He had left a note on the hall table saying he was taking some days off to prepare lecture notes for a medical conference and had decided to work at Stonecrest.

First I'd heard about any medical conference. But, to be fair, Haydon's shop talk often went in one ear and out the other. Actually, I was relieved. My stint at Desiree's was proving to be hard graft, not relieved by my mixed feelings about the woman. Her sad admissions about the failure of her marriage struck me as perfectly honest, stripping away my initial repulsion towards 'the widow' who, in order to steel herself against Max's persuasive charms, had given the impression of hardness, which I guessed had put Kennedy's back up for a start. And Max? Who would have believed it? I tried to picture Max at the gaming tables, my only imaginative prop being vague recollections of glamorous scenes in James Bond movies. But Max? Max a persistent lone gambler? I gave up and took myself off to bed early with a supper tray and a historical romance.

The telephone jangled. Zoe glanced at the clock: just after midnight. It was Haydon.

'Sorry, love. Did I wake you? Didn't realize how long I'd been working.'

'Time flies when you're having fun.' Zoe plumped up her pillow. 'How's it going?'

'OK. A rehash of a talk I gave in April. New slides, a couple of fresh case histories and, hey presto, Rio here I come. How are things progressing with Max's stuff?'

'Like untangling spaghetti with chopsticks.'

'That bad? And the wicked widow?'

'As a matter of fact I was wrong about Desiree. And Max. I've come to the conclusion I'm a rotten judge of character. You're not hiding any nasty bits from me, are you, Haydon?' she added with a chuckle.

'Not my style, my darling. What gives with Desiree then?'

Zoe belatedly remembered her promise to Desiree to keep Max's gambling a secret and prevaricated, vaguely citing a change of heart after working with her so closely.

'Intuition? Or a feminist plot to gang up on poor old Max's shade?'

'Neither. Still, I must admit my naive admiration of the old rogue was slightly off-key. Anyway, enough of my boring day; what's the news at Stonecrest?'

'I've tipped Saba out.'

'Jolly good. She's at Roddy's?'

'No. I talked to Rod and we decided it might not pan out. If Saba's no good at book-keeping, Roddy's in a better position to give her the push if she's not squatting in his guest cottage.'

'Sounds sensible. Where's she gone?'

'I've persuaded her to move into the semi attached to Bert's. Mrs Clack used to live there, but she kept complaining about the dogs and decided to move in with her cousin in the village, which suited us.'

'Is it still furnished?'

'Basically. But I've arranged a charge account at French's in Ashford and she's going there tomorrow to pick up a few kitchen things and stuff like that. I said she could help herself to whatever else she needs from the house.'

'Saba's really fallen on her feet then. How's Bert taking it?'

'Loves kids, so having Ali bobbing about suits him fine.'

'Ali's better?'

'In great form. He's a smart little tyke, too

121

molly-coddled by Saba, of course. She never takes her eyes off him, but Fay Betteridge has decided to make Saba her new project.'

'The fallen woman?'

'Doubt whether Saba's confessed her murky past to our bossy vicar, but it suits everyone if Saba's got a friend in the village. Keeps her out of my hair and Fay's no pushover – used to be a social worker in Leicester before she got the call. She's trying to get Saba to loosen the apron strings a bit, let Ali go to the Sunday school, get to mix with other little boys.'

'I think Saba's a Muslim.'

'Really? Oh well, that's Fay's problem. You missing me, sweetie pie?'

'Mm. The bed's full of crumbs and that Elizabethan bodice ripper you recommended just makes me horny.'

'Come down here then.'

'I can't. I've got to hang about for the insurance man, and anyway, I've promised to give Desiree till Thursday evening. Hey, guess what? You remember that estate agent guy we met on New Year's Eve? – Freddie McPherson. He's going to handle the sale of Max's house. He's coming on Thursday to measure up.'

'The widow's no slouch, is she?'

'Get you! In no time flat you've pushed Saba out to one of the gatehouse cottages, fixed her up with a job and shoved her into the arms of the Church of England. That's what *I* call moving.'

They chatted on for a while, Zoe nuzzling down under the duvet, the phone pressed close to her ear, Haydon's gravel tones soothing as any lullaby.

McPherson presented himself on Desiree's doorstep bang on two o'clock Thursday afternoon, a middle-aged secretary in tow, her world-weary appraisal taking in Max's overdecorated hallway with the glance of one who has seen it all before. Desiree rushed forward to take their coats.

'No photographer?'

'We decided that to give your house its due he needs daylight. A full day, in fact. Roger's a perfectionist. He would like to telephone to make an appointment to suit you, Mrs Loudon-Fryer. He'll be bringing his assistant, of course, and you did mention there was no immediate hurry to place the house on the market, didn't you? November's not the best time to sell, what with Christmas coming along, but properties of this calibre are always in demand, so I see no problem there. I've brought some brochures to show you – to give you an idea of the sort of presentation we have in mind.'

Zoe heard their voices recede into the sitting room and she continued preparing a file for Desiree's accountant.

It was growing dark when McPherson and

his secretary breezed into Max's study. Zoe was crouched over the desk under a pool of lamplight, her head glossy as a blackbird's. She shot round, surprised.

'Hey, Freddie! You still at it?'

'Last two rooms. Ruth and I are nearly through. Would it bother you if we continue measuring up?'

'Absolutely not. I could do with a break.' She stretched her arms and stood. 'Tea? Coffee?'

'Two coffees, black, no sugar,' the woman snapped, clearly all too keen to get the job over with.

Freddie butted in, taking the pad from her hand. 'Don't you move, Zoe. Ruth knows just how we like it and she sussed out the kitchen first round.'

The woman left the room, Zoe throwing Freddie a flirty grin. He relaxed.

'Take no notice of Ruth; she's a bloody good typist, just a bit rough at the edges.'

'Boring job, though, trailing behind you with a tape measure.'

'It has its lighter moments and I get to meet lots of rich widows. Last week we busted into the cloakroom at this house in Eaton Square and found the butler and the Filipino maid in flagrante. Ruth never batted an eyelid, just closed the door and stalked into the next room without so much as a blush.'

Zoe giggled. 'While you're here, Freddie, could I ask a favour? My workshop's flooded out. I've got to move. Could you keep an eye open for a shop or a studio or something not too far off the map? To rent. Must be cheap, but I don't mind a short lease or tackling improvements.'

'Fine. Call in at the office and we'll see what I've got on the books. I might have to ask around. Would an office do you?'

'Possibly.'

He passed over his card just as Ruth came back with a tray loaded up with Desiree's best china and a silver coffee pot.

'I brought milk and sugar for you. The man in the kitchen said how you take it.'

'That's Jason.' Zoe poured the coffee and passed Freddie's cup. 'You have met Desiree's security man, I take it?'

'Wise lady, Mrs Loudon-Fryer. These bad lads read the obituary columns you know, make a beeline for the house while the funeral's taking place and clear everything out while the family's away dabbing their eyes.'

Zoe regarded Freddie, unblinking. He was perfectly serious. She blew her nose, masking a terrible urge to giggle. The man was a perfect twit.

Haydon rang again that night, earlier than before, just as she got out of the shower, in fact.

'I'm off for a quick bite with Roddy,' he said. 'Don't ring back; I'm thinking of camping out in the conservatory with my shotgun when I get home.'

'What?'

'My Sherlock Homes bit. I've been seeing a chap lurking down by the gates after dark a couple of times. With binoculars. I've warned Bert to keep his eyes open, but it's a big area for one man to cover on his own.'

'You be careful, Haydon. It's not worth getting involved. Why don't you ring the police?'

'You must be joking. They're undermanned as it is and seeing as I've got my own "gamekeeper", as Bert is laughingly termed, the police would reckon I must be paranoid requesting surveillance on the strength of spotting what was probably only a bird-watcher.'

'In the dark!'

'Nightingales? Owls? These nutty twitchers have night-sight glasses, ninny.'

'Haydon, you know sod-all about bird-watching. You're just trying to calm me down. Look, if you see this bloke hanging about again, ring 999 and get a patrol car out.'

He laughed it off and they reverted to their usual pillow talk, Haydon's voice, Zoe had to admit, being the sexiest this side of a cinema screen.

Sixteen

The post next morning brought a pile of bumf for Haydon and a cheque for Zoe from Mr Gilbert's office – a generous cheque that certainly brightened the prospect of waiting for the insurance assessor to turn up.

The workshop was gloomy and smelt badly, not only of damp but of chemical cleanser, a bottle of which had been accidentally broken during the frantic efforts of Saba and Nick to mop up the water. She sat at the table watching the rain course down the window overlooking the street. Then the insurance inspector arrived and she snapped out of her reverie to let him in.

Mr Patel was a decent sort, no more than thirty years old and with soft brown eyes still capable of compassion despite a job that could only bring him into daily confrontation with disasters. She made some tea and explained the nature of her work, the absolute necessity to maintain clean and dry conditions for the protection of the valuable textiles. He made short work of his tour of inspection, noting the damage to her equipment and smiling encouragement as he jotted figures into his file. He expected her claim to be processed within weeks, he said, and foresaw few problems, outlining his own increased workload as a result of the flooding, which had affected claimants throughout his area.

After Mr Patel had driven off, Zoe decided to make a clean sweep of it and arranged for a scrap dealer to empty the workshop on Saturday, loading up any total rejects into the skip, which was still standing at the kerbside awaiting collection.

Feeling in need of some commiseration, she drove over to the museum to chat with her old friends in the conservation department. Everyone was sympathetic, Zoe's courage as a freelance putting her on a pedestal with the salaried workers who, over the years, had almost come to envy her independence; but going it alone was a risk, and a so-called Act of God in the guise of a flood was a stab in the back no one deserved.

'You could always come back here, Zoe,' the head of department confided. 'I badly need someone with experience. These young girls straight off their degree courses need constant supervision. Think it over.'

Zoe drove back to Haydon's flat with more than enough to think over. Could she buckle down to being part of a team again? Could she afford to set up from scratch, even with the cushion of the insurance payout to look forward to? And in the meantime? She could, on reflection, beg from Haydon. Haydon was a generous soul – never one to begrudge handouts, as his acceptance of Saba had all too clearly demonstrated. But deep down Zoe knew such an appeal to Haydon would be impossible. It would put their relationship on a different footing altogether, destroy the fierce independence she had always guarded, place her in the same slot as the wretched Saba, in fact: an amateur prostitute.

At six she phoned Haydon to tell him the result of her meeting with Mr Patel, glossing over any misgivings about re-establishing her business, enthusing about Gilbert's plump cheque.

'And what's with you? Lecture notes all wrapped up?'

'Hit a few blips, but nothing too serious. You will get down in time for supper, won't you, darling? Saba's put together a real blowout – set the table with flowers and candles, the lot.'

She jerked to attention. 'Saba's cooking for you? I thought she'd moved out.'

'All but. Starts work with Rod on Monday. You sound cross. What's the problem?'

'Nothing. Sorry. Just a bit fed up, I

suppose. I can't drive down tonight, Haydon. I've ordered a scrap dealer to clear the workshop in the morning; there's still a terrible mess down there. You and Saba'll have to have that romantic supper yourselves. Save a doggy bag for me.'

'Tomorrow night then? I could book a table.'

Zoe hesitated. 'Look, Haydon, I really think it would be better if I gave this weekend a miss. I'm not good company just now. What with this flooding on top of what is probably delayed shock after finding Max's body, I need a bit of time on my own. You understand, don't you? Anyway, it'll give you a chance to polish off your lecture notes and we can be together in London next week.'

'Actually, I've taken next week off; I've decided to stay on at Stonecrest for a bit of a break. Venetia's reorganizing my diary.'

'Never known you to be so keen on country air. Why now?'

'Life's more than just work, Zoe!'

'You've been talking to Roddy.'

'Don't worry. I'm not about to chuck it all in to breed pigs. Anyhow, at this time of the year Stonecrest's pretty cosy – ideal for letting the dust settle – and I've still got some work to do on this bloody lecture.'

'And you've got Saba to keep you company. What more could a man ask?'

'Since you've brought it up, Saba's been bobbing about a bit too much for Mrs Clack.'

'No contest there. Brenda Clack's ugly as sin and has the tongue of a viper.'

'Well, Saba certainly gets the rough end of it.'

'Your Mrs Clack prefers to have you all to herself. She misses having someone to fuss round, as we're away most of the time. Did the previous family live there all year, not weekenders like us?'

Haydon ignored this, pressing her to join him. They argued for a bit, Zoe making various excuses, pleading a necessity to trawl some agencies to find new premises. In truth she *was* feeling blue and didn't trust her current touchy mood to survive a whole week in the country with Haydon without a quarrel. Perhaps Roddy was right: perhaps they weren't so well suited as a couple after all. Being in love with a man was one thing; accepting such different aspirations was something else.

Saturday was spent finishing off the clearout. After the scrap dealer had departed with his loot and the skip had been taken away, Zoe finally realized it was the end. She wandered round the empty rooms, turning off lights, stacking the kettle and the rest of the kitchen items in her car. She looked at her watch: just after six. Perhaps this would be a good time to pick up the tapestry.

Jason, Desiree's bodyguard-cum-butler, answered the doorbell, Desiree hovering behind in the hallway silhouetted in the half-light from the sitting room, her hair a bright halo, her face a white mask.

'Oh, Zoe, it's you. Wonderful. I thought it might be that horrible police inspector again.' Jason shut the door and Zoe found herself unexpectedly clasped in Desiree's tremulous embrace.

'Kennedy? He's still sniffing round? What for?'

They sat on the sofa, the flames of a log fire bringing a needful liveliness to the big empty room. The television flickered, its sound muted, Zoe guessing that the widow's 'bad vibes' were getting to her, sitting alone in Max's house. She wore a long velvet skirt and a chiffon blouse, Zoe in her inevitable jeans and sweatshirt.

'I won't admit anything to the police about Max's gambling, of course, and you mustn't mention it either, Zoe, but that beastly detective's been questioning people in the trade. A friend of Max's rang me, a big noise on the committee, and told me Kennedy had been to his office making enquiries. Max was very proud of his standing with the Association; these innuendos would have mortified him.'

'Does Kennedy have any grounds for

these enquiries? When I spoke to the Coroner's Officer, he gave the impression the file was all but closed.'

'Oh yes, I'm sure it is. I was told the body is likely to be released next week, but it will be awkward if this inspector person implies at the inquest that Max's dealings were in some way questionable. Really, it would be too cruel to cast aspersions on his honesty now! Can't they leave the poor man in peace?'

'I'm sure you're worrying about nothing, Desiree. Kennedy's no sort of financial genius. He probably finds it difficult to comprehend that a man with all Max's assets – an unmortgaged house furnished with priceless art objects – would kill himself over money. Yes, I know he had a cash-flow problem, but his gambling debts were covered and Max wasn't on the brink of bankruptcy, was he? Lots of dealers are experiencing a rough ride just now, but the trade's flexible, used to ups and downs. In Kennedy's rat-like brain the figures just don't add up, that's all. Our Inspector Plod likes things nice and tidy and there being no suicide note leaves him room to wonder. Try and forget it, Desiree; it'll all work out in the end. Tell you what, let's treat ourselves to a night out. Haydon's away and I've had a lousy day clearing out the last of my stuff from the workshop.'

Desiree perked up, patting her hair in an idiosyncratic gesture Zoe recognized as one of her less endearing traits.

They drove to Chelsea in the runabout, Zoe choosing a bistro off the King's Road, where early diners jammed in with the first-showing cinema crowd and where Zoe's admittedly work-stained jeans were of no consequence. Desiree glanced round wide-eyed, her unfamiliarity with the seedier end of town clearly firing her imagination. Service was brusque but cheerful, but they were into their main course before Zoe relaxed sufficiently to share her anxieties about setting up on her own again.

'Won't this doctor friend of yours put up the money?'

'Sure to. If I ask him. But I'm used to being independent, see? I'd rather keep my options open. Haydon's staying in the country at present, and it gives me a chance to sort out my priorities. Saba's looking after him.'

'Max's housekeeper?' Desiree squealed.

'Sure. Why not? Haydon's fixed her up with a cottage on the estate, and she starts a new job on Monday.'

'But I thought she was beautiful?'

Zoe laughed. 'Well, yes. Absolutely gorgeous. But so what?'

'Do you trust him alone with her like that? In the country with no other live-in staff?

It's Max all over again, Zoe. You should get rid of that girl; she's bad luck.'

'For heaven's sake, Desiree! What on earth gives you that idea?'

'A rich older man? A man of experience? Max and I came from the same background but, if I may say so, you're an artist, not the sort of girl to be moulded into a trophy wife. Does your Haydon always choose unusual lovers? Has he ever been tempted with a black girl before?'

'Saba's not really black. And she's not some sort of oriental temptress. You're being old-fashioned, Desiree. I don't expect Haydon to marry me, you're right. I wouldn't fit in with his stuffy medico fraternity; his sister Meriel has hinted as much dozens of times.'

'Why hasn't he married before?'

'Too busy carving out his career, I suppose. He's not bi-sexual, if that's what you're thinking. Haydon's had lots of girl-friends before me – just doesn't want to settle down. Actually, you're right about one thing: he must be attracted to oddballs to live with me.' She laughed, leaning back to let the waiter remove the plates, shoving Desiree's novelettish notions to the back of her mind.

The rest of the meal progressed with no more contentious subjects coming up; Desiree insisted on paying.

'Please. Let me, Desiree. A thank-you for

that generous cheque I got from Mr Gilbert this morning.'

Desiree brushed aside Zoe's remonstrations, beckoned the waiter, then delved into her handbag and made out a cheque, which she passed across the table.

'For you, Zoe dear, to cover the cost of taking Max's tapestry to Paris. It was his last transaction, poor love.'

The waiter came back with the bill and Desiree gave him her platinum card together with a fiver as an extra tip, her smile sweet as a nut.

'You really are too kind, you know. Can you really afford these mad gestures?'

Desiree patted her hand. 'Trust me. Now where were we?'

'Look, while we're being so frank with each other, are you sure Kennedy's not still worrying about that hammer? The blood-stained hammer found in Max's car?'

'It wasn't human blood, for heaven's sake.'

'No, the Coroner's Officer told me. But a hammer, Desiree? Honestly, it does *not* sound like Max, does it? Whose was it?'

'Oh, it was Max's all right. I told that nice man from the Coroner's office why Max always kept a hammer in his car and he said he would strike all mention of it from his report. It's irrelevant to the inquest and—'

'Irrelevant?'

'Quite irrelevant,' Desiree went on. 'You

see he was in a train crash a couple of years ago. A serious accident – many people were killed – you must have read about it at the time. Poor Max was travelling to the West Country for a sale and got trapped in the wreckage for over an hour. Fire broke out. Traumatized the man for life. Afterwards he vowed never to go by train without his own hammer in his briefcase so he could smash his way out if ever it happened again. Kept it in the car at the ready.'

'Now why didn't our Inspector Kennedy think of that?' Zoe said with a grin.

Seventeen

Zoe spent the day driving around the inner suburbs following up some tips Nick had thrown out about possible workshops. One was definitely tempting: a unit in a co operative set-up in a former laundry. The tenants were all connected with arty projects, including one man, a decorative metalworker, she had known at college. There was adequate parking in a cobbled yard, a caretaker who did all the dirty work and locked the big iron gates each night, and a group of independent jobbers who were

137

people she felt sure she could get along with. Trouble was, the rent was twice what she had been paying in Dyson Street and the unit did not include living accommodation, which clearly threw her in with Haydon on a permanent basis, a prospect, that she guessed would make for tension all round.

She drove over to McPherson's agency and collected the sheaf of possibles his assistant had put aside for her. Zoe sat on a bench by the window, sifting through the brochures, growing more depressed by the minute. She strolled over to a display board and examined the selection of properties for sale. No doubt about it, Sherbornes was an agency well out of her league. She thanked Freddie's girl and walked back to the car; but just as she was about to start the engine, her mobile phone jangled the demented call tone she kept meaning to zap: the 'Flight of the Bumblebee' was something that in her present depressed state of mind was no longer amusing.

'Zoe, thank goodness you're there; I thought you might have gone to Paris. It's Desiree. Could you come round? I can give you lunch. Inspector Kennedy's just rung through to say he's coming over and I just can't face up to him on my own.'

'Desiree, calm down. He's probably only making a social call. Just to let you have the

138

date of the inquest, I expect. Why are you so scared of the man? He's got nothing on you.'

'Well, I haven't been entirely frank about Max's gambling, have I? Perhaps he's found out. Perhaps he's checked on Jason and knows I employed Mr Perry to investigate Max for myself, thinks I'm hiding something and—'

'OK. OK. Cool it, Desiree. I'm on my way.'

Desiree was certainly agitated, raking her fingers through her hair at a rate of knots. They went into the sitting room, the remains of a log fire now only ashes in the grate, a vase of drooping roses scattering petals on the dusty surface of the coffee table.

'Isn't it time you got a temporary cleaner, Desiree? I expect Jason could fix something if he asks at the corner shop. A real Mr Fixit, that newsagent – knows everyone who works in the street.'

Desiree looked shocked, nervously glancing round at the room as if the disorder was something she hadn't noticed before.

'Oh no, Zoe. I couldn't possibly have a stranger in the house, not with all Max's lovely things about.'

'Well, something's got to be done: you'll be showing prospective buyers round next. And what about the funeral? Are people coming back here afterwards?'

'Oh yes. Of course. It's on Friday. I fixed it up today. I've been meaning to phone you, but there's been *so* much to think about.' She drew Zoe to the sofa and rattled out a whole raft of arrangements she had made, including booking the caterers.

'You're expecting a crowd?'

'Absolutely. Didn't you see the announcements in today's *Times* and *Telegraph?* Max had so many friends I'm sure the church will be packed.'

'I don't check the obituaries. You'll still need a bit of a spring clean, Desiree. Can I help? I'm really quite handy with mops and buckets these days.'

'Oh no, dear; don't worry about it. I'll get my woman who cleans the flat to pop over. Someone I can trust.'

Jason came in with a tray of sandwiches and a pot of coffee, but clearly Desiree had already been at the gin and, when he had gone, she pressed Zoe to join her in an aperitif.

'Jason gets these sandwiches for me at Harrods. I phone through and he collects my order each morning with any other shopping I need. He's really a sweet boy; I shall miss him.'

'How long can Mr Perry spare this bodyguard-cum-butler of yours?'

'As soon as the funeral is over I shall move

back to my flat.' She shivered. 'This house gives me the creeps and once Jason's gone I would be here alone.'

'The agency will take care of viewings for you?'

'Mr McPherson has promised to deal with it personally and after the inquest, when everything's settled, as soon as Mr Gilbert gives the go-ahead, I shall dispose of all Max's special treasures, just leave the house looking lived-in. It *is* a nice house, isn't it, Zoe? I was very happy here once.' She topped up her glass and Zoe passed the plate of sandwiches, anxious that Desiree's drinks should be mopped up before Kennedy dropped in.

'What time's the inspector due?'

'Not till two, but I needed to see you, Zoe. Did I drag you away from your work?'

'I'm in limbo at present. No work. No place to work. No Haydon.' She went on to explain Haydon's continued absence from London, admitting a certain anxiety about the state of play at Stonecrest.

'The regular housekeeper, Mrs Clack, is not happy. Saba's been making herself useful about the house – too many cooks spoiling the broth, I imagine; and if Mrs Clack gives notice, it will be just like Haydon to offer the job to Saba on a permanent basis. She's already bedded down in the cottage adjoining Bert's – the bloke who

141

looks after the house when we're not there. Saba's an expert at fitting in anywhere...'

Her voice trailed off on a vague note of complaint, the exact nature of her disquiet far from clear even to herself.

'Didn't I tell you so?' Desiree crowed. 'Didn't I say that woman was bad luck? See if I'm not right. By the way, you never told me how Max found her, did you? She doesn't sound like the usual agency staff I'm used to. And with a child in tow, too – poof!' Desiree's cheeks puffed out in comic dis-approval and Zoe pressed her to accept a cup of black coffee, saying, 'Take no notice of me; I'm just a bit fed up today. Tell me about the funeral.'

Desiree elaborated, even down to detailing the menu.

'Three o'clock on Friday at St Mark's in the Square. Full mass, of course, followed by—'

'I didn't know Max was religious.'

'Well, I suppose he wasn't, but my family will expect it. Very high church,' she said with a lift of the eyebrow. 'We were never divorced, Zoe, just separated. Max was what they call "lapsed", as it happens, but Father James has been generous, accepted my proposals with enormous kindness. Friends will come back here for the buffet, and I shall go home at the weekend. You won't desert me when all this is over, will you,

Zoe? We will remain friends? Perhaps you and Haydon will join me for dinner at the flat when the inquest is over and done with? See me in my *normal* surroundings. I shall be better then, shall pick up my little routine, be able to put these last days in perspective, draw a line under my life with poor Max.'

'Actually, once the inquest is over and I'm free to go, I shall have to take the tapestry to Paris without more delay. Monsieur de Vries is getting impatient. In fact, I may stay on in France for a few days, do the rounds of the foreign dealers I know. And there's my father, of course. I've been neglecting him lately. Not to mention Christmas looming up, by God.'

'Your father lives in London?'

'No, Wales. Poor man's in this nursing home in Wrexham. Alzheimer's, sadly. Mother left us when I was four and a half and so Pa and I have propped each other up ever since. Till I left home to go to college, that is.'

'I am so sorry, Zoe. And there's me going on about my own troubles. Is your mother still alive?'

'No idea. She was what she called "a free spirit". Actually a drugged-up hippy, I imagine. I remember her, of course, her weird clothes and all that vegetarian food she used to serve up, lentils and tofu mostly.' She laughed. 'Suddenly Mother took off to India, to find herself, as they say – joined some nutty commune and never sent us so much as a postcard after that.'

'Poor little scrap you must have been.'

'Not really. Pa was a teacher, so home in the school holidays and always a rock. That was his trouble: not exciting enough for Mother. But even so he didn't deserve to end up in a local authority home with a lot of geriatrics.'

'You couldn't have him live with you and Haydon?'

'No way. But the home's very "homely", and Pa always seems content when I visit. Not often enough, of course, but as he rarely recognizes me when I do arrive, I don't feel *too* guilty.'

'He has no lapses? Times when he remembers what used to be?'

'Not so often now. I expect he's tranquillized when I visit, but I go away feeling he is as happy as he can be and physically he seems fine. His old pupils sometimes call in and funnily enough he remembers their names more easily than mine.'

The doorbell rang, Desiree jerking up, spilling coffee in her saucer. Jason did the honours, showing Inspector Kennedy into the sitting room with a flourish, clearly his stint in the Loudon-Fryer household giving him airs.

144

Zoe excused herself, taking her coffee into the study, giving Desiree a thumbs-up behind Kennedy's back as she left the room.

His chat with Desiree was brief, barely ten minutes at most, and Zoe tensed, hearing his voice in the hall, waiting for Jason to show him out. But Kennedy was not leaving. He knocked on the study door and entered before Zoe had a chance to catch her breath.

'Miss Templeman. Glad to catch you. Just a quick word.'

Zoe half-rose, feeling her throat tighten, her response, when it came, strangely hoarse.

'We're just tying up the loose ends for the inquest. You will be called to repeat your statement for the Coroner, of course. Thursday week is a tentative date to put in your diary.'

He wore a different suit. Tweedy. Baggy at the knees but with the undeniable air of a good tailor having had his hand in it somewhere. Zoe wondered if the inspector trawled the better-quality charity shops in Kensington, where she herself had seen racks of dead men's suits for sale just like this one.

'How can I help you, Inspector?'

'I'm surprised to find you still here, Miss Templeman. And so friendly with Mrs Loudon-Fryer too. Hardly your type, if I may say so.'

Zoe coloured, losing her carefully constructed cool; but before she could extirpate this barely concealed cynicism, Kennedy continued, his eyes steely.

'I'm still baffled by the lack of a suicide note. I gather from Mrs Loudon-Fryer that there is to be all but a requiem mass for the deceased on Friday. Presumably his widow's keen to buy him a place in Heaven. In my experience, religious qualms sometimes provoke relatives into mistakenly believing themselves to be protecting the reputation of the suicide victim by destroying the suicide note – the man's dying confession, perhaps. Do you know of any such cover-up, Miss Templeman? As an old friend of the dead man and a new friend of his wife's I hope you would not have been so silly as to involve yourself in such an illegal act as burning important papers, for instance? There were fresh ashes in the grate when I arrived that our lab people have regrettably been unable to reconstruct, but I would hate to think an intelligent girl like yourself would get involved in any conspiracy with the widow.'

'What do you mean, conspiracy?'

'Let me sketch out a little scenario. You arrive here early, Miss Templeman, to find your employer dead at the end of a rope, the room littered with papers including a letter addressed to his wife. You telephone the wife whom, contrary to your statement, you had in fact met on several occasions, and she tells you to open the letter. It describes various activities the family would not wish to emerge in a public investigation, these alleged improprieties backed up by correspondence littering the room. Mrs Loudon-Fryer, a quick thinker, orders you to burn the letter together with anything else that could blacken his reputation. Only then do you rush out to ring the bell at the front door and rouse the housekeeper, Mrs Raz. By the time the police arrive, the evidence is destroyed, Mr Loudon-Fryer's reputation is intact and the widow generously rewards you for your swift action.'

Zoe leaned back, giving the inspector a slow handclap.

'Very good. You should give up sleuthing, Kennedy, and write screenplays for those ghastly cop shows on television.'

'You deny everything?'

'There's nothing to deny. I came here. I found Max's body and I rang 999. I never set eyes on Desiree until after his death and any money she paid me was for my services since the tragedy plus a settlement for my outstanding account, including expenses to transport the tapestry to Paris.'

He sighed. 'The Coroner's Officer is satisfied, but I have to admit to you, Miss

Templeman, that I remain sceptical.'

'Next you'll be saying he was murdered.'

'Not as fantastical as you might think. If a victim is drugged, constructing a hanging to seem like suicide is by no means impossible. But no, I'm not suggesting he was murdered. What I am concerned about is lack of motive. Money troubles? Certainly. But not insurmountable in Loudon Fryer's financial bracket. A death wish following a doctor's diagnosis of a fatal illness? Entirely ruled out: the man was good for another twenty years. His doctor is adamant that no such bad news drove the man to hang himself. And no, he was not druggy – not even drunk. Your late boss was sober, calculating and, to my mind, had planned his exit meticulously. You, Miss Templeman, upset the apple cart by not calling in for your tapestry the day before, as he had arranged. Arriving *after* the suicide opened up a whole new set of possibilities, and this case will remain in my mind, whatever the Coroner decides, as a suspicious death.'

'Look, check the outgoing phone calls that morning if you think I blew the whistle to Desiree before ringing 999.'

'We've done that. There only remains your mobile phone. Next on my list.'

Zoe drew back. 'The number's on the business card I gave you.'

Thoughtfully, he tapped his temple with

his pen.

'Your workshop flooded, I hear. Bad luck. Expensive business, I bet. Fortunately, you've got a new rich ladyfriend to lean on.'

'Desiree's alone here. She hasn't anyone else.'

'Still think it's a funny sort of friendship: an all-but penniless art restorer and a middle-aged widow.'

'I thought they gave police officers lessons in tactful questioning these days. Loose talk like that could get you into trouble, Kennedy. If I were you I'd stop badgering the witnesses and get on with improving all those crime clear-up figures the government's shouting for.'

He smiled wearily, buttoned the tweed jacket and, turning away, raised his hand in a mock salute before closing the door behind him.

Zoe slumped into Max's chair, wondering what all that was about. Desiree burst in, wild-eyed.

'What did he want?'

Zoe roused herself, smiling wanly. 'Just loose ends, Desiree. Nothing to worry about. He hasn't anything new, just making sure his case is watertight before the inquest. Look, I've got to go. Ring me on my mobile if you get any more fall-out. Better still, ring Mr Gilbert, let him handle it.'

Zoe grabbed her coat and bag from the

bench in the hall and made a swift exit, her mind still churning with Kennedy's ridiculous twist on events.

She busied herself for the rest of the week searching out suppliers of new equipment and viewing premises, estimating the astronomical cost of starting from scratch again. Well, not quite from scratch. 'Still got all my contacts,' she comforted herself, 'the goodwill of people like de Vries.'

On Thursday night, after a long, exhausting day, she almost forgot to ring Haydon at Stonecrest. But there was no answer.

It was four a.m. before she heard his voice, his words stabbing her awake in an instant.

'You must come straight away. There's been a terrible accident. Bert's cottage is gutted.'

'What?'

'The firemen are sifting the wreckage now. He's dead, Zo.'

'Christ! How did it happen? What can I do?'

'Just get down here for God's sake.'

'And Saba? Is she safe?'

'Saba and the kid were here all night. Their place is damaged too, but Bert's was a fireball, they say.'

'Why?'

'I just told you. Some sort of accident. A fag end, most likely.'

'No, I meant why wasn't Saba sleeping in

150

the cottage? She could have raised the alarm.'

'She was scared. Some sort of premonition, I suppose. Bert mentioned about me seeing that man hanging about and she bottled out.'

Zoe felt an icy finger touch her spine.

'Zo? You still there?'

When she found the words, they came slowly, with careful deliberation.

'I have to be here, Haydon. There's nothing I can do. It's Max's funeral today and I promised Desiree I'd help. I'll drive down first thing Saturday morning.'

He slammed down the receiver, his response, she admitted, being more than fair. But why was Saba not in her own bed? And if Bert had accidentally set light to the cottage, why couldn't Haydon, a man professionally inured to emergencies, deal with it on his own?

Eighteen

Max's funeral was, as Desiree predicted, well attended, including those who normally made a quick start for their weekend retreats staying on to give the old scoundrel a decent send-off. Even the sun put in an appearance, the last wintry rays gamely penetrating St Mark's plain windows, shafting dusty columns of sunlight on to the bier.

The hymn-singing was ragged, the congregation a mixed bag of dealers, runners, picture framers and auctioneers, plus a smartly dressed coterie bunched around the widow who, Zoe concluded, could only be this high church family circle of which Desiree boasted.

Zoe sat at the back with Jason, who had been ordered by his boss, Mr Perry, to keep his eyes peeled. Quite what sleuthing experience Jason would gain from his surveillance of this motley crowd was not altogether clear, but as Inspector Kennedy had also found time to mount a similar and, to Zoe's mind, equally pointless appraisal of the mourners, perhaps there was something in it after all.

Fortunately, Kennedy did not trail along after the others to the house later, but slipped away as the coffin was being borne off to the burial plot for a brief ceremony.

The house had been spruced up with fresh flowers and a liberal dose of beeswax, the studio door locked against the curious and a covey of waitresses flitting from room to room with trays of drinks. The decibels rose and Zoe retreated to the study, where men in dark suits wandered about in twos and threes eyeing Max's furniture and pictures with barely concealed avarice. The house was brightly lit against the darkening afternoon and, as the wine circulated and the guests relaxed, the air of gloom lifted, the atmosphere being lightened not least by Desiree's determination to make Max's farewell a success.

She wore black, of course, but widow's weeds only seemed to accentuate her English-rose complexion, the pale oval of her face framed by hair smooth and golden as a helmet. Desiree left her haughty relatives to fend for themselves and fluttered from room to room greeting Max's associates with a warmth that might have puzzled Kennedy had he dared to infiltrate this inner circle, his preconceived notions about the bereaved wife being challenged by a performance that was patently sincere. Jason hovered at her elbow, speaking to no one, his presence never explained, his duties construed as being a cross between butler and Rottweiler.

Zoe filled her plate at the buffet table and found herself beside Larry Buxton, a north-country dealer with whom she had done business from time to time.

'Hi, Larry. Well off your usual beat, aren't you? Making a weekend of it in the big bad city?'

'Saucy cow. We provincials aren't stuck in primeval mud, darling. I was in town collecting some nice stuff from a pal of mine in Notting Hill and he suggested we gave poor old Maxie a bit of a wake.'

'Tremendous turnout. Had you known Desiree before?'

'Never met her. I thought they were divorced.'

'Not quite.'

'No kids?'

'None. I've been helping Desiree tidy up. She's taken a bad knock over this, Larry. Don't be deceived by her smooth manner.'

'And you too, poppet. Jimmy tells me you found the body. What do you think tipped him over the edge?'

'God knows. Money troubles, most likely. Did you hear about my workshop being flooded?' She told him the whole story.

He listened attentively, his manner grave. 'What beastly rotten luck. Still, you'll have no trouble picking up the pieces, will you? Not like that poor bastard Chris Mayhew.'

'The Chester dealer? He's had a flood at his shop?'

'Worse. Didn't you read about it? I suppose random muggings don't rate much coverage down here.'

'I never seem to get around to buying papers. He was mugged, you say? Badly hurt?'

'Murdered. Stabbed while out jogging one morning. Mind you, he was always a flash bugger, decking himself out with a gold Rolex with diamonds studded round the watch face and a fancy bracelet. We used to pull his leg about it, called him Goldfinger – just asking for it these days, running about the woods sparkling like a Christmas tree. Didn't you ever do any jobs for Mayhew, Zoe?'

She shook her head. 'Saw him around pretty often – he used to bring clients to the West End previews quite a bit, foreign buyers mostly.'

'Not wishing to speak ill of the dead, but Chris Mayhew wasn't too popular with us lads in Cheshire. All matey one day and cut you dead the next. Getting too big for his boots. Still, being stuck like a pig and left to bleed to death on a muddy track at six in the morning's a miserable way to go.'

'When was this?'

'Couple of weeks ago. Made big headlines in the local press at the time.'

'No arrest?'

'A police mate of mine working on the case tipped me off on the q.t. to watch my back. Big-time dealers might be considered easy targets if they get clean away with this one.'

'Just for a pricey gold watch?'

'No. Tyre tracks near the mugging tie up with matching tracks outside his cottage. The place was turned inside out. Seems the robbers pinched his keys off the body and did the house while they were about it.'

'Much stolen?'

Larry shrugged. 'No idea, apart from a few items for the trade to watch out for listed on a police handout. But the cops will soon catch up with them once the killers try to sell the stuff. All museum quality, at a guess. Chris had done deals with agents in the States, was getting quite a reputation for himself for such a young guy who crowed about having started out as a double-glazing salesman.'

'Not married?'

'Lived alone – not gay from all accounts, but not much of a one for the ladies. Meant to spend all his hard-earned cash strictly on himself.'

Zoe changed the subject, attacked by an urgent desire to escape all this death talk. First Max. Then Bert. And now this Chris Mayhew person. It was as if she were caught up in a ripple effect spreading in ever-widening circles, killing people she hardly even knew.

She spotted Freddie McPherson signalling to her from the hallway and excused herself, hoping to find a more cheerful companion than Lugubrious Larry.

Freddie grabbed her arm, steering her to the bench in the hall. He wore a black tie and a serious expression and her hopes of the mood lightening evaporated.

'Nice to see you here, Freddie. Your feet under the table with Desiree already?' she tartly added.

'It's no joke for the poor woman hostessing a funeral when your ex has hanged himself.'

'No ex. Just separated.'

'Yes, I know; Mr Gilbert filled me in. She asked me to come today to lift the load a bit.'

'Me too. But I must admit I've been steering clear of the relatives. A deadly-looking bunch, only here to size up Desiree's assets, if you ask me. But let me introduce you to some of the dealers, Freddie. They're nice people, and since the wine's been circulating they've brightened up no end;

you'll like them.'

'Actually, I'm not stopping, thanks all the same. I just wanted to have a word with you about this terrible fire at Stonecrest.'

'You heard?'

'I got a phone call – I am the agent, remember. The owner rang to ask me what was going on.'

Zoe looked blank. 'The owner? What *are* you talking about, Freddie?'

'The owner. Mrs Redford. Stonecrest's owner.'

'I thought Haydon had bought the place.'

Freddie lowered his voice. 'Haydon didn't want it broadcast, but he just rents. Mrs Redford asked him to occupy it for her – for a peppercorn rent, jammy blighter. He never told you?'

Zoe shook her head. 'I'm going down there tomorrow.'

'I'd steer clear if I were you, Zoe. And tell Haydon: if he's got any sense, he'll do the same.'

'But the police are there. The security man died in the fire.'

'It was arson.'

'What! Who told you that?'

'Mrs Redford. She's got feelers everywhere. Someone poured some sort of accelerant through the door; the cottage went up in minutes. That poor sod didn't stand a chance.'

'But who would do such a thing? Bert was no threat to anyone.'

'The prime suspect is a farmer from the village, apparently. Suspected Haydon's man was having it off with his wife and beat her up on a regular basis. This chap – I forget his name – and Haydon's caretaker had words about the wife and the police are questioning him at the station.'

'Hell fire. No wonder Haydon wanted me down there straight away.'

'He told you?'

'Only that there'd been a fire and Bert had died in the blaze. But that was early this morning; Haydon wouldn't have known about any arson or love-triangle complication then.'

'Have you two not spoken since?'

Zoe looked embarrassed. 'We have been a bit semi-detached lately. He tells me to jump and I instinctively baulk at the fence. Sheer bloody-mindedness on my part but,' she shrugged, 'that's me all over.'

Freddie frowned. 'On second thoughts you'd better get down there, Zoe, and tell Haydon yourself – he's *got* to clear out. It's really dangerous, believe me. He should have realized that the deal Mrs Redford was offering was too good to be true. She just needed a nice respectable tenant to sit on the nest for a while and I was merely called in to tie the ribbons on their agreement.

Look, Zoe, call in and see me next week when you get back and I'll let you know if I find out anything else.'

'Where is this Mrs Redford?'

'Rio.'

'Is she coming back?'

'No chance. Just take my word for it: Stonecrest is bad news. Tell Haydon to get out quick and let Mrs Redford handle the police – she's got plenty of experience, I promise you.'

Nineteen

I didn't stay long after that. Desiree seemed to be coping more than adequately and it looked as if the wake was shaping up to continue all night. I even caught Larry sidling up to Desiree and pulling her aside to discuss a crystal epergne he'd set his heart on and I bet he wasn't the first to get his bids in while the tears were still fresh on the widow's cheeks. I left a message with Jason to say I had an emergency at home and would ring Desiree later, deciding, despite Freddie's admonitions, to stick to my original plan and postpone driving down to Stonecrest till the morning.

Truth was, Freddie's indiscretion about the

real ownership of Stonecrest had knocked me for six. Not that I cared twopence about the place, but why had Haydon lied about it? Also, a maggot of suspicion wriggled in my brain about Saba's lucky escape in all this. Why was she sleeping in the big house? Had she been involved in setting the fire? – tipped off the potential thieves that the place was guarded by a security man and that once he had been dealt with Stonecrest would be wide open for a full-scale robbery?

I needed time to get my head around this and you know how it is once you know your man has lied to you: mistrust strains the heartstrings.

Zoe drew up at the main gates just before ten next morning, the drive blocked by a police car.

'Yes, miss?'

'I'm Doctor Masure's girlfriend. He's expecting me.' She gave her name and Haydon's London address.

'There's been an accident, Miss Templeman. I'll have to phone through.'

Eventually she was allowed to drive on after the constable had noted the number of her car, but only as she passed the smouldering ruins of Bert's cottage did the full impact of the tragedy hit home. She wondered about the dogs, but who could possibly take them on even if they had escaped the blaze?

161

Two more cars stood in the drive, unmarked police vehicles, she assumed. She opened the front door with her key and heard voices issuing from the library, Haydon's and two others, their interrogation of the poor guy all too audible. She fled to the kitchen, which was mercifully empty, and made herself a pot of coffee.

After half an hour Haydon appeared in the doorway, his face haggard, his exhausted features striking her as showing his age, something that had never bothered her. She could almost swear that there were grey strands at his temples that had not been there before; but would shock strike so cruelly overnight? She rose and held out both arms, and they clung together for a long moment, unspeaking.

She poured a mug of coffee for him and he slumped at the table. 'It was arson, Zoe. Petrol poured through the letter box they say.'

'Where's Saba?'

'Fay Betteridge burst in as soon as she heard the news and whisked Saba and Ali back to the vicarage.'

'The police let her go?'

'Sure. Why not?'

'I just thought...'

'Saba's got nothing to do with this, Zoe, so put that right out of your mind. The poor kid's hysterical – seems to think the arson was aimed at her, that the bomber just picked the wrong cottage by mistake.'

'Good excuse to scoot off with Fay, wouldn't you say? The police presumably bought this cock and bull story? And why wasn't she in her own bed last night, tell me?'

Haydon's mouth tightened. 'I don't know what's got into you lately, Zo; you're seeing demons round every corner. The police already have their suspect at the station: a bloke called Cundey; his wife works in the farm shop. Cundey accused his wife of having something going with Bert. He's a very jealous type, apparently, and Bert wasn't the first one to rouse his suspicions.'

'Was there anything in it?'

'Don't ask me. Wouldn't blame the woman if there was; she was beaten up most Saturday nights after he got back from the pub and stupid Bert confronted him in the village one night and threatened to break his legs if he didn't lay off the poor bitch.'

'Who told you all this?'

'Who d'you think? Gabby Fay knows all the village gossip, including the latest episode, but even Saba got to hear about it at work – she's been temping for Roddy all week, working in the office behind the shop and came home full of it. Not that Mrs Clack was impressed – told Saba in no uncertain terms to mind her own business.

Made Saba cry. Saba's complained to me before about that old harridan getting on at her. For two pins I'd give Clack her cards; I can't stand women fighting in the kitchen.'

Zoe withheld an acid response and pressed Haydon to fill in the details.

'I was dozing in the conservatory, woke about three hearing shouts and rushed outside with my gun, thinking Bert had nabbed that intruder I'd seen.'

'You did tell the police about your so-called birdwatcher?'

Haydon impatiently brushed this aside. 'Of course I bloody well did, but by the time I got down there I could see Bert's cottage was all but gone, sparks and smoke pouring from the chimney like a steam train. I called the fire brigade on my mobile and tried to get inside, but the flames beat me back. You've never seen anything like it, Zo; the whole place went up like a tinderbox and not a sign of Bert. I prayed he was out on one of his nightly rounds, but the dogs were howling in the kennel block and I didn't think he'd risk patrolling without them. The roof of the wooden shed where he keeps them was already beginning to catch fire, so I let the dogs out and they ran off God knows where. I told the police and they're getting a dog warden out to comb the woods.'

'Have they found Bert?'

'The firemen went in and dragged him out, but it was too late. Poor bugger had gone to bed. Let's hope it was quick.'

'Do you think it was Bert you heard shouting?'

'Probably not – the shouts I heard sounded like two men outside and Bert was trapped upstairs with the windows shut.'

'And the fire investigator is sure it was a petrol bomb?'

'Yes. Wicked sods – what an insane thing to do. It must have been that lunatic Cundey.'

'I thought you said two men?'

'Don't quibble. I've been questioned till I'm blue in the face and after they've asked you half a dozen times you can't even swear to your own name.'

'The police have no evidence?'

'Not so far, but it looks black. They say Cundey's wife took the kids to her mother's after a row when he got back from the pub last night. She knocked up a neighbour to borrow his van to drive to Essex and took off while she still had a head on her shoulders.'

'Cundey's that vicious?'

'So they say. Never met him myself. Apparently he has a smallholding beyond Roddy's pig field, a run-down farmhouse and a few acres of soft fruit and vegetables. Barely makes a living except in the summer, but known to the police, who were called out in August following a complaint about a fracas outside the Red Lion – some sort of family birthday celebration that went wrong and Cundey allegedly gave his wife a broken arm. But she refused to press charges – said she'd tripped on the kerb – so they must have made it up.'

'And I thought the countryside was a nice safe haven for one and all. No wonder Saba wants to run back to the smoke.'

'Fay'll calm her down. Still, you can't help feeling sorry for her, can you? Being that close to an arson attack.'

'I'll drive over to the vicarage and try to smoothe her down.'

'Would you, darling? I can't move till the police have given clearance. Do you mind staying while all this is going on?'

Zoe paused, deciding this was not the moment to pass on Freddie's warning about Stonecrest and certainly not the moment to air her grievances about Haydon's lies about the real ownership of the house and his mysterious association with this Mrs Redford. And Rio? A medical conference in Rio? A bit of a coincidence and a half.

'I'll go now. There isn't much I can do while the fire investigation's going on.'

Zoe found Fay locked in fierce combat with Saba over her desire to make a run for it.

166

'You can't spend the rest of your life on wheels, Saba,' she insisted, her figure planted four-square in front of the willowy dark girl whom Max had scooped from a notorious red-light district.

'Oh Zoe, you're here!' Saba wailed, breaking into fresh tears, the boy clasped in her arms like a hostage. 'You'll drive me back to London, won't you? Or I'll call a taxi.'

Fay threw Zoe a conspiratorial glance, her patience clearly in shreds. Zoe took Saba's arm and drew her aside.

'Let's sit down, shall we? Let's all relax. You've had a terrible fright and poor little Ali doesn't know what's happening. I've got some sweets in my bag; how about letting Ali loose on Fay's Sunday school box? He's magic at tidying up, aren't you, Ali?'

His huge dark eyes sought Saba's as Fay, light on her feet as plump women are, leapt upon a plastic storage hamper stashed under her desk and snatched the half-eaten packet of chocolate beans Zoe offered. Ali knelt beside Fay's box of tricks, his bony little hands flicking through the piles of colouring books and building blocks accumulated for the nursery class. The women moved over to the sofa at the darker end of the room, Saba sniffling into a man's handkerchief that Zoe, green-eyed, recognized as one of Haydon's.

Fay got in first. 'Now, let's thrash it out,

shall we? Saba's got this nice new job in the farm-shop office; Ali's asthma is much better here in the country; I've offered Saba a home here with me until she finds a little place of her own, and she's *still* trying to make a bolt for it.'

'What are you afraid of, Saba?' Zoe put in sternly. 'Come out with it. There's something you're not telling us, isn't there? Bert's cottage catching fire was nothing to do with you, was it?'

Saba bit her lip, casting an anxious glance at Ali already absorbed with colouring in a picture of Moses in the bullrushes.

'But it was. I can't stay here! It's very kind of you, Fay, but they would only come after me. I shall never escape. You would end up like Bert: everyone who comes near me is as good as dead and Ali *must* be kept safe.'

Zoe looked sceptical, but Fay urged her on.

'Anything you say will be safe with me, Saba. I am bound as a priest to keep any secret you share with me. Would you prefer us to be alone?'

Saba shook her head. 'Zoe had better hear this too. She may be in danger. You see I have had to lie to see my boy safe. And I've got to keep on running, for ever if need be. My husband and my uncle are out to kill me. They will *never* give up; Ali and I are

168

hunted down like dogs. I'll tell you everything and then you will understand why it is better if I get right away from here.'

Twenty

Saba rose from the couch and stood with her back to the window, her face in shadow. After a long hesitation she started to speak, her voice low but with a growing cadence, as if the words had been smothered like fire smouldering underground.

'First of all you must understand that I was born here, went to school here and grew up with the same silly fads and longings as any other English teenager. But I belong to a very traditional family, very close, very loving in the normal way and my affections were never divided. I did well at school and was planning to train as an accountant. My father owned a newsagent's but died of lung cancer when I was fourteen. After that my uncle took over as head of the family and my mother and my sisters came entirely under his control.'

'Where was this?' Fay gently interjected.

'Keighley.' She paused, watching Ali at the other end of the room, the child entirely absorbed in his drawing. Then she continued.

'I have three younger sisters I love very much, but I shall never see them or my mother again. When I was sixteen I was tricked into visiting Pakistan with my uncle and a cousin, another girl a little older than me. It was supposed to be a holiday to strengthen my links with my culture and I suspected it was a ruse to get me away from my English boyfriend, but I thought I could handle that. I was not unwilling; Aseefa and I were excited at the prospect of meeting our grandmother for the first time. But as soon as we arrived at the village my uncle's attitude changed. He introduced us to several men and after a few weeks, when Aseefa and I could get no answer to our anxious questions about going home, my uncle announced that we would be staying in the village until we agreed to marry. There was no escape. My grandmother made it clear that it was our duty to obey him and our terror of never being allowed home to England left Aseefa and me with no choice. I had taken my O Levels, for goodness' sake, I had a normal life in Keighley, wearing ordinary clothes, having friends from different communities – can you guess what living in that backwoods without so much as a telephone did to us? We were gradually reduced to two scared little girls and even I, the naughtiest in the family, was browbeaten into agreeing. It was the only way out, the only way, my uncle said, I would be allowed to fly back home.'

'You were married? Out there? You *and* your cousin?'

Saba nodded. 'As soon as I set eyes on my husband-to-be I knew I could never love him. But Aseefa and I agreed we would have to go along with it. My uncle said that as soon as the ceremony was over we would travel back, and Aseefa and I, silly girls that we were, thought we would be able to sort it out as soon as we got back to England. Perhaps the wedding would be invalid, we argued; perhaps it was just a paper marriage and we would never see our new husbands again. I thought about my English boyfriend, Sean, and decided to say nothing about it to him when I got home. My uncle said the two men chosen for us would remain in Pakistan for the present and he promised that my mother would be happy that I had fulfilled my destiny. Can you believe it? In this day and age?'

'So you came home to Keighley and went back to school as if nothing had happened?'

'The new husbands were forced to stay behind while they applied for entry visas. My uncle insisted I left school and worked in the shop seven days a week, forcing me to wear traditional clothes, threatening to beat

171

me if I caused trouble. My mother is a simple woman and entirely dependent on the family, anxious for me to conform. She warned me that if I did not accept my birthright I would be cast out of the Asian community into what my uncle called a racist mob. After all those months in Pakistan and being closely watched at the shop and at home, never allowed to mix with my schoolfriends, never permitted any phone calls, the brainwashing bore fruit. I received no wages for my work, I had lost confidence in my ability to break free and my mother made it plain that my little sisters would suffer if I continued to rebel. I lost heart.'

'What happened to Aseefa?'

'She went home to Bradford and for a long, long time I was unable to contact her. But later I found out she accepted the husband who had been chosen for her and, when he eventually arrived in England, they settled into some sort of life together despite the fact that the man spoke no English, had no job and beat her.'

'How long did this limbo of yours go on for?'

'Three years. But I was sly, sending messages to Sean through a friend who came into the shop, and once my uncle was convinced I had accepted the situation, I was allowed a little freedom – visits to the library and to take my mother to the doctor's if she needed an appointment. He even let me enrol at an evening class for bookkeeping, provided I was accompanied by his chosen minder. He knew, of course, that my husband would be dependent on me when he arrived, and any skills I acquired would be useful in the family business. Uncle owned two other shops in town, all staffed by family members, each receiving, like me, a pittance for their long hours. Then the day I dreaded came. My husband flew into London and the house was decked out for a welcome celebration. In the excitement I managed to escape. I stole money from the till, phoned Sean and together we took a train to Leeds, where he had a friend willing to hide us till the hue and cry died down.'

'That was very brave of you.'

Saba smiled bitterly, her response ironic. 'Yes, wasn't it? But Sean regarded it as all a bit of a lark; he never realized what he'd let himself in for and thought my running away would be the end of it. Sean got a job as a bricklayer and earned good money.'

'You were safe?'

'At first. But soon Ali was born and we moved on, warned by an Asian friend – a minicab driver – that enquiries about me had been circulating, cabbies asked to keep a lookout, leaflets printed up with my photo and offering a reward for this "missing person". The net was closing. That was probably how my uncle traced me here.'

'What do you mean?'

'I used a minicab service Haydon paid for, but it was booked in my name.'

'Your Pakistani husband's name?'

'No, my maiden name. But the firm was owned by Asians, which pleased me at first, and Ali loved riding into town in a taxi. The poor kid's led a very narrow life with me, and the cab drivers all made a big fuss of him, of course. But little boys chatter. Too much. I think one of the cabbies tipped off my uncle, told him where I was hiding out. There's a network nationwide, believe me.'

'After all these years? You're still hunted?'

'You don't understand, Zoe. The honour of the family was destroyed when I abandoned the role that had been set out for me. Running off with a white man and bearing his child was the ultimate disgrace.'

'What happened to Sean?'

Saba turned away, her shoulders twitching with emotion. At last her voice emerged from the shadows. 'He was killed a few months ago. A hit-and-run accident. No one was ever charged, but *I* know who murdered him. That was when I ran to London with Ali, and Max found me. But it's no use, they will never give up. I sent a desperate message to Aseefa through a friend and she managed to make a phone call to my lodging at King's Cross. Aseefa has two children now. She loves her kids and will never leave, whatever misery she has to accept. She warned me that Fawaz, the man I married in Pakistan, wants to marry a young girl he's met in Keighley, needs me to be dead, don't you see? My uncle's control over my mother and my sisters is complete; my defection was an insult to his authority, which he can never forget, and now Fawaz is determined to have a new wife, one like the village girls back in Pakistan, not an unfaithful bitch with a half-caste bastard thumbing her nose at traditional values.'

She turned to face them, her features set. 'Now do you see? I must get right away immediately, Fay. I have some money – Zoe arranged a savings account for me through Mr Gilbert and Roddy paid me a week's wages on Friday. Ali and I will manage.'

'Where will you go?'

Saba frowned. 'Could you give us a lift back to London, Zoe? We are safer in crowds and I shall be able to disappear again.'

'Oh no you don't!' Fay shouted, causing Ali to look up in alarm. Saba signalled warmly to the little boy and he settled back with his colouring book as she dropped on to the arm of the sofa, eyeing Fay with suspicion.

Saba's new protector took over, her

patience exhausted.

'I've listened to all this, Saba, and, let's face it, the Asian community is a wonderful shelter for those who accept the rules, but your story is hardly unique. Girls and boys born into traditional homes but educated as regular English teenagers find their loyalties split and, from my own experience working in this field, tragedies sometimes occur and girls like your cousin either conform or, like you, rebel and run away. Yours is, of course, a terrible situation, but there are other ways of tackling it than running away. Let me help you. I can arrange for you to see a sympathetic lawyer and get instant legal protection for you and Ali. Later we can take steps to nullify this marriage of yours.'

'Legal protection won't be good enough.'

'Oh yes it will. Believe me, yours is not the only arranged wedding forced upon a young girl; there are loads of people out there, Saba, fighting on your side. Give me a chance and I will prove to you that there is a civilized way to escape this manhunt you imagine is under way. Has it not occurred to you that you may be imagining all this? That your husband merely needs to see you to gain a divorce so that both of you can get on with your lives?'

'Aseefa says—'

'Aseefa may not have the whole story,

Saba. Why not give it a try? I'll stand by you.'

Saba stared at this stoical figure in her dog collar and flowery dicky who was holding out a hand of possible deliverance, and her obduracy wavered. She glanced at Zoe, who nodded encouragement, and these two unlikely supporters stood firm.

At last she agreed. 'OK. What do you suggest?'

'There's a condition.'

'There would be,' Saba retorted, her trust receding. Fay ploughed on undeterred.

'No, hear me out. I'm your best bet, Saba, and Ali needs you to give it a try. You've got to come clean with the police about all this. A man, possibly innocent, is likely to be charged with firing Bert's cottage, and if you honestly believe the attack was a failed attempt on *your* life, you owe it to Cundey to give them your uncle's address so they can make a full enquiry.'

'And if I don't?'

'If you don't, you're free to go on your way. Start running right now.'

'And you won't tell the police what I've told you? Inform on my family?'

'I don't even know your uncle's name and, even if I did, I promised you my silence as a priest.'

'You too, Zoe?'

Zoe shrugged, unsure whether Saba's

177

secret was hers to keep. 'You must decide for yourself.'

Fay put her arms around Saba's thin shoulders. 'Could you live with this if Cundey is innocent? Isn't it time you faced up to your family, Saba? Even an animal will turn on potential attackers to defend its cub. Ali deserves better than a life on the run. Show real courage, Saba, and let me help you.'

Saba nervously laughed, breaking away from the embrace. 'You do realize that by placing myself under the protection of a Christian priest I will have put myself truly beyond the pale? If I do go to the police, tell them what I believe happened – that my uncle and my husband fired the wrong cottage by mistake – I will not only have betrayed my community but also placed myself on the side of the "enemy", as my uncle sees it. I shall become an orphan.'

'It's worth it,' Zoe insisted. 'And Fay's offer is the best you're likely to get. Think it over. I've got to get back to Haydon. Please don't run, Saba; even Cundey deserves a chance. And you may be wrong: Cundey may be as guilty as hell, but if you don't speak out now, you will be looking over your shoulder for the rest of your life.' She gave Saba a meaningful glance and added, 'Just say how you got the job with Max from answering an ad you saw at the corner shop – no need to go into details, OK? They already have enough background stuff from the statement you gave to Inspector Kennedy before, remember.'

Zoe left them to it, her confusion at this astonishing turn of events compounded as she pulled up on the drive at Stonecrest and saw Kennedy emerge from his mud-spattered car.

Twenty-One

Haydon was unable to leave while the police and the fire inspection team were still investigating Bert's death. I'm ashamed to say, I chickened out and drove straight to Roddy's, thus evading Kennedy, whose arrival on the murder scene would put not only myself but Saba into his sights.

I was nervous about Saba. Even with Fay and myself to back her up I was far from confident that she would get her story straight, or convinced that her tale of woe was actually true.

When it came down to it, how well did I know her?

Roddy was working in the office behind the shop, sorting his receipts and tapping away at the computer. The girls in the shop fell silent as Zoe passed through, clearly embarrassed by the interruption of an avid dissection of the drama at Stonecrest. There were no customers, an almost unique state of affairs on Saturday afternoons at the farm shop, to which weekend shoppers drove in from miles around. Presumably the police and fire inspection presence had frightened them off.

The shop had gradually expanded since being set up and now not only sold organic meat and vegetables but also boasted a specialist cheese counter and home-made bread and cakes made by a local farmer's wife.

Zoe strolled into the back office, quietly closing the communicating door. Roddy looked up and smiled, rising to pat her cheek and pull up an extra chair to the table.

'You OK, Zoe? You look all-in.'

'Yeah, well it's been a terrible couple of weeks and I'm beginning to think I must be harbouring some sort of incubus, and causing random havoc at every turn.'

Roddy was not amused, his narrow features grave as he dragged out the full story.

'And Fay Betteridge has clasped Saba to her bosom?'

'Going to get Ali made a ward of court, I shouldn't wonder. Do you believe all this family vendetta rubbish, Roddy?'

'Saba being forced into a teenage marriage, you mean? Then sought by her murderous clan in revenge?'

'She believes her boyfriend was run down and killed by them and that it's only a matter of time before they catch up with her.'

'Sounds fantastical but may well be true, you know. If Fay believes it, who knows? Have the police been told?'

'That's Fay's trump card. She's offered to organize legal protection for Saba and the boy, but only if she tells the police that she suspects her family were behind the arson attack – got Bert's cottage by mistake.'

'Whew!'

'There's another complication. The inspector who was in charge of Max's case has turned up here. He must have heard about the fire and the extraordinary coincidence that the same characters, including yours truly, are involved. Kennedy probably can't believe his luck, a chance to reinvestigate the background; he's never been convinced he got the full story and is likely concocting some incriminating tie-in right now, putting Haydon through the mill for starters.'

'And what about you?'

'Kennedy hasn't caught up with me yet, but it's only a matter of time. Funny thing is, I was warned to keep away from here only yesterday. By Freddie McPherson, the estate agent. Do you know him?'

'I do. He represented the owner when I signed the lease.'

'Mrs Redford.'

Roddy sobered. 'Haydon told you?'

'About not actually buying Stonecrest? No, he didn't, the lying bastard. I found out from Freddie; a small deception but hurtful nevertheless. I can't think why Haydon couldn't be straight with me; it's not as if I would have cared one way or the other.'

'Perhaps Mrs Redford asked him to be discreet.'

'You know her?'

'A bit. She's no lady to argue with, believe me. Hard as nails, and not acting alone, of course.'

'What does that mean?'

'It's no secret. If you'd been less unworldly, my darling, you would have picked up on the Redford–Mullins story years ago. It made headlines in all the papers.'

'Well, I've been a bit busy carving out a miserable pittance from mending old bed-covers and stuff to follow the news. You knew about Mrs Redford letting the house to Haydon all along, didn't you, Roddy? Why didn't you tell me?'

'Thought it none of my business, which, of course, it isn't. I tried to nudge Haydon into coming clean with you over it once or twice, but he shrugged it off. And frankly, Zoe, why worry about it?'

She made a face, and scraped back her chair to rise. 'Why don't we go back to your place, Roddy, and make some lunch? There are questions buzzing round in my brain like wasps in a jam jar and I don't feel comfortable with your girls flapping their ears next door in the shop. Can you leave this?' she said, waving vaguely at the accounts strewn across the table.

He grinned. 'No sweat. As it happens, that gorgeous female you dumped on me's a genius with figures.'

'Saba?'

'Yes, Saba. Only been here a week and got my books in apple-pie order. I'd hate to lose her if she takes flight again.'

'I think Fay's got her tethered.'

He packed up his papers, flung on a windcheater and took her arm, steering her through the farm shop and across the car park to his cottage. Once safely inside he set a gas poker under wood laid in the grate in his sitting room and poured two glasses of wine. Zoe followed him into the kitchen and watched his deft movements with fresh interest, realizing something that had scarcely crossed her mind before: apart from being a mate, Roddy Meirs was undoubtedly a smashing-looking bloke, his air of unhurried calm underlining a masculinity that, in normal circumstances, would have struck her long ago. He slapped some bread, ham and cheese in a sandwich grill and within minutes they were seated in front of a blazing fire with plates of croque-monsieur on their laps.

'Right, Zoe. Fire away.'

'Mrs Redford?'

'No mystery about Bobby Redford. She's the one-time live in lover of Jimmy Mullins and looks after Mullins' interests while he's away.'

'Away?'

'Away in prison. Currently away on the run and rumoured to be in Northern Cyprus, where there is no extradition arrangement. The police try to tag her, but she's no fool, and I suspect they find it more useful to watch her movements than to pull her in on some trumped-up charge.'

'What did Mullins do?'

'Apart from doing time in Parkhurst? Two security-van hold-ups plus a few hundred safety deposit boxes in another raid. He escaped five years ago and lets La Redford run the shop while he's otherwise engaged. She looks after his "family", as he calls it – members of his gang who are either in clink or on the run like himself. Cash and jewellery worth millions are still unaccounted for. The police presumably think that if they keep their eye on the Redford woman she will eventually put a foot wrong and they'll be able to nab the big boss and, with luck, recover some of the money.'

'But they caught them – his gang, I mean?'

'Not all. I don't know the details, but my guess is that Bobby Redford keeps them sweet until it's safe to share out the loot.'

'They must be getting pretty impatient after five years.'

Roddy nodded. 'But if anyone's capable of keeping all the balls in the air, Bobby Redford is.'

'You still see her?'

'Not lately. We used to come across each other from time to time when I was still on the party circuit before I took up pig-keeping. Freddie McPherson introduced us. If you want to know more about her, Freddie's your man; she's based in London between stints on the more exotic holiday venues. He warned you to keep away from here, you say?'

She nodded, describing their hurried conversation at Max's funeral. Roddy looked grave.

'Why don't you push off back to London right now, Zoe? I'll explain things to Haydon. There's no sense in you getting embroiled in this filthy investigation; you weren't even here, for God's sake.'

She sipped her wine, the half-eaten sandwich cooling on the plate. 'I don't think I can do that, Roddy. It would be unfair to Haydon to leave him without a word. And I feel I owe Fay some back-up; she's taken Saba on and, believe me, she hasn't heard all of it by a long chalk.'

She rose, gathering up her coat, and leaned across to give Roddy a hug before leaving.

'Thanks a million for putting up with my moans. I won't tell Haydon you put me wise about Mrs Redford and the house – it was Freddie who spilt the beans. Let's pretend our little heart-to-heart never got serious, shall we?'

He kissed her cheek. 'Play it by ear, sweetie. Just be extra careful.'

They walked towards the customer car park. As she opened the car door she turned and said, 'I'm still terribly confused by all this, Roddy. Until I've had a chance to talk to Haydon I feel as if I'm treading on thin ice here, tottering about on the rim of a disaster.'

Twenty-Two

Haydon Masure was unused to being circumscribed in his own house. In fact, Haydon Masure had never before found himself at the beck and call of anyone, let alone the police – a situation he found less than amusing. The doctor's fabled good nature frayed, his irritation falling mostly on Zoe's head; her tardy response to his distress signals phoned through in the early hours of Friday morning still rankled.

He spent a miserable weekend, Saturday broken up by repeated interviews with not only the local fuzz but also the fire inspector and Inspector Kennedy who, to Haydon's mind, had no business to be there at all.

'Is he following *you*, Zoe?' he fumed, the two of them at bay in his study on Sunday morning, reluctant to face the curious glances of the regulars in the local pub agog with the arson attack at the big house.

'Kennedy thinks we're still holding something back. About Max's death. If he's following anyone, it's Saba, not *me*.'

'She was frogmarched down to the nick,

you do realize? As a result of the interference of two women who should have known better.'

'So what? You got something to hide, Haydon? Keeping your fingers crossed that Saba doesn't blab about goings on up here? And you were the first to hear from her about her bloody relatives, if you remember? That Saba guessed *she* had been the target of the fire not Bert, and all the time she just happened to be safely tucked up in your bed. The police probably think it funny you didn't come out with that little nugget of information before Saba decided to come clean and volunteer her side of the scenario to add to the investigation.'

Haydon turned ugly at that, his temper rising in a whoosh of sparks.

'You think *that*? You really believe I'd stand in line after that dirty old man, Max, with a slapper like Saba?' He grabbed her arm, refusing to let go. 'Zoe, you're insane! As it happens I was freezing my butt off in the conservatory till three that night hoping to catch my burglar – hardly rolling in satin bedsheets with Max's cast-off.'

'You still haven't explained why she wasn't in her own place!'

Haydon paused, releasing his painful hold and stepping back, his rage doused as suddenly as it flared up. He looked puzzled. 'Actually, I'm not sure either. What did she tell you?'

'Nothing about that, but I bet Kennedy won't let it go. He suspects her of something – gut instinct he'd call it – but Saba sings a very sweet song.'

Zoe gave him a rundown on the family saga that had allegedly driven the girl to run away.

'And her boyfriend was killed in a hit-and-run?'

'So she says. Again there's no proof that it was her uncle and this husband of hers, but at least Fay's forced her to go to the police. Do you think Cundey is innocent?'

Haydon shrugged, shuffling round his desk like a blind man, finally sagging in his chair clearly all but done-in. 'Has Kennedy asked for you yet?'

'He's gone down to the station to be in on the second interview with Saba. Fay rang me yesterday afternoon and confirmed that the girl is willing to testify against her people, if it comes to it. Fay's sent one of her tame solicitors along to protect Saba's interests. I know you don't much like our lady vicar, Haydon, but you must admit she's managed to pull the coals out of the fire with this one, forcing Saba to come forward, giving that poor sad bastard Cundey a possible escape from prosecution.'

'That sad bastard, as you call him, is a wife beater for starters and is, in all likelihood, lying through his teeth.'

'Well, that shouldn't bother you, Haydon – a man who wouldn't recognize the truth if he fell over it.'

He stared, his exhausted gaze focusing on the slight figure confronting him, her eyes sparking with anger.

'Go on. I presume there is some point to this?'

'You lied to me, Haydon. You lied about owning Stonecrest. You lied about your private arrangement with Mrs Redford, and for all I know you are lying about this medical conference in Rio, which just happens to be handy for an assignation with this dubious female chum of yours. Did you know she's a stand-in for her partner, Mullins, while he's on the run?'

'You taken to reading the gutter press all of a sudden, Zoe?'

'No. Freddie McPherson let the cat out of the bag about you renting the house from Mrs Redford and I made Roddy tell me the rest. Roddy filled me in about Mullins being on the international Most Wanted list; but what bothers me, Haydon, is why you of all people got yourself involved with these characters in the first place.'

He leaned back, propping his feet on the desk and crossing his arms, his eyes steely.

'For a simple girl you seem intent on weaving a mystery out of all this, Zoe. It's perfectly simple: Bobby Redford is a patient of mine. As a favour she asked me to house-sit for a year or two while she's abroad. It was an offer I couldn't refuse,' he said with a grin. 'She needed a trusted friend to take the place over and to keep the staff. I baulked at employing a security guard, but she was adamant and, to be fair, I only intended to spend weekends here and the place would have been wide open to theft and vandalism when it was unoccupied. We argued the toss for a bit and I eventually agreed to keep Bert on if she paid his wages. She explained he was an ex-con she felt sorry for. Bert needed a job and a place to live and he was, I admit, tailor-made for the job.'

'Have you spoken to Mrs Redford since the fire?'

'Briefly.'

'Will she come back to explain your agreement to keep Bert on at her expense?'

'No need.'

'Then why Rio? You still plan to go ahead with a meeting on her home ground?'

He laughed. 'Brazil is, believe it or not, the nip-and-tuck capital of the world, apart from the States. Some of the best cosmetic surgeons operate in Rio, it's the perfect venue for an international conference and yes, I may take the opportunity to speak to Bobby about all this when I'm there – not that there's anything I can add to what she already knows. Do you know, they even have bank overdrafts allowing all and sundry to go under the knife? It's practically a national obsession. Anyway, I shall probably cancel the trip if they can find someone else to fill in. I'll phone through on Monday.'

'But why lie about all this, Haydon? Why not tell me about renting Stonecrest, about you coming to this weird arrangement with the Redford woman to keep Bert on the payroll? The police will think it odd that you told all the locals you'd bought the place.'

'Bobby Redford was offering a package, a strictly on her terms take-it-or-leave-it offer. I agreed and she insisted for private reasons we kept up the pretence that Stonecrest had been sold off. McPherson was warned to be discreet and being economical with the truth was not such a big deal, was it? It was all fixed before you and I got together and I saw no reason to bother you with the details.'

'You didn't know how long I'd be around, did you, Haydon? It wasn't worth breaking your word to Mrs Redford by sharing the secret with a clueless girlfriend who might just be passing through. I *believed* you, Haydon, and all this dishonesty makes me wonder what else you've lied about. If it hadn't been for me getting friendly with McPherson I suppose none of this would have come out.'

'Freddie McPherson would be wise to keep his mouth shut. Bobby Redford has nasty friends.'

'So I heard.'

Zoe moved round the desk and stood behind him, hugging his shoulders and resting her chin on the top of his head.

'Let's bury the hatchet, darling. Let's try to get through this weekend at least without any more fighting. I love you, Haydon. And, whether you admit it or not, you've got yourself into one hell of a mess and will need all the friends you've got.'

The day dragged on, Haydon spending most of it locked in his study making phone calls. It was Sunday evening before Kennedy called to speak to her, a brief conversation merely to confirm what he knew already, almost a social call, in fact.

She led him into the dining room, her mood frosty. The inspector, on the other hand, seemed pretty pleased with himself. They sat on either side of an enormous mahogany table, the antler heads lining the walls seeming to watch them with their glittering glass eyes. He pulled off his raincoat, perspiration breaking out on his upper lip as the overheated atmosphere of the house kicked in.

'Let's get straight down to business, shall we, Inspector? I gather Saba's filled you in about her family troubles.'

'Very public-spirited of her, coming forward like that, wasn't it, Miss Templeman? She could have run back to London with her boy and left us to follow our noses with Mr Cundey.'

'The jealous farmer?'

'Cundey's been temporarily released for lack of evidence. Trouble is, the Raz family are also in the clear. My colleague here, Superintendent Collins, has checked them out. A cast iron alibi. Saba's nonsense about being hunted by a vengeful husband turned out to be a figment of her imagination.'

'The family knew nothing about her whereabouts? The wicked uncle doesn't exist?'

'I didn't say that. Fawaz Abbas managed to track her down through a network of contacts.'

'Minicab firms?'

It was Kennedy's turn to look surprised. 'Yes. How did you know that?'

'Lucky guess. Go on, Inspector.'

'The husband, Abbas, wants a divorce. The uncle, a man called, if I remember, Shajar Raz, and a posse of cousins all hate your friend Saba right enough, but the suspects she named were definitely witnessed in Keighley on the night in question. Cundey can't claim such a copper-bottomed alibi, but we're working on it.'

'So you're back to square one?'

'May I ask you, Miss Templeman, if you were aware of this background story when the young lady was employed by Mr Loudon-Fryer? Was he under the impression he was protecting her in some way?'

'It never came up. Max was a very kind man. If Saba appealed for his help, he wouldn't hesitate to give it, I'm sure; but it wasn't a subject we discussed. As I've said before, my association with Max was purely business. We were friends but not intimate friends, if you see what I mean. As a matter of interest, what happened to the dogs?'

'The dog warden roped them in and, as far as I know, they've been put in a dog pound. In fact, the dogs may have provided us with vital evidence. They caught up with one of the intruders after Doctor Masure let them loose. A bloodstained shred of clothing was found by the perimeter fence. It may lead to nothing, of course, but the chances are we can link up the blood sample with our suspect.'

'Mr Cundey?'

'The lab are testing it now.'

Zoe was stunned, impressed by the fact that, despite the combined efforts of the fire inspection team and the police, it might well be Bert's dogs who had nabbed his killer.

He rose, holding out his hand to her. She led him through the echoing, panelled hall, the silence in the empty house bearing down like a pall.

'You're staying on here, Miss Templeman, should I need to get back to you?'

'Yes.'

'Alone?'

'Doctor Masure has driven back to London, yes. He has to rearrange his appointments, but he will be back tomorrow night. While the investigation's continuing he thought it best to commute, but I shall be here for the present.'

'No new workshop?'

'Still looking.'

Kennedy buttoned his coat, eyeing her sympathetically. 'Perhaps you would be wise to stay with a friend tonight, Miss Templeman. A big house like this? And you, unprotected ... The doctor did mention anxieties about a possible intruder sighted at the gates recently and—'

She laughed, opening the door wide. 'Anyone planning a robbery here would be less than bright to break in while the village is still swarming with bobbies, wouldn't they?'

'Even so. This house has a poor history, I'm told. Attracts misfits of all sorts.'

'Should suit me fine then, wouldn't you say, Inspector?'

She waved him off, the darkness closing in on a bitter winter's night, the air sharp as a knife.

Twenty-Three

Haydon was back at the surgery, returning late each evening, his mood jumpy. The Kent police had pursued him even to his consulting rooms, their arrival giving Venetia palpitations in her efforts to rearrange his appointments, smoothing the feathers of his rich patients being no joke. The reputation of Doctor Masure was starry, his clientele drawn not only from UK residents but including, most impressively, a number of foreign VIPs wishing to keep their cosmetic surgery out of the gossip columns.

Venetia loved her work, her own botoxed visage smooth as a baby's bottom. She probably loved the doctor equally but with the adoration of a movie fan, realizing that proximity at work was a barrier to any closer relationship. Venetia had watched the charming doctor's girlfriends come and go, the latest, the arty one, lasting much longer than most, perhaps only because she was so unlike any of those who had gone before. Possibly because of her confusion about Zoe's social appeal in the fashionable circle in which the doctor moved, Venetia felt protective of her, and a certain rapport had built up between them.

Zoe found that time hung heavily at Stonecrest. There was little for her to do and the grounds were still being searched for further clues, making any solitary walks an ordeal. Occasional curiosity seekers stood at the gates, gawping at the burnt-out cottage, speculating on the lifestyles of people who lived in houses like Stonecrest. Villagers had been admitted to lay bunches of flowers on Bert's doorstep, his gruff friendships with the local suppliers who frequented the farm shop only now appreciated, his threats to Cundey about any future wife-beating being taken in good part. There seemed to be no support for Cundey's suspicions about his wife's infidelity with Bert, Bert's attitude to her abuse being traceable back, according to the press, to his own brutal childhood.

Zoe made brief sorties into Ashford, avoiding the farm shop and its gaggle of nosey-parkers. She wished Haydon would abandon Stonecrest so that they could both settle back in London, but he seemed even more determined to stick it out, enduring the rush-hour traffic each night, his obstinacy fuelled, Zoe suspected, not by any civic duty to be available to the police but by an inexplicable fear that deserting the horrible house would bring some sort of biblical retribution, to which Bert's incineration was only the intro.

She constantly tackled him about this, but his mind was set. There was nothing to stop her leaving herself, but despite all the lies and despite a very real apprehension, loving Haydon left her no choice. If she went now it would be the end, and she couldn't face that.

They sat in the gloomy dining room on Wednesday evening picking at a chicken curry Zoe had concocted from leftovers in the fridge. The conversation was stilted, of the 'How was your day, darling?' variety, the atmosphere choked by a feeling of impermanence, as if they were waiting for something to happen. Zoe plucked up courage to touch on the investigation.

'Have the police given you any more information? Anything new?'

Haydon shrugged. 'Keep whittering on about Bert's terms of employment. Was he supposed to be a gamekeeper? Did I know he had a record for GBH? Was I aware that his bank balance showed a healthy input from a lady called Roberta Redford? Did I pay him in cash? Who paid his insurance stamps? And so on and so on...'

'Well, you must admit it was an odd way of keeping staff.'

'Redford's boyfriend, Mullins, is the thing that really sticks in their guts. The inference is I am in cahoots with the guy and if they badger me long enough, embarrass me at the surgery, I will co-operate.'

'Co-operate? How?'

'How the hell do I know? Do I look like a bounty hunter?'

'They offered a bribe? Offered you money to put the finger on Mullins through Mrs Redford?'

'Not directly, of course they bloody well didn't. Have some sense, Zoe! Why would I need a few hundred quid as an informer? – even if I could put Mullins in their pocket, which I can't.'

'You were a fool to get embroiled in Stonecrest in the first place.'

'Hindsight's a wonderful thing, my darling.'

'But why?'

'I've already told you! Bobby Redford's a patient. She asked me to help her out and at the time I stupidly thought a nice country house would be fun. You've enjoyed it, haven't you?'

'Not much. The only nice thing to come out of all this is meeting Roddy Meirs.'

Haydon pushed away his plate. 'Let's go to bed; I'm fed up with going over and over all this, first with the police and then, when I do get away, you bloody well can't leave it alone either.'

Next morning she decided to tackle Fay's

altar cloth. It would give her something to concentrate on, something she was actually good at. She had just filled the butler's sink in the scullery with warm water as Mrs Clack bundled in, her cycling cape and pixie hood dripping with water. Zoe and Brenda Clack had come to terms, the housekeeper's mood distinctly improved.

'I won't be in your way, will I? Just giving this cloth a wipe over – I'll dry it in the ironing room.'

'Use the old wringer first, then it won't drip all over the floor. Want any help?'

'I think I can manage. Still raining?'

'Cats and dogs. Never known a winter like it. I remember when I was a kid seeing this film about India. *The Rains Came*, I think it was called. Made a big hit with me – all lovely romance, not like the stuff on the telly these days. Anyway, this film was all about the monsoon – just poured and poured, drowning hundreds of these poor people.' She laughed. 'P'raps we'll get used to monsoons here before long. I bet that Saba's in her element.'

'Saba's not Indian.'

'Ain't she? Well, it's all the same to me. She's moved in with the vicar, so I heard down the post office. Got a real talent for squeezing in where she's not wanted, that one. My Arnold used to say they should all be sent back.'

'Back where?'

'Back where they come from.'

'But Saba's British. She was born here, Brenda.'

'I know we're not supposed to say this, but don't you be taken in by these immigrant people, Zoe. Only out for their own ends, you see if I'm not right. Now she's gone I'll give you the real story. That Saba was making eyes at the doctor the moment your back was turned, and at Mr Meirs an' all, hedging her bets, looking for a nice rich husband to take care of her like that poor old man you worked for, dear – the one what hanged himself.'

Zoe turned away to submerge the soiled parts of the altar cloth in the treated water, but the Clack continued, relentless, her manner kindly on the face of it, no spitefulness involved.

'She used to make excuses to be behind him like a shadow, running his bath, finding his glasses for him, letting that little boy of hers bother the poor doctor when he was trying to test out his slides.'

'Ali meant no harm. He probably thought putting slides through the projector was a new game.'

Brenda Clack leaned against the wall watching Zoe gently dunk the embroidered silk up and down in the suds. The silence grew. The arrow found its target.

'She slept with him, you know. I can always tell. I changed the sheets.'

'Why are you saying this?'

'Because I like you, see. You're not like the others. Doctor Masure may be a very clever man but he don't know right from wrong – been spoilt all his life, shouldn't wonder, like my sister's boy Derek, a right little brat who ended up a con-man, cheating widows of their money. Got six years for the last one. Six years? Should have strung him up, if you ask me. This silly woman lent him her life savings to invest,' she said, bunching her fist to her heart at the very thought, 'and now her life's ruined. But in a couple of years Derek'll be out on the streets again chatting up more silly women, you see if he don't.'

Zoe let out the plug and the water gurgled away like a death rattle. Haydon had slept with Saba? Had sex with her? Had lied ... But what if Brenda Clack was the liar, had concocted this terrible story just to cause trouble? Zoe couldn't believe that. Why would the woman make it up, risk losing her job if it was untrue?

She helped Zoe squeeze out most of the water and they lifted the sodden mass into a laundry basket to transfer it to the mangle. Together they put it through the rollers, Zoe wordless while the other continued chatting away as if nothing of any importance had been said at all. Perhaps she thinks I knew already, Zoe argued. Maybe I did, sub-consciously – just couldn't bring myself to believe it. The only thing would be to con-front Saba and have it out; accusing Haydon would only result in yet another denial.

She drifted back to the library and sat at the big table, hearing the rain patter against the leaded lights. The phone rang. It was the administrator of her father's nursing home.

'We wondered if you would be coming to see us soon, Miss Templeman? I wouldn't bother you like this – I know how busy you young people are – but Charlie's had a bit of a fall. Nothing serious, but he keeps asking for you, getting himself in a state.'

'I'll come straight away, Mrs Glover. What happened?'

The conversation was brief, the minor accident less alarming than the old man's uncontrollable anxiety to see her. Zoe felt bad, knowing that being inundated with her own troubles had been no excuse. She should have telephoned, spoken to the old boy at least.

She went into the kitchen and explained matters to Brenda Clack, realizing as she did so that her sudden departure might be misconstrued, taken as an excuse by the housekeeper, whose disbelief shone like a beacon.

'I've ... I've left a note for Haydon,' she

stuttered. 'I don't know how long I shall be away, but if anyone rings, they can reach me on my mobile.'

Brenda Clack's expression hardened. 'Yes, of course, miss. I'll tell him tonight, shall I? I'll get some sausages from the farm shop for his supper.'

Zoe scuttled out, furious with herself, furious with Brenda Clack and, most of all, furious with Haydon. If Saba admitted sleeping with him, that would finish it. Really finish it. But she would bide her time: having a row with him on the phone was not sensible, especially on the dubious say-so of a woman like Brenda Clack, who had likely imagined the whole thing. Ending a relationship as enduring as she believed theirs had been deserved better. Having a reason to get right away for a few days was a blessing in disguise.

Twenty-Four

Zoe drove to Wales on autopilot, her confusion about Haydon's equivocal attitude both to herself and to Mrs Redford and Stonecrest leaving more questions unanswered. She had thought she knew Haydon, a clever man with a simple view of life: work hard, live well and let the detail take care of itself. Quite where she fitted into this equation was now unclear. His lies had unnerved her – paltry lies about the renting of the house but possibly serious dishonesty about his attraction to Saba. But, looking at Saba, who could blame any red-blooded male? A beautiful girl like that, with an endearing vulnerability.

She arrived in the early evening and managed to book into a small hotel near the nursing home. The place was warm, the welcome friendly and Zoe had a shower and relaxed, it seemed, for the first time in days. She ate dinner in a dining room otherwise occupied only by two couples, the reception desk littered with cut-price offers for the Christmas holiday.

'Hell fire, Christmas!' she said to herself as she waited for coffee in the lounge. 'I'd better get something for Pa, just in case I don't get down here again before then.'

The prospect of Max's inquest was still in the air. She wondered if Kennedy would attempt to delay procedings, to somehow link the fire at Stonecrest with Max's death, a coincidence the Coroner might be interested in despite the lack of any tangible evidence. Trouble was, she loosely featured in both untimely deaths, as did Saba, of course. The whole thing was a mess.

Next morning she rang the home and arranged to call in at eleven. The administrator invited her to stay for lunch, but Zoe declined, knowing that Pa's attention span would be cruelly stretched by a prolonged visit. 'Perhaps I might come back for tea?' she suggested. 'That would give my father a chance to have a nap in the afternoon, wouldn't it?'

Zoe walked to the shops and bought a sweater, some socks and a big box of chocolates; she reluctantly dismissed the temptation to take a bottle of whisky for the old boy, unsure if booze was allowed. The parcels were gift-wrapped in the shop, the jolly ribbons and shiny paper oddly depressing, reviving memories of all those Christmases when Pa had been the one to make everything magical for his little girl.

She arrived at the nursing home with thirty minutes to spare, reluctant to walk back to the hotel for her car. A woman in a nylon overall showed her into the waiting room. 'Charlie will be right down – he's just getting his hair cut, miss.'

The waiting room was brightly furnished, a vase of paper poppies glowing in the fireplace. It was oppressively hot and Zoe dropped her packages on the floor and un-zipped her ski jacket, sniffing the peculiar cabbagey smell which seemed always to hang in the air here whatever the time of day.

She picked over a stack of magazines on the coffee table, selecting a dog-eared county weekly already weeks old. She sifted through several pages of local news, reviews of amateur dramatics, wedding pictures and supermarket ads before turning to the centrefold, which was entirely taken up with a fatal stabbing. The victim's picture struck a chord and, with a pang of recognition, she realized it was a full-blown account of the murder of Chris Mayhew, the Chester dealer whose mugging had been described to her at Max's funeral. Just as she was about to read all about it, there were foot-steps in the hall. She stuffed the paper into her bag and smiled nervously at the nursey type who had come to fetch her.

'How is he?'

'Charlie? Pretty fit, all things considered. The sprained ankle's a bit of a nuisance, but falls are a regular event in this place – lucky it wasn't more serious.'

'But in himself? Is he better?'

The nurse regarded her with sympathy. 'Your father's not going to be *better*, Miss Templeman. We just hope to keep him as cheerful as possible, and physically he's in good shape for a man of his age.'

'He knows I'm coming?'

'We've been reminding him since Mrs Glover spoke to you yesterday, but don't be too disappointed if he's a bit vague. More gets through than we might think.'

They arrived at the lounge area where a few card tables were laid with tea cloths at one end. The atmosphere was noisy, two helpers keeping a dozen patients cheerfully occupied at the big table, others watching television with scant attention. All the residents were elderly but not all as dependent as Charlie Templeman, whose happy disposition probably disguised the cloudy recollections that visitors stirred up.

He was sitting at one of the card tables, his eyes bright, his new haircut painfully military-looking, tobacco-stained fingers playing restlessly with an empty pipe. Zoe hurried forward, ditching her Christmas parcels as she bent to hug him, feeling the rough heathery touch of his tweed jacket.

'Pa! It's so lovely to see you. Sorry it's been so long but—'

'Ah, Chrissie! I knew you'd come. My own love! But why have you cut your hair? Your wonderful long black hair...'

'It's Zoe, Pa. Your wee girl – you remember.'

'Where've you been, Chrissie, you naughty wifey – off with the raggle-taggle gypsies again, I shouldn't wonder.'

His blissful misrecognition was too fragile a dream to break. Zoe touched his knee, a tear trickling down her cheek. Was it necessary to insist on the truth all the time? If poor Pa thought Chrissie had come home from her wanderings, why not let it go?

She took the pipe from his hand and tucked it into his top pocket, dropping the gaily wrapped gifts into his lap. As he struggled with the ribbons, a girl brought two cups of coffee on a tray, together with a plate of chocolate biscuits. Zoe smiled and thanked her, leaning back to watch the old man unwrap his parcels. No doubt about it, he *was* looking well cared for, his shirtfront unspotted, his fingernails, she was ashamed to admit, cleaner than her own. She wondered about the pipe, having the impresion that smoking was banned here, the danger of smoking in bed too difficult to oversee; but perhaps they relaxed the rules for one or two, Pa's craving for a smoke maybe worth the extra trouble.

He held up the sweater, beaming all round, and called the tea girl over to look, pressing the box of chocolates on her, his wordless pat on her hand as charming as Haydon's. Charlie rattled on about old pupils he had seen recently, their names flowing effortlessly from an isolated pocket of memory. Her presence was cherished, his proud insistence on introducing 'Chrissie, my beautiful wife, you know – she's been abroad, you see' greeted with awe by the curious fellow-residents, who crowded round to admire his early Christmas presents. The girl gently shooed them back to the big table, leaving Zoe and her father alone again.

'You do like it here, don't you, Pa?'

He stared, his rheumy eyes puzzled. 'Oh yes, my dear – it's a lovely hotel and the staff are very obliging but,' he said, leaning across the table to whisper in her ear, 'I do find it a little confusing. Our room number, Chrissie – do you remember what it is? I seem to have mislaid our key.'

She squeezed his arm. 'Don't worry, darling. I'm here now; we shan't get lost.'

He settled back, closing his eyes, his mouth gentle, clearly dozing off for a moment. Someone started to play the piano, banging out old tunes, the livelier ladies and gents joining in a singsong. Zoe found herself quietly continuing a one-sided conversation, the other people in the room receding like characters in soft focus.

'I wish you could talk to me, Pa. I've been so wretched. Everyone seems to be lying to me and I don't know which way to turn. I thought Saba was just another victim, but I'm not so sure she hasn't been manipulating us all, Haydon included. But then Haydon is so enmeshed in his own lies he doesn't know when he *is* telling the truth, I'd swear. And I'm here as a sort of lie, aren't I? You think I'm Chrissie back from God knows where, possibly back from the dead and haunting us both with her witch's curse and I can't break the spell for either of us. You can't make things better for me any more, can you, Pa? And I can't help you. We are both adrift and all I can hope is that we shall eventually emerge from all this. But how? I don't know what to do and you can't tell me. Never mind, my darling, we'll just wait for the wind to turn. That's what you used to say, wasn't it, Pa? When I got into one of my tizzies and the whole world seemed black you would say, "Well, sweetheart, we'll just have to wait for the wind to turn." And it always did.'

She slipped away after that and left him sleeping, the new socks and sweater draped over his knees. She had a short conversation with the administrator, but there wasn't much to report, Charlie Templeman's progress being currently in limbo. Zoe lunched at a sandwich bar in the High Street and mooched around the shops until three o'clock, when she returned to the nursing home for tea.

It was not until she was back in the hotel that night that she remembered the newspaper she had filched that morning. She settled in the bar downstairs with a drink before dinner and showed the page to the barman.

'Jesus, I remember that,' he said, swivelling the newspaper to read the headlines. 'Poor devil nobbled in that beauty spot just outside Staithsbury and the villains stripped out his cottage. Knew what they was after, if you ask me. A big-shot antique dealer he was – got a shop in Chester up on the Rows.'

'I knew him slightly,' Zoe said, telling how she had only just heard about the killing.

'Sad about the dog, though, poor mutt.'

She looked up, startled. 'What dog?'

'This bloke Mayhew used to go out jogging every morning, same place, same time. Took his dog along for a run.'

'It didn't go for his attackers?'

'Might have – nobody knows – but unlikely. It wasn't no German shepherd, just a pet, some sort of pointer, I heard. Anyway, the dog must have run round in panic when they ambushed the poor guy; it got run over when the muggers reversed out of the lay-by. They left tyre tracks.'

'They deliberately ran over his dog?'

'Well, that's what all the local animal lovers are upset about – never mind the poor sod with a knife in his ribs. That's the trouble with this country, if you ask me: everyone up in arms about fox-hunting and animal research laboratories but muggings barely get half an inch in the papers, let alone on TV. Only the fact that he was a local got it a mention in the press at all. Didn't get reported in London, I bet.'

'Probably not.'

Zoe sipped her gin and tonic, mulling over this philosophical argument. 'He was a local, you say?'

'Not actually living round here these days, but born and bred in Wrexham – went to the local school, even spoke Welsh, so we took a special interest, see? He had a place about twenty miles outside Chester, a little spot called Howfordham. Mayhew converted the old forge at the edge of the village, made a good job of it by all accounts.'

Zoe sat in bed that night trying to decide how to spin out her trip. She would go to the nursing home in the morning and hope that Charlie's misty recollection would clear sufficiently to remember his daughter on a third visit. It was all a put-off, she had to admit, a reluctance to drive back to Stonecrest and endure another miserable weekend with her doubts about Haydon unresolved and the police still hanging about. At least she was safely out of range here and had a decent excuse to stay away. Why not take advantage? After all, there was the inquest looming ahead; in all probability she would be going back to London the following week to give evidence about finding Max's body. And Kennedy? Would Kennedy be on the warpath looking for her?

In her present mood she was unwilling even to phone Haydon, rationalizing this reluctance by resort to the fact that he hadn't phoned her either, so what the hell? She would ring in the morning.

She studied the news story about the Mayhew mugging, the gory details sparse, the bulk of the article made up with photographs of his shop and cottage and a rehash of the victim's successful career. But then the paper had appeared straight after the killing, when presumably clues were still being followed up; perhaps the muggers had even been caught by now, or were at least being tracked down by the police. She rather doubted it. Her friendly barman would have filled her in if he'd had any more gossip to share, and presumably the CID in this country area was stretched very thin.

She ran down to the car and fetched a

road map. Howfordham. The barman was right: the village was only a short trip up the main road. A pleasant rural route suggested itself and a nose around Mayhew's neck of the woods would fill in most of the day. She decided to make a weekend of it and drive back to Stonecrest on Sunday night, by which time Haydon would be more like his usual self and her confrontation with Saba might no longer seem so imperative. So what if Haydon had been tempted by a one-night stand with Saba? Wasn't it partly her own fault? She had thrown them together, had avoided joining him when he had asked her down that week, hadn't she? Excuses, excuses, excuses.

But the desire to avoid the issue seemed more and more beguiling, warming with the half-bottle of vodka that she took to her lonely bed.

Twenty-Five

'Hi! It's me. You not out of bed yet, Haydon?'

Zoe kept the tone light, eight o'clock on a Sunday morning not being Haydon's highlight of the week.

'Yes, sure. Of course. Well, actually no,' he added with a laugh. 'I'm thinking about it, though. Be honest. You're missing me, aren't you?'

The banter blew back and forth across the airwaves, Zoe ruefully admitting that her weekend had not been an unmitigated joy.

'What's with the early start, sweetie?' he said, interrupting her lowdown on Charlie's state of health. 'You're chucking it in and coming home now?'

'No, I can't do that, Haydon. I've promised to make a final visit after lunch,' she lied.

'But if the old chap doesn't know you, what's the difference?'

'It's complicated. He thinks I'm my mother. Look, Haydon, take it from me, I've got to stay another day; I'll be back tonight.'

'Promise?'

'Don't wait up, I may be late – depends on the traffic. Any news on the Bert front?'

'Yes and no. The superintendent guy dropped in yesterday. The blood sample doesn't tie up with Cundey and he hasn't got any dog bites.'

'Really? That puts him in the clear then.'

'Not yet. They're now looking for a second man, possibly a drinking pal of his, who may have been treated at an accident and emergency unit over the weekend. And local doctors are being questioned too, just in case a man's been asking for urgent tetanus injections.'

'You did say you thought you had heard two men, didn't you? When the row woke you up.'

Haydon demurred. 'Couldn't swear to it, especially with Bert's dogs racketing on. Still, it's the only lead they've got.'

'But if Cundey had an accomplice and is temporarily in the clear, then Saba's uncle or husband could be back in the frame, couldn't they? Supposing they got two other relatives to do the dirty work? Saba says the uncle, being head of the clan, so to speak, is in a position to command family loyalty. Do you believe all this vendetta stuff?'

'I'm not sure. According to Fay Betteridge, it happens often enough in these close communities, and from their point of view I suppose Saba and her boyfriend deserved all they got.'

'To the point of setting fire to her in her bed?'

'Don't ask me, Zoe; leave it to the police. They're still searching for more bits of bloodstained clothing or even fag ends. That other detective, Kennedy, was telling me they could link an intruder with something as innocuous as a discarded cigarette butt or a half-eaten apple. The wonders of science!'

'Talking of the wonders of science, were you able to get out of the Rio conference?'

'They couldn't find another speaker at such short notice, so I agreed to stick with it. I'm not altogether sorry; it's a chance to meet with some of the top people in my field, exchange news of current break-throughs in technique and do a little net-working.'

Zoe paused, unwilling to break up the relaxed tone to ask whether networking included the tiresome Roberta Redford. 'Ah yes, sure, I see your point. Next week, isn't it? A chance to get away to the sun sounds heaven.'

'Do you want to tag along? A short break for both of us wouldn't come amiss.'

'Haydon, you know I can't. There's Max's inquest coming up.'

'Bad luck. Incidentally, I brought back your mail from the flat, lots of bumf from the estate agents and an official-looking envelope from the Coroner's office. Shall I open it?'

'No. Throw it in my drawer; I'll check it out this evening. I've got enough to worry about down here. Anything else? Saba still under lock and key at the vicarage?'

He laughed. 'Did you really think she could escape Fay that easily? This is all very nice, my darling, but I've got to be up and away. Roddy's coming for me at nine. We're invited to a clay-shoot at a farm belonging to one of his City friends. Sounds promising. According to Roddy this bloke's celebrating a massive end-of-year bonus, so it might be interesting.'

'Who's driving?'

'Roddy's farm labourer, the pig boy. I'll see you later then?'

Zoe put down the receiver with more than a little regret. Had she known Haydon would be in such a good mood she wouldn't have lied about filling in her day with visiting Pa. Still, he wouldn't be home, would he? And spending an empty day at Stonecrest would hardly have been much fun, especially with the fire-investigation team still on site.

She called in at the home to spend half an hour with Charlie before setting off towards Chester. The old man was less alert, but despite the confusion behind his welcome he had no difficulty in recognizing her as his daughter, making no reference to his dream-like recollection of Chrissie coming home. Perhaps he often had such hallucinations. Zoe hoped so. Even an imaginary visitation from Chrissie seemed to bring more animation than her own very real presence, a grown-up daughter so different from the black-eyed little girl in the photographs at his bedside.

The day was bright, the bare trees on the horizon gaunt and spectral against a clear washed sky. She intended only to nose round the picnic area in the forest where Chris Mayhew had met his assailants and then perhaps, if she had no new ideas about filling in the day ahead, to wander on to Howfordham and peer at the dead man's cottage.

Zoe felt reluctant to examine this wholly uncharacteristic curiosity. Perhaps the shadow of death, which seemed to be attached to her every step on the way since discovering Max's body, could be shaken off by this examination of the scene of the violent killing. Whatever was driving her on, she felt it was the only way forward, a secret rendezvous too shameful to confide to Haydon — or anyone else, come to that. It was as if she was drawn by a voyeuristic magnetism to face yet another bogeyman and thereby eradicate the demons. One man hanged, one man burnt in the flames and the last brought down by a knife. Except that Mayhew was not the last victim, was he? Mayhew had been the first to die and the three men were utterly unconnected except that each could loosely be described as her friend. Extraordinary.

The forest was gloomy and to Zoe's mind no beauty spot. The area had been planted with commercial pine, only the edge of the plantation disguised with deciduous trees. Sandy paths crisscrossed the forest in a geometrical pattern, occasionally opening out into a rough clearing, the perimeter pitted with lay-bys where joggers and weekend family parties could dump their cars to walk their dogs or unload children's bikes and move on to the picnic areas set out with rustic tables and benches: an unlovely venue, in Zoe's view, the canopy of evergreen unchanging through the seasons. Even so, the place was popular at weekends and to its credit was clean, safe from traffic and smelled wonderfully of pine needles crushed underfoot.

From the newspaper description, the crime scene was not difficult to pinpoint, with tatters of plastic ribbon tied to tree trunks to section off the actual spot and blowing in the cold wind like frayed streamers. Several ramblers were about, even joggers, all clearly undeterred by the recent violence. Zoe wandered around, straining to hear birdsong, which was curiously absent.

The murder spot was only fifty yards from a secluded lay-by, the same parking space where the police had found tyre tracks identical to those outside Mayhew's cottage. Zoe almost felt herself an expert in this scenes-of-crime business, having absorbed the minutiae that Kennedy had impressed upon her as being important. Presumably the fire officers investigating Bert's death had even more specialized methods of detecting criminal involvement, an expertise Zoe could not bring herself to contemplate.

A dog-walker approached on the path, his spaniel pulling on the lead, its nose glued to the ground. She turned away, feeling nauseous, and hurried back to the car. It was past midday and she decided to stop off at a pub before continuing, hoping the cheerful atmosphere of a bar would dispel the gloomy apprehension the dark forest had only made worse.

An hour later she drove slowly through Mayhew's village, past the church, finding the old forge at the end of a muddy side road just as the barman had described. The cottage stood back from the lane, its forecourt paved over, ranch-style gates wide enough to admit a full-size lorry, something Zoe guessed would frequently have featured in Mayhew's deliveries from sale rooms.

She parked under some trees a little way past the entrance and walked up a track that skirted the cottage and its numerous out-buildings. A back gate stood ajar, several dustbins and black plastic bin liners bulging with refuse put out ready for collection. Just as she was about to walk on, a woman struggling manfully with yet more rubbish stuffed into cardboard boxes suddenly appeared from behind a shrubbery.

Zoe hesitated. 'Can I give you a hand?'

The woman looked up, grey hair escaping from under a bandanna, her exhausted eyes red-rimmed and yet hopeful. She smiled. 'You must be an angel from heaven. Would you?'

Zoe took the larger box and stacked it with the others, following the woman back and forth to the kitchen door, where the remains of a major turn-out had been piled up. Finally, they stood back, eyeing the tottering stack with nervous satisfaction.

'I should have ordered a skip, shouldn't I?' she said. 'You've been so good. Won't you come in for a cup of tea?'

'You sure? You look all-in.'

She took Zoe's arm, guiding her through a kitchen and on into a sitting room. 'I'd be glad of some company, to be honest. My brother died and there's no one else to do this.'

'You're Chris's sister?'

She looked up, startled. 'You must be a neighbour.'

'No, a friend. My name's Zoe Templeman. Chris and I knew each other in London – I'm sort of in the trade.'

'From London?'

'I was up this way visiting my father – just passing – and I felt I owed your brother something of a salute. I only heard about his death a few days ago, you see. I suppose I missed the funeral. Being in the area I thought it would be nice to raise my hat in passing. A belated gesture of sympathy...' she ended lamely.

The woman pulled off her bandanna and held out her hand.

'What a charming thought! My name's Penny, by the way. Penny Drysdale. I owe you a cup of tea, at least. Sit down, I shan't be a moment – I'll just put the kettle on, shall I?'

Twenty-Six

While Chris Mayhew's sister was making the tea, Zoe gazed round the dead man's living room, the makeover of what had been a country forge quite an eyeful. The room had, she imagined, been the original workshop, the end that had opened up on to the lane being glassed in with an enormous picture window shaded with blinds. The window had presumably been shut off from prying eyes since the murder, the room now in semi-darkness with the curtains firmly closed against the world, the only illumination being an overhead light and a bright table lamp on the desk.

The floor had been expensively resurfaced with polished oak boards and dotted about with rugs. Two sofas flanked a wide fireplace and numerous side tables displayed statuettes and enamel snuff boxes. Zoe wondered why the thieves had not pocketed these, but perhaps, during the turn-out, the sister had unearthed some of the more valuable items to take away.

Penny returned carrying a tray of teacups,

226

and lurched into the seat beside her new friend, her exhaustion all too apparent. She smiled and passed a steaming cup to her visitor.

'Sorry, no cake, but the milk's fresh.'

'Isn't there anyone to help you with all this?'

'Unfortunately not. I'm divorced and Sunday's my only free day. I've been at it since last night, the first weekend I've had the chance to sort out, though, to be honest, I have been putting it off. How did you hear about poor Chris?'

'A friend told me. Another dealer from around here. You may know him – a chap called Larry Buxton.'

She shook her head. 'I didn't take much interest in Chris's business, and the funeral was a very quiet affair – just family. Mr Buxton told you the whole story?'

'Only what was in the local paper, and even my latest information is out of date. I expect the police have made progress by now, haven't they?'

'Absolutely none. No witnesses. No traceable fingerprints and the few items that disappeared have not, on the face of it, been offered for sale anywhere. There were tyre tracks which apparently indicate that one of the back wheels had a brand new tyre, though the rest were badly worn. Luckily, the ground was soft and the police were able to take casts. Hardly pinpoints the vehicle, though, does it? My own car's got a mixed batch of tyres, as have millions of others.'

'Just tearaways, I guess. An opportunistic hit.'

'No, not at all. The inspector is quite certain Chris was targeted. His watch and gold bracelet were stolen, but they didn't stop there. This cottage is piled high with antiques – Chris used it as a sort of staging post for things for the shop – but very little was taken.'

'They must have been disturbed.'

'Possibly. But the strange thing is, Zoe, the stuff they did take was minimal, when one looks around here.' She brushed a hand in a wide gesture. 'Chris's assistant checked the contents against recent purchases and found the only things missing were a couple of Colombian vases, a bronze mask and a Venetian glass paperweight.'

Zoe gulped, a nasty taste of déjà-vu rising in her gullet.

'But,' Penny continued, 'the most puzzling move was their search of the filing cabinet using the keys on his keyring. Luckily, we had spares.'

'Did Chris use it for locking up small items? A sort of mini-safe?'

'Frank, his assistant, says not. But he's sure some correspondence was taken. Receipts, provenance certificates and so on.'

'That sort of paperwork would be invaluable to anyone wanting to sell a stolen object. Without such back-up questions would be asked by reputable dealers. Did Frank know exactly what was gone?'

'No, he's only the shop assistant. Chris handled all the buying himself and did his own typing. My brother was a self-made man, Zoe, and distrustful. He didn't make friends easily and liked to keep his deals to himself as far as possible. But I expect you know all that.'

'He never married, did he?'

'No, more's the pity. A wife would have been a godsend. Chris's interests were narrow, making pots of money being his chief aim in life. He was much younger than me, of course, so we were never really close, but no one deserves to be attacked so brutally, killed that way ... And his dog too. He loved that dog, you know.'

Penny quickly rose to fetch a framed snapshot of a shaggy looking beast with a lolling tongue. She passed it over to Zoe, who visibly brightened.

'Oh, it's a spinoni,' she said with a laugh. 'A friend of mine has one. They're lovely dogs – quite scatty, of course. Roddy's dog's always running off and getting himself into scrapes.' She returned the picture.

Penny stared at the photograph, her face grave. 'Poor old boy. Chips, Chris called him. Took that dog everywhere with him, even left it in the car at auction sales. Not that Chips was any good as a guard dog. It was run over by the other car, you know. Silly dog must have been diving round in a panic during the attack and got in the way as they drove off.'

'Yes, I heard. Bad luck.'

'Though if Chips had survived, goodness knows what I'd have done with him. I live in a flat.'

Zoe placed her empty cup on the tray and rose to go, holding out her hand. 'Anything more I can do before I go, Penny?'

They walked to the front door and picked their way past the pile of detritus heaped in the side lane. On impulse Zoe felt in her bag for an envelope and scribbled down her phone number.

'Here,' she said, pressing it into Penny's hand, 'give me a buzz if ever you're in town. We'll have lunch.'

'Lovely. When all this is over I may treat myself to some shopping in London. You've been kind. Thank you. You popping in like this has cheered me up no end. I had no idea Chris had friends in the business who cared about him. He was so *driven*. It tended to put people off.'

Zoe accelerated away, a niggle of anxiety working away at the back of her mind, the cause of which danced further out of focus the more she thought about it. She thrust it aside, concentrating on getting back on route, the dark already closing in, the winter afternoons getting shorter and shorter.

She arrived back at Stonecrest earlier than she had expected, the traffic thin on this Sunday night, weekending in the country being less attractive in bleak November.

Haydon was in a good mood, his clay-shooting excursion with Roddy having been just the thing for taking his mind off the police investigation. He had got back only an hour before her, but was already showered and eager for an extended evening.

'What happened to Roddy?'

'Too much booze. My guess is he's retired to bed with a headbanger. This pal of his had invited a crowd of investment brokers and some other City types down for a day's shooting and, believe me, no expense was spared.'

'Boys only?'

'Very laddish. Not at all like my sober medical colleagues, my love.'

'You seem pretty perky. Went easy on the champagne? Or just got more stamina than poor Roddy?'

He grabbed her, putting on his caveman act. 'Yeah! And there's plenty left over for you, my little trixy belle.'

Zoe relaxed, knowing that there was no soft pedalling with this mood of his. They went out for a bite to eat at an Indian place up the road and spent an hour or more picking over the bones of her weekend. She said nothing of her meeting with Mayhew's sister and skated over the sick-visiting bit, knowing Haydon's boredom threshold to be low when it came to descriptions of geriatric establishments. Nevertheless, she managed credibly to fill the gaps and pressed him for details about Roddy's affluent friends, on which subject he was happy to elaborate.

'These guys are seriously loaded, Zoe. The numbers are just mind-blowing.'

'You talked business all the time? I thought it was supposed to be a fun day out.'

'Money *is* fun, honeybunch. Maybe I should have gone in for banking – do you think I'd have been good at it?' He wasn't altogether joking.

'Undoubtedly. Still, Roddy took to his heels quick enough, didn't he? The stress factor must be enormous.'

'And you think reassembling faces is stress-free?' he retorted.

'No, of course not.' She patted his hand. 'And the burns cases you treat are a million times more valuable than piling up money in crazy deals.'

When they got home, Zoe stretched out on the sofa, the day's travails suddenly taking over. Haydon passed her a glass of brandy together with her post he had recovered from the flat. She sifted through the estate agents' guff with little enthusiasm and reluctantly opened the official-looking envelope that was, as she feared, requiring her attendance at the Coroner's Court the following Wednesday morning. She passed it over, and Haydon read it and grimaced.

'You still going to Rio next week?' she said.

'Uh-huh. Venetia's booked a flight on Tuesday. Just as well she didn't book an extra one for you; evading a coroner's summons is probably a hanging offence.'

'I shall only be required to make a brief statement. Stupid, isn't it? I could be lying on the beach with you instead of dancing attendance in court. You do realize I shan't be at Stonecrest while you're away; I don't relish being stuck here on my own all week. I might as well move back to the flat for a few days and suss out possible workshops.'

'Just as you like.'

'But that means the house will be unoccupied. What would your Mrs Redford say about that?' she wickedly added.

'We've already discussed it. She's sending down a security team – two muscle men to look after the place – just as soon as she's able to fix it.'

'There's nowhere for them to sleep! Bert's cottage is burnt out and Saba's is uninhabitable. Apart from peripheral fire damage it was soaked by the hoses. It'll be damp for weeks.'

'They'll be bringing a caravan. The police say it will be OK. They've scaled down the search in the grounds – just a patrol surveillance to keep an eye on comings and goings. They're still questioning Cundey about a possible accomplice, but until they turn up more evidence he's up and away.'

'And Saba's tribe?'

'Similarly being badgered, I imagine, but the police have to tread carefully – don't want to be accused of racial harassment. Roddy tells me Saba's going back to work tomorrow.'

'Well, it's one way to escape Fay for a few hours,' she said with a chuckle.

'You may be bitchy about that girl, Zoe, but Roddy says she's a bloody good book-keeper.'

'And?'

'And what?'

'What else is the delectable Saba bloody good at?'

'Now you're just being jealous. If Roddy gets his leg over, good luck to him, I say. He leads the life of a monk with those pigs of his. About time he got himself a bit of skirt.'

'Is your crudity saved only for your friends, Haydon? I bet your lady patients have no idea what a sex-crazed beast you are under that white coat.'

'I don't wear a white coat.'

'You don't call yourself "Mister" either, do you, Haydon? I thought all surgeons dumped the "Doctor" bit when they moved up the ladder.'

'It's an English thing. Most of my patients are foreigners; they trust a "doctor". If I started calling myself plain Mister Masure, they might think I'd something to hide.'

'Been struck off for naughty thoughts?'

'Seriously, Zoe, it's simpler to hang on with a handle they're used to. In Europe half the politicians call themselves Doctor Something-or-Other. It's unimportant. I call myself whatever I choose.'

She let it drop, realizing that she had accidentally touched a raw nerve.

'OK, Haydon. Let's go upstairs and play doctors and nurses, shall we?'

Twenty-Seven

After Haydon left on Tuesday morning Zoe packed her bag and spent an hour sifting through the estate agents' offers. It was all very depressing: either office premises way out in the suburbs or empty shops, way over budget. A unit in the laundry complex was still the most appealing; it looked as if she would have to bite the bullet and resign herself to a workshop without living accommodation.

Trouble was, the longer she had to refuse work the more likely her regular clients would take their business elsewhere. Haydon had suggested she use the old stables at Stonecrest, move out of London, save on rent and have all the space she wanted. He even offered to pay for the refurbishment, but to accept would be to place herself entirely in Haydon's pocket, and what if Mrs Redford decided to sell up after she had put all her savings into re-establishing herself out in the country? Also there might be problems with setting up business in the grounds of a private house; she would have

236

to ask Roddy's advice about planning permission, Roddy being in with all the council bigwigs.

The phone rang. She picked up the receiver at the side of their bed and a gruff voice on a crackly line assaulted her eardrums.

'Donny there?'

'You've got the wrong number.'

'Don't piss me about, darlin'; just put him on. Donny Masure.'

'Doctor Masure's away. Are you a patient?'

'Yeah. It's urgent. What about the surgery?'

'You could try, but he's flying out to a conference this afternoon. Can I take a message?'

'Who's this?'

'Look, either you want me to take a message or you can try his consulting rooms. Please yourself.'

'Now ain't you the stroppy one!' he said with a laugh. 'You must be the girlfriend. The police still hangin' about?'

She hesitated, the voice at the other end of the line sounding most unlike that of any of Haydon's patients. 'The place is crawling with them, day and night,' she lied.

The interference on the line grew stronger as if the man was calling from a submarine at the very least.

'Who shall I say called?' she persisted. But

the line went dead, leaving her holding the receiver away and frowning in disbelief. Obviously this was no patient, but who *was* it? Close enough to ask for 'Donny', at any rate. She laughed, picturing Haydon wincing at this, no one ever to her knowledge having dared use such a familiarity. Perhaps it was one of Mrs Redford's heavies clocking in. She donned her ski jacket and lugged the weekend bag downstairs, dropping it in the hall before going in search of the house-keeper.

She was in the kitchen loading up the washing machine. 'Hi, Brenda – I'll be off then. Back Friday night.'

'Right you are. Any shopping?'

'Order some croissants for the weekend, if you wouldn't mind. I'll bring some fish back from town myself; Haydon likes fresh tuna and I can call in at the market before I leave. He arrives back on Saturday. One other thing, Brenda: if anyone rings up, or anyone asks you in the village, would you mind pretending the police are still here all the time? I had a funny phone call just now; he didn't give his name and I don't like to let people know that we've no one on call at present, especially when the place is unoccupied overnight.'

'The doctor said you was getting some new security men in shortly.'

'Yes, but it may take a week or two to

arrange. They'll be living in a caravan so shouldn't be a nuisance to you up here, but in the meantime mum's the word, OK?'

Brenda looked pensive. 'They let that Cundey out I heard.'

'Innocent till proved guilty,' Zoe wryly remarked. 'You're not nervous, are you, Brenda, being here on your own?'

She smiled grimly. 'No way. Got used to it, 'aven't I, since Mrs Redford sold up.'

Zoe's eyes widened. 'You must have known her, of course. What was she like?'

'Oh, very glamorous in a splashy sort of way, if you take my meaning. Bottle-blonde and gold charm bracelets jangling like bunches of keys – you could hear her coming a mile off.'

'Any children?'

'Not likely – would have cramped her style. Thought herself no end of a catch. Beats me why she stuck to that ugly brute Mullins; stands to reason it'd only lead to trouble. I bet she's found herself a new sugar daddy by now; no point in 'anging about for *his* ship to come home no more, he's been on the run for years.' She tapped the side of her nose in a knowing gesture and turned back to loading the machine.

'Oh, before I forget, Brenda: I've ironed the altar cloth and laid it out on the bed in Saba's old room, if the vicar calls in for it. I'd better push off; I've got two appointments this afternoon. Ring me on my mobile if there's any emergency.'

By the time she had unpacked her things at the flat and made herself a sandwich, it was time to make tracks. She hadn't spoken to Nick for over a week and until she had made up her mind to rent a new workroom it was impossible to calculate whether she would even be able to afford to keep him on. Perhaps she would ask if he would be willing to commute to Stonecrest if she decided, as a last resort, to take Haydon up on his offer to set her up in the stables. Economically it made sense. If she worked from Stonecrest she would even save enough money to employ a full-time assistant and have more of a work area into the bargain. The pros and cons battled it out in her mind all day, her reluctance to put herself entirely into Haydon's debt being, if she was honest, the real stumbling block.

Inspector Kennedy rang her at the flat that evening and reassured her that her appearance at the Coroner's Court would be a mere formality.

'It's kind of you to call, Inspector. To be honest, what with all the trouble at my boyfriend's house, Max's death seems ages ago. I hope I don't let you down.'

She dressed carefully next morning, choosing a black trouser suit enlivened by a Hermes scarf Haydon had tucked inside a chocolate egg as a surprise at Easter. Haydon was brilliant at surprises, his enthusiam at Christmastime putting her own panic-buying to shame. He had phoned early Wednesday morning to say he had arrived, that Rio was stupendous and that, joking aside, it was just as well she hadn't flown in to reveal her skinny white legs on the beach, as the sight of all those stunning and minimally covered beauties would have had her scampering back to the hotel room.

'Thank you for those words of encouragement, sweetheart, but these skinny white legs you are so rude about are just about to take me off to court. Wish me luck. Oh, by the way, someone asking for "Donny" phoned before I left. Wouldn't give his name and sounded something of a rough diamond, so I told him to ring the surgery. Did he reach you?'

'Er, yes,' Haydon replied curtly. 'A patient. Anything else?'

'Really? He's really a patient of yours? Crikey! I was pretty rude, too. And I lied about the continuing police presence at Stonecrest.' She giggled. 'Honestly, Haydon, I thought he was just another villain "casing the joint", as they say.'

Haydon didn't think this was funny and rang off in a huff, Zoe admitting that, for all his nice side, this live-in lover of hers had no sense of humour.

The courtroom was thinly attended, Zoe appreciating the friendly wave of Trevor Simpson, the Coroner's Officer, as she took her seat. Proceedings had already started as Desiree slipped in, her face half-hidden by a silver-fox hat that covered her ears augmented by a mohair stole pulled around her chin to create a picture of a Russian refugee, albeit a refugee of aristocratic status. Zoe discreetly raised a hand and Desiree's eyes under the fur brim swivelled nervously in response.

The hearing trundled along, Kennedy's promise of a swift outcome adequately fulfilled. The Coroner's Officer's work had been proficient, Kennedy's evidence was succinct, and Zoe's brief résumé of her part in the event was kindly received. A suicide verdict – no problem there – and, to Desiree's relief, no elaboration regarding Max's money troubles. Zoe joined her in the street outside, squeezing her hand in sympathy. Desiree's eyes brimmed, the veneer of estranged and unfeeling wife stripped away.

'Will you come back with me, Zoe? I've got to pick up a few things from Max's house first, but if you have time, it would be a comfort to have some company for an hour or two. At my flat, of course. I asked my help to put up some sandwiches for lunch. Do come. Please?'

They waved down a taxi and bowled along

to Bisley Road, Desiree asking the driver to wait while they went inside. The locks had been changed since the funeral, she explained, 'And Mr Perry urged me to update the burglar alarm system too, just in case.'

'But you are selling?'

'Oh yes. Freddie McPherson has keys; I leave it all to him. I'm so glad to see you again, Zoe; it seems ages. Jason said you'd had trouble at the doctor's country house: a fire. I don't take a newspaper myself — too depressing for words; but I hope you haven't been caught up in it. One suicide in a lifetime's enough for anyone. A man died, I heard.'

'Yes, the caretaker. But it wasn't suicide; they suspect arson. It's a terrible business. But don't let's talk about all that, Desiree. What is it you came for?'

They hurried into the study where a sizeable cardboard box lay on the desk, vividly taking Zoe back to that other deserted house where another sad woman, Penny Drysdale, had had to face the boxed-up reminders of a dead man.

'As we're here, Desiree, could I ask a favour? You know all those old catalogues we checked against Max's purchases? Do you still have them?'

Desiree looked blank, her blue eyes bright as cornflowers under the fringe of her fur hat. 'All that paperwork? I suppose so. I told

Jason to bag up the correspondence and store it in the cellar until after the sale of the furniture and contents in case the auditor wanted to double check. Why?'

'Could I possibly borrow some catalogues for a few days? A check on textile prices would be useful to me. Would you mind?'

Desiree frowned. 'No, of course not. Take the lot, if you like; I can always say we threw them out. Max didn't buy much lately, as I remember from our stocktaking, but he always noted prices. Goodness me, if Max kept every single catalogue we'd be snowed under. Here's the key; help yourself.'

Zoe felt her way down the unfamiliar cellar steps, the empty wine racks seeming to emphasize Max's cash-flow problems in that last year or two – a man who had prided himself on the quality of his cellar. The lighting was poor, casting shadows along the cement floor and into the arched niches, the atmosphere as chill as a crypt.

Plastic bags were stacked at one end, all date-labelled. She opened the relevant sack, rifled through the contents, pouncing on the latest sale room lists as if she had found fifty-pound notes in the street, and stuffed them into her bag. She ran back upstairs, locking the cellar door behind her.

Desiree stood in the hallway, the cardboard box at her feet, her eyes closed as if in prayer. Zoe helped lift the box into the taxi and they arrived at Desiree's mansion block just after one.

As they rose in the clanking old lift, Zoe ventured to ask about Max's car.

'Oh, it's gone. I told Jason to get rid of it. Max wasn't at all interested in cars, you know, and Jason said it needed an MOT certificate. Mr Gilbert said it could go, so I told Jason to deal with it.' Her fingers trembled as she placed her key in the lock. 'I'm not very good at that sort of thing, and what would I do with a big old car like that? I find it easier to use taxis, don't you, Zoe dear?'

Twenty-Eight

Having Haydon's flat to myself was a mixed blessing, the emptiness aggravated by all his things dotted about, his exercise bike lumbering up the spare room, the lingering scent of aftershave in the bathroom.

I had thought I needed some time to myself, but as soon as I determined to set my mind to facing up to my problems with work, not to mention my relationship with Haydon, the thoughts skittered away like frightened mice.

Perhaps it was stress, like everyone insisted I

must be feeling; but I rather doubted it, 'sheer funk' being the words I'd have chosen.

Zoe did eventually pluck up courage to ring the consulting rooms to speak to Venetia, quizzing her in as discreet a manner as she could summon up about her rough-speaking caller.

'Oh, that must have been Mr Benson – sounds a right old tramp doesn't he? Yes, he did ring, but Haydon had already left for the airport – wanted to know which hotel the conference was booked into.'

'And he really is a patient?'

'Oh yes, a long-standing one – still has the odd tuck from time to time. Haydon's going to meet up with him in Rio.'

Zoe swallowed hard. 'Is this roughneck a friend of Mrs Redford?'

'Don't think so. Why?'

'Oh, er, nothing. Just that I hear that Mrs Redford is in Rio too at the moment. She's a patient as well, isn't she?'

Venetia reluctantly agreed, judging that discussion of the doctor's special patients was moving into deep water.

'Look, Zoe, I've got to get on. Lots of catching up to do.'

She rang off, leaving Zoe feeling uncomfortable, as if she had taken advantage of Venetia's goodwill. But she had every right to enquire, hadn't she? After all, Haydon had left her with the Stonecrest enquiry round her neck, had asked more or less that she should keep an eye on the place for him, hadn't he? To look out for any possible intruders. Perhaps she should have stayed put in the country – done the decent thing and kept watch in his absence.

He phoned her each day, briefly outlining conference sessions but saying nothing about meeting up with Benson in Rio, or even Mrs Redford, who was presumably pumping him for details of Bert's death and the continuing investigation of the fire.

Zoe put down the phone after each of these perplexing conversations increasingly worried about Haydon's state of mind. His usual hearty manner was uncharacteristically subdued, her questions brushed off with excuses about a busy schedule, cocktail parties and 'pointless debates about skin grafting'. Zoe couldn't help wondering if accepting this last-minute invitation to address the conference had been an excuse to fly to Rio, Haydon's contempt for his lesser colleagues normally enough to make him avoid professional get-togethers of this kind, his unassailable position as a leading light in his field in London being a discouragement to possibly denting his own self-esteem by hobnobbing with the competition. Zoe knew her man – or thought she did – and his professional egoism, albeit well founded, was a human failing she accepted.

She telephoned de Vries at home on Thursday evening just to assure him that she was now free to bring the tapestry to Paris. A woman answered, her low-voiced response immediately switching to English as Zoe introduced herself.

'Ah yes, Miss Templeman; my father has often spoken of you. He has a very high regard for your work. This is Anne speaking.'

'Would it be convenient to deliver the de Maurnay tapestry one day next week, mademoiselle?'

'But of course. But my parents are away at present. In Bermuda – my mother's rheumatism demands it,' she added with a chuckle. 'You could leave the tapestry at the gallery with Xavier, no problem.'

'I'd rather not.'

'It will be perfectly safe, I assure you.'

'No, that's not in question – of course not. It's just that Monsieur de Vries is anxious to see the work I have done, requires me to indicate the exact nature of my repairs. I need to see him in person.'

'In that case, may I suggest a delay? They will return to Paris in time for Christmas, are expected home about the fourteenth, I think.'

'I had better leave it until he gets back. I'll ring again later then, shall I? But would you mind telling your father I rang? Or shall I leave a message with Xavier – a new man, isn't he? I haven't met Xavier before.'

'*Mais non*,' Anne de Vries hurriedly intervened. 'Xavier *is* new, and rather forgetful, I think – or so Papa complains. I expect the poor man is nervous at being left in charge of the gallery at such a busy time of the year; but *Maman* insisted, you see – insisted her life was at stake if their usual winter break in the sun was postponed.'

De Vries's daughter sounded nice, Zoe decided, not at all the brusque Parisienne she was used to encountering on her gallery excursions. The dealer had never mentioned having a daughter living at home, but maybe she was flat-sitting. Feeding the cat? Taking the chance to move back home for a week or two and do her Christmas shopping in comfort?

She drove to Kensington the following afternoon, hoping to catch Desiree in, and rang the doorbell. It was her lucky day: Desiree was playing bridge with three of her ladies. She drew Zoe into the hallway, all smiles, all traces of the sad Russian refugee erased.

'My dear, how lovely to see you. Do come and meet my friends.'

Zoe grabbed her arm. 'I don't want to spoil your afternoon, Desiree. It's the tapestry. I wondered if I could borrow the keys and collect it from Bisley Road?'

Desiree glanced at her watch. 'No need; Freddie's there now. If you hurry, you'll catch him. He said he was showing round two sets of viewers this afternoon. I'll ring him on his mobile, shall I? Tell him you're on your way? Come through.'

'I'll wait here,' Zoe whispered, anxious not to be caught up with Desiree's bridge trio. Desiree disappeared into the kitchen to make the call, emerging to assure her that the estate agent would be there till four.

'Are you off to Paris then, dear?'

'Soon. I just thought I'd better pick it up while I'm in London. Things are pretty frantic at Haydon's country place because of the murder; I'm not sure when I'll be able to get back to town.'

Zoe made a swift exit, glad to have escaped yet another likely heart-to-heart with Max's widow. Much as she had grown to like Desiree, the older woman's keen interest in her 'romance with that lovely surgeon' bordered on the Mills and Boon and, in her present frame of mind, dissecting her love life was the last thing she needed.

She drove to Bisley Road at speed, hoping to catch Freddie McPherson between clients. He opened the door before her second bang on the knocker, his eyes taut with apprehension.

'Quick! Come in. My next lot are due any minute. What's up? You wanted to see me urgently, Desiree said. More trouble at Stonecrest?'

He shut the door behind her, stiff as a man awaiting execution. Fresh flowers bloomed on the hall table and the aroma of fresh coffee wafted from the kitchen.

'Calm down, Freddie; nothing's blown up yet. Haydon's gone to Rio, on the face of it to attend a conference, but I think his main concern is filling in Mrs Redford with all the bad news.'

'Let's hope she stays there.'

'Really? You're probably right. Frankly, I'm too confused to care at present. Desiree put the wind up you for nothing; I only came to collect my tapestry. It's in the studio. Would you give me a hand? My car's outside.'

He visibly relaxed, blowing out his cheeks in comic relief.

They lifted the consignment on to Max's trolley and wheeled it out to the car, Freddie watching with amazement Zoe's deft bundling of the heavy tapestry into the boot.

'I'll return the trolley when I get back from Paris.'

'Don't bother. Desiree's still got stuff to chuck out once the place is under offer; the trolley's no use to anyone else. Keep it, why don't you?'

'You sure? I'll ask Desiree, but you're right: it's really of not much value except to me. I'm still looking for a new workshop, by the way.'

'None of those I sent to you any good?'

'Too pricey. I'm seriously thinking about renting a unit in a co-operative in Fulham, if nothing else turns up.'

'Let me give it the once-over for you before you sign. I might be able to do a deal for you. Who's the agent?'

Zoe had just started to natter on about the old laundry project as the limousine bringing Freddie's second set of prospective buyers drew up at the kerb. She broke off, shutting the boot with a thud and waving goodbye as he turned to greet his new clients – Hong Kong Chinese, by the look of it, the lady diminutive but well upholstered in a puffa jacket, her partner equally tiny but dressed in a lightweight suit, seemingly oblivious to the chill wind, his eyes swivelling from Zoe's battered runabout to his own chauffeur-driven Mercedes.

She left the tapestry with the caretaker at Haydon's apartment block, who promised to lock it safely away in his storeroom, Zoe cheerfully admitting to herself that a fortnight's grace before de Vries expected her in Paris was an unexpected bonus.

By then the nagging persistence of an

unnamed dread lurking at the back of her mind since her trip to Chester would sensibly have blown away.

Twenty-Nine

Haydon rang on Friday saying he would be driving straight down to Stonecrest from the airport on Saturday morning.

'You will be there, won't you?' he said.

'Sure, if that's what you want. But wouldn't it be less tiring if you stayed in London for the weekend? – I presume you are back at the surgery Monday morning.'

'I can't talk now; just take it I need to be down there as soon as I can. I'll explain later.'

He sounded irritable and rang off before she could ask about his trip. Haydon hated flying – that must be it.

He arrived back just before lunch, his face grey and his mood stony. Zoe had buzzed down to the country with high hopes of a return to their former relaxed relationship, but clearly the continuing police surveillance was getting on his nerves.

'Still searching the grounds, are they?'

'Off and on. When they can spare the

manpower, I guess.'

Haydon flopped on to one of the library sofas, clearly all-in. She perched on the arm of his chair.

'Guess what? I've been cooking. Home-made chicken soup, the nearest thing to a love potion.'

Zoe's skill in the kitchen was a running joke, Haydon being by far the more adept at the chopping board, showing a deftness with the knife that made her wince.

'Why don't you have a nice relaxing bath and I'll bring you some of my magic broth on a tray? An afternoon in the sack and bye-bye, jet lag. I've lots to tell you.'

He squeezed her hand. 'Yeah, me too. Actually, what I really need is a whisky. Then the bath. *Then* the bloody soup.' He threw her a weak grin, a phantom of the old Haydon she knew.

'Was the conference a terrible bore?'

'One or two interesting things turned up and my lecture was a hit, but you're right: on the whole it was a waste of effort.'

'No time for romping on the beach, then?'

He ignored this, rising stiffly to pour himself a drink. 'Something for you?' he said, raising an eyebrow.

'Not yet. Later. I thought we might send out for a Chinese. I expect you've had enough of airline catering.'

He swigged the double Scotch like

mother's milk and, tucking the decanter under his arm, trailed out of the room and upstairs to run a bath.

Zoe slid down on to the sofa, troubled by his strange mood. Haydon was generally the last to admit to depression, his sunny disposition honed by years of professional cheerfulness. She shrugged and moved into the kitchen to put the soup on to simmer.

Later that afternoon, while Haydon slept, she walked over to Roddy's cottage and knocked at the door. No reply. She looked in at the shop to seek him out, but only Saba was in the back room, tapping away at the computer. Zoe brightened.

'Hi! Long time, no see – you working overtime?'

'End-of-year accounts.'

'I was hoping to catch Roddy.'

'He's up in the field with Terry, seeing to one of the sows. Taken Ali with him to round up the piglets.'

Saba looked radiant, her crankiness all washed away, her white rollneck sweater gleaming like a detergent ad.

'You look happy, Saba. Everything working out at the vicarage?'

'Fay's been wonderful, and as soon as I've saved a bit more cash I shall find myself a couple of rooms in the village. The girls in the shop are keeping an eye out for me.'

'You've decided to stay, then.'

'Fay's organized a solicitor to look after us and the police seem to think my family had nothing to do with the fire, so I've decided to stop running – for the present, anyhow. Ali's in the nativity play! Just loves it. Fay wangled a place for him in nursery school and I'm hoping he can start proper school after Christmas. Sean would have been so proud. Can I get you some coffee or anything while you're waiting for Roddy? He won't be long.'

'No thanks, I'm trying to cut out some of the caffeine hits; all this worry about the fire and Max's inquest has made me jittery as a hair trigger.'

'It went well, the inquest? Roddy said there would be no problem.'

'Went through like a dose of salts. I told you there was nothing to worry about, didn't I? Kennedy was just trying to make two and two make five linking Bert's accident with poor old Max. Do you mind if I smoke?'

'Roddy's given up, did you know? He was worried about Ali's asthma.'

'Really? Well, that's it. I've simply got to take to the nicotine patches, no messing; but, until the smoke clears on this current catastrophe, I just can't summon up the will-power.'

Zoe lit up and moved to the window, staring out at the bare winter fields. Saba started tapping away again, her dark hair falling like silk around her shoulders. Zoe turned to face her, encouraged by Saba's upbeat air to raise a question that had been gnawing away at her for days.

'Saba, I know talking about Max is painful, but could you cast your mind back? All the time you worked for him, did Max ever stay away overnight?'

She looked up, puzzled. 'Max? Oh Zoe, it all seems so long ago. I can't remember.'

'Think back. He always said he liked to sleep in his own bed if he could, but apart from his foreign buying trips he seemed very much the home bird.'

Saba frowned. 'I was only there a few weeks, Zoe, but actually, now you mention it, there was one time. It must have been about a week before he ... er ... you know...'

'Can you remember exactly?'

'It was a Thursday, I'm sure. I had expected him back and had left a shepherd's pie in the fridge for him. Max preferred simple food like that – never took to takeaways or pizzas and stuff. When he had been out working late, I always left something ready and he put it in the microwave when he got home. He was a lovely man, Zoe – never wanted to disturb me in the evenings.'

'Then what?'

'Next morning I got up early and found the supper untouched. I knocked on his bedroom door – he was an old man, Zoe; I was worried he had been taken ill. But he hadn't slept in his bed and the car was still gone. I threw the shepherd's pie in the bin, and when he returned that night, I offered to make something fresh. But he brushed it aside and shut himself up in the study, said very sweetly he'd already eaten; but I didn't believe him. Poor old Max just didn't want to cause me any trouble.'

Hearing Roddy and the excited chatter of Ali in the shop, Zoe stubbed out her ciggy and got up to greet them. Ali was like a jumping jack, leaping into Saba's lap as she opened her arms to him. Roddy grinned, saluting Zoe and announcing the good news with a flourish.

'This clever little boy can now count, you know! Totted up the new piglets without even using his fingers. A real chip off the old block, aren't you, old man? Be working the computer next.'

Saba beamed, hushing Ali's outpourings with a kiss and setting him down while she shuffled Roddy's accounts back into a box file.

'I'll finish this on Monday, shall I?' she said, wrinkling her nose and pointing at the ashtray. 'But I'll get back now before Ali starts wheezing. Only a joke!' she added, giving Zoe a playful push and striding out through the shop, the child clinging to her long woollen skirt like a monkey.

Haydon slept like the dead until well after seven o'clock that evening, Zoe nervously lighting up all the rooms in the house like a power station, suddenly aware of the quiet without Bert's dogs to enliven the night air. This weekend she would pull out all the stops to persuade Haydon to abandon the house. It definitely had a jinx and, since the police had scaled down their presence, the loneliness of this monstrous pile of masonry seemed to crowd in on her. Why keep up the pretence? Haydon was no real country lover; nor was she. And even if the clangour of traffic in London sometimes got wearisome, it didn't mean they had to continue to maintain an ancestral country seat, did it? A weekend cottage would do. But then, as Meriel so often pointed out, a thatched love nest in the backwoods was hardly an appropriate setting for an eminent surgeon, was it?

Haydon staggered downstairs in his dressing gown, the empty decanter in his hand, a day's stubble shadowing his chin, his eyes blurry with sleep.

'Good God, is that the time? Why ever didn't you wake me, Zoe? I'll never sleep tonight.'

'So what? I've got other plans for filling in your bouts of insomnia, Doctor Masure.'

She pulled him to her, running her cold

hands over his chest. 'Soup working yet? Supreme aphrodisiac, according to the witch's handbook.'

He pushed her away, replacing the whisky decanter on the side table.

'Sit down, Zoe. I've got something serious to discuss with you.'

Thirty

To say that alarms started ringing would be to pretend that Quasimodo swinging on Notre Dame's biggest bell was temple chimes tinkling in the breeze.

This was it: Haydon had decided to end it. After years of a see-saw relationship, he was finally tipping me off. Was I surprised? Numb with dreadful expectation, more like. I moved to one of the club chairs as far away from him as I could and waited for the ultimate stroke of the clapper.

But I was wrong.

'Listen, Zoe, we've got to pack up in a hurry. We're leaving here pronto.'

She listened, open-mouthed.

'You did hear me, didn't you? By Monday we have to clear out with all our stuff.'

Her voice came out in what could only be described as a squawk. 'Why?'

'Because I say so.'

That broke the spell. She laughed, leaning back against the leather, her expression one of genuine glee. 'Haydon, I'm not five years old. I haven't heard that phrase since Pa refused to let me go to India in my gap year.'

She lit a cigarette, a move guaranteed to rile him, and Haydon sighed, sifting his words as if he were sorting mouldy grapes in a bowl of fruit.

'OK. Mrs Redford's selling up.'

'Immediately?'

'Absolutely. She's already e-mailed McPherson to get on his horse.'

'Why the sudden change of heart? I thought she intended to return here some time – that you were only keeping the place warm till she got tired of jetting around. Presumably she warned you we were being kicked out without notice when you were in Rio.'

'You don't know this woman, Zoe. She clicks her fingers and we all jump.'

'Not me I don't.'

'You refuse to leave?'

'Just you try to stop me! In fact it was on my mind to beg you to split from here. As it happens, I couldn't agree with her more. The fire did it, I suppose, or maybe she's superstitious about Bert coming back to haunt her.'

'She's not that sort of lady, believe me. On a practical level she's arranged for two heavies to move on site with their caravan on Monday morning.'

'Sounds sensible. Tell me one thing, Haydon: as an intelligent man, why did you get involved with this person in the first place? She doesn't sound your type at all.'

Haydon shrugged. 'It was a brilliant opportunity, a chance to try the life of a country gent without the hassle of ownership. The woman tempted me.'

A mental picture flashed into her mind: the de Maurnay tapestry, Eve offering the apple, the bedazzled Adam taking it and then whining to God afterwards, 'The woman tempted me.' But who was the snake orchestrating this little scenario from behind the tree? Were all men the same? The clever and the stupid ones? Each motivated by a juicy offer?

'OK. Where do we start?' she said.

The next day passed in a flurry of activity, Zoe, having installed few of her personal belongings over the years, concentrating on boxing up the textiles salvaged from the workroom. Haydon's things were scattered all over, and he seemed helpless in parting the good from the inessential. Where was he to put it all? he wailed, and Zoe, strapped for storage ideas herself, started to panic.

Roddy invited himself over for supper Sunday night, bringing Saba along for the ride. Zoe greeted her with a marked lack of enthusiasm, until the wonderful girl produced a huge casserole of coq au vin and proceeded to take charge of the kitchen. Zoe bobbed at her heels, laying the table, making small talk.

'Is Fay babysitting?'

'Sort of. She's got a parish meeting, so you could say Ali's got twelve beady-eyed carers.'

'He doesn't mind you going out?'

'Got used to it, didn't he? When I was working the streets in King's Cross I had to leave him in my room on his own; blow jobs on kerb-crawling perverts need no home comforts.'

Saba delivered this small aside as if girl talk of this kind was normal Sunday-night chat. Zoe wondered if Saba came out with casual references to her brief career as a hooker in *Fay's* kitchen, but decided to let it pass. After all, she was moving out, wasn't she? Leaving Saba to cosy up to her new friends in the village.

They ate in the kitchen, Roddy claiming that the stags' heads on the dining-room wall put him off his food.

Having Saba and Roddy round was a bit of luck, their cheerful repartee fuelled by Haydon's desire to persuade his guests to

263

drink up as much of his wine collection as possible before Monday morning. Saba rarely touched alcohol and her discreet takeover of the hostessy bit caused Zoe not a flicker of jealousy in what was technically still her house. But she did find herself watching Roddy's response, then watching Haydon's, searching for any hint of past intimacies.

There was nothing. Absolutely nothing. The foursome sat round the table, laughing and teasing each other like old friends, which, apart from the lovely Saba, they were.

Later, as the talk mellowed, Haydon touched on Rio and his meeting with their mutual 'landlady', the real owner of Stonecrest.

'Does she have a house in Brazil, Haydon?'

'Search me. She insisted we met in a hotel suite. I got the impression she wasn't resident – no women's potions in the bathroom; in fact nothing personal about the rooms at all.'

'She wanted the low-down on the fire?' Saba asked.

'Not really. She seemed to have been fully briefed before my plane hit the tarmac. But she was certainly rattled; I've never seen her so jumpy.'

Roddy was riveted. 'Any mention of

Mullins, her Most Wanted boyfriend, or has he been dumped?'

Haydon lurched away from the table to fetch another bottle and by the time he had fiddled with the corkscrew and refilled their glasses the talk had moved on.

Zoe suspected Haydon was drinking much less than the rest of them, his mind still chipping away at the crisis Mrs Redford had precipitated. Had they had a big row, she wondered? Had Haydon's charisma lost its charm? Maybe La Redford had suddenly tired of England, and decided that keeping an expensive country house on the back burner was an embarrassing burden, now that the police were conducting a murder enquiry there.

'I'll store your stuff, if you like,' Roddy put in. 'The guest cottage is warm and dry and I'm not inviting anyone down till after Christmas. I'm too busy with the shop, turkeys coming on line next, and there are my retailers in London to worry about. Orders are pouring in.'

'Oh Roddy, would you?' Zoe said. 'I'll take my fabrics off your hands as soon as I get a new workshop, I promise.' She glanced at Haydon. 'What about your things?'

'There's always the storeroom in the basement of my block. But unless Zoe and I decide to rent another weekend place, most of my clobber will be redundant.'

Looking into this void sobered him and, after another pass with the bottles, Haydon pleaded secondary jet lag and the party broke up.

She slept heavily, curled against Haydon's spine like a backpack, her last thought being the reassurance that this would be their final night at Stonecrest.

A series of bangs broke into her dreams like a car backfiring, and she reared up in the darkness, casting about for Haydon like a blind woman, realizing in an instant that he was gone. She flew to the window in time to see running figures crossing the lawn, clearly silhouetted in the moonlight. Her trembling fingers dialled 999 and she screamed for help.

'They're back at Stonecrest! The Masure place on the old Church Road. Haydon's out there with his gun. For God's sake hurry!'

She flung on her boots, grabbed a raincoat from the wardrobe and flew downstairs, the devil at her heels. The night was clear and cold, a hint of frost in the air. Shouts rang across the garden from the woods where the dogs had caught up with the intruders last time. The break-in must have bypassed the gates, which, since Bert had gone, had remained permanently locked, traffic using a little-known back lane that skirted the stables.

In her panic Zoe was on top of the figure curled up in the shadow of the big cedar before almost stumbling over it. A shotgun lay in the grass nearby and the realization hit her like a blow between the eyes. She knelt down, cradling his head.

'Haydon! Haydon, you fool, why couldn't you leave it alone?'

His jeans were soaked with blood but the wounds were in his chest, the fall having crushed his legs under him, his arms being flung wide. But he was still alive.

As Zoe held him close, his eyes widened as if in disbelief.

'She said they would be ... back...' he murmured.

He tried to speak again, but a bubble of mucus rose on his lips before gushing out in a thin stream of blood. Sirens shattered the night air, shouts and sounds of crashing undergrowth blending in Zoe's head like the reverberations of hell.

He died in her arms.

Thirty-One

Her screams rose on the air like the howling of a wounded dog, but it was several minutes before patrolmen found her in the dark under the cedar tree. One forced her away while the other shone his torch over the body. Whistles blew behind the screen of trees and the sound of a fight breaking out amid a screech of brakes added to the mayhem. One of the constables called for support on his mobile, walking away to describe Haydon's injuries to the ambulance service so as not to alarm the lady even further.

She already knew the worst, however, her hysteria now reduced to muted sobbing as she clutched her coat to her amid the chaos. Car headlights pierced the darkness through the belt of conifers masking the back lane; shouted orders and the sound of vehicles reversing at speed augmented the racket.

Zoe barely registered all this, her mind numb, the inert figure huddled on the grass the focus of her misery. An ambulance bumped over the lawn accompanied by a second patrol car, and more lights sprang up as if from nowhere. A WPC tried to lead Zoe away, but she flung off the sympathetic hand, insisting on waiting until Haydon had been lifted on to a stretcher and the ambulance had moved off. It all took a very long time and the freezing temperature had permeated her very bones before she recognized the familiar voice in her ear. It was Roddy's.

'Come away, sweetheart. There's nothing we can do.'

He supported her back to the house as the police focus moved to the knot of vehicles grouped in the lane.

'Did they catch them?' she whispered.

'I think so. How many did you see?'

'Two, I think. Yes, two – but there may have been others – it was all so sudden – I was asleep. I didn't hear Haydon get up.'

'He may have been lying in wait – you couldn't have stopped him, love. Haydon was determined to nab them if they came back.'

'He said she warned him they would – the prowlers I mean.'

'Who said?'

'The Redford woman. It was the last thing he said, Roddy.' She started to weep again, leaning against his shoulder, the terrible events running back and forth in her brain like the faulty projection of a strip of film.

They sat in the library, waiting for the police to complete their search of the crime scene. Roddy tried to persuade her to sip the brandy he pushed into her cold hands, but she shook her head, struggling to clear the sequence of events in her mind.

'I heard the police sirens,' Roddy said. 'I got up and saw all the lights and I knew something had happened but, seeing no fire, thought it was probably a false alarm. But—'

Just then the door opened and several officers entered, the senior man casting a wary eye on the girl before greeting Roddy. They moved aside to quietly access the situation out of earshot. Roddy had met the superintendent before in the course of the preliminary enquiries following Bert's death, and the two men seemed quickly to have established some sort of rapport. Roddy outlined the conversation at the previous night's supper party.

'And Doctor Masure admitted being worried about these prowlers. Worried enough to stake them out with a shotgun?'

'Mrs Redford, the owner of the house, had wound him up, I think. Haydon met up with her in Rio to put her in the picture regarding the arson attack. The victim was, as it happens, Mrs Redford's employee, put here to guard the property. Naturally, she was anxious about security, her tenant, Doctor

270

Masure, being here only at weekends and there being no live-in staff on hand.' Roddy waved a hand around the room. 'As you can see, all this would be attractive to burglars.'

'Very persistent burglars, though – to try the same place twice and in such a very short space of time. However, we picked up the injured man and—'

'Haydon shot one of them?'

'Oh yes, didn't I say? One man was winged and was trying to reach the getaway car as the second man was revving up in the lane. We nabbed them both and hope to get the full story from the horse's mouth. It's murder now, of course, although the weapon has yet to be retrieved. My men are searching the woods. It's only a matter of time.'

'Do you know what they were after? Weekends would seem the least likely period for getting away with a robbery; midweek, Stonecrest is wide open, now that poor old Bert's not around. Maybe they heard on the grapevine that tonight would be their last chance before the new security guards moved in.'

The superintendent looked startled. 'What?'

'It was common gossip in the farm shop. Mrs Redford was sending two new men here starting Monday – this morning now, of course – so tonight was the last slot between Bert going and the new men coming.'

'As one of Mrs Redford's tenants yourself, do you have her current address?'

'The agency handles her affairs – a Mr McPherson at Sherbornes in Brompton Road would be your man. The doctor's meeting with her in Rio was fortuitous; he was attending a conference there and she was, so I understand, on holiday.'

They were interrupted by the sergeant coming in to call the superintendent away. He returned after a minute, rubbing his hands and smiling.

'Good news, Miss Templeman – the man Doctor Masure shot is willing to make a full statement.'

'And the second man?'

'Can probably be persuaded once he hears what his mate has admitted,' he replied darkly before leaving.

Zoe looked dazed, wrapping her arms around her in a shivering embrace, although the room was, as always, grossly overheated. Roddy made a phone call before turning back to the girl and putting his hand on her shoulder.

'I've rung Brenda Clack; she's on her way over. You need someone here with you, Zoe, and I can't stay long. Try and get some sleep; tomorrow can't get any worse.'

But he was wrong: Monday morning was indeed worse. The newspaper headlines screamed:

EMINENT SURGEON GUNNED DOWN BY
PROWLERS
SECOND TRAGEDY AT HOUSE OF TERROR
MORE POLICE PRESENCE CALLED FOR IN
PUBLIC OUTCRY
IS THIS GANG WARFARE?
HAVE-A-GO DOCTOR SHOT DEAD
DEFENDING HIS PROPERTY

Fortunately Zoe saw none of this, but Mrs Clack sent her niece into Ashford to buy all the newsprint she could lay her hands on, the village shop having immediately sold out.

The superintendent came back next morning to interview her, undeterred by Brenda Clack's best efforts to keep her charge away from all the rumpus. Saba telephoned, but was brusquely dissuaded from barging in as also was the vicar, Brenda inventing an official blanket ban on visitors – apart from that nice Mr Meirs, of course.

Zoe ranged about like a caged tigress, waiting for permission to see Haydon one last time. Meriel arrived soon after ten, accompanied by her apology of a husband, an ineffectual little man who reminded Zoe forcefully of Mr Gilbert, Desiree's solicitor. There wasn't much comfort she could offer Haydon's sister, his determination to see off the intruders with his shotgun a piece of bravado she herself found it impossible to comprehend.

'Such a stupid waste, Meriel. Senseless. I could have stopped him if I'd been sober,' she cried, twisting a sodden tissue in her fingers. Brenda Clack came up trumps, bundling the hapless relatives down to the library and ringing for Haydon's doctor to 'come and help poor Miss Templeman. In shock, you know. Come as soon as you can, Doctor.'

Roddy returned at lunchtime, seating himself beside her in her room.

'I've got some news: they've charged both the men, though clearly only one pulled the trigger. They've confessed but say the shooting was an accident; they hadn't expected Haydon to open fire, and when he bloodied one of them, the driver fetched his own shotgun from the car and retaliated before trying to drag his mate away. Self-defence, they said; believe that if you like. But the police were on the scene right away, thanks to your emergency call, Zoe, so it was a fair cop. In fact, there's a chance they'll prove a connection with the arson attack. One of the villains has dog bites.'

'You mean *they* burned Bert's cottage. I thought they were just the prowlers Haydon had spotted before – nothing to do with the fire.'

'Could be a coincidence; being bitten by a

dog's not proof by any means. They'd have to match up the bloodstained piece of trouser leg, or whatever Bert's dogs got their teeth into.'

'But why?' Zoe persisted. 'Why target the place when it's been under surveillance since Bert died?'

'They're probably the usual lowlife – doesn't mean they had wonderful powers of deduction. My guess is that they thought it was their last chance. The men are known criminals, currently under investigation in an effort to prove they were members of Mullins's gang when the bank robberies happened, so my nice superintendent whispered in my ear.'

'But wasn't that years ago, those bank robberies?'

'Yes, but not all of them were caught. Mullins is on the run and known to have masterminded the heists, but these other two thugs are now suspected of being part of it, waiting all this time to share out the pickings – millions of pounds' worth of jewellery and cash.'

'Whew! Well, they must have run out of patience big time to risk coming here twice.'

'The police are working on the theory that they know where it's hidden.'

Light dawned. 'You mean Mullins's girl-friend has been fending off these guys until Mullins says it's safe to divide up the spoils, and they just got tired of waiting? Deliberately killed Bert to give themselves a clear run?'

'You've got it.'

'And the police think they'll give up the lot in exchange for information about the gang and a possible lightening of the charges? This is *murder*, Roddy, double murder, and getting poor Bert out of the way was even more wicked than shooting Haydon, which you *could* call self-defence, an act of panic after the first man was injured. Bert's death was cruel and premeditated and he certainly didn't attack them first like Haydon with his stupid popgun.'

'Look, Zoe, just let the police sort it out. There's no proof yet to connect them with the fire; they're still working on it. By the way, I've spoken to the man in charge and he's happy for you to leave here if it upsets you. Why not come and stay at my place for a few days? Is there anyone you'd like me to ring? Anyone you'd like to come over?'

She shook her head. 'I've been thinking of nothing else for hours, Roddy, and you know what I think? I think this bloody Redford woman had some hold over Haydon, was blackmailing him. He wasn't the sort of man to take orders from a brassy cow like that and yet she says, "Get out of my house by Monday morning," and like a lamb he comes home from Rio and tells me we're packing up. It just doesn't make sense. And why was he out there in the garden ambushing these prowlers, playing Gary Cooper with his gun at the ready? It wasn't his property he was defending, it was hers. Think about it, Roddy. Could Haydon have known all along that this stuff was buried in the grounds here? Was he in on it with her from the start? Had he promised to hold the fort till her two new security men turned up to take over? A share in millions of pounds is a temptation even to someone like Haydon.'

'Personally, I don't think Redford's security team were booked to guard you two or the house. Strictly between ourselves, Zoe, I think they're coming to sit in and wait for the heat to die down, and then they'll remove the booty themselves and transfer it to another of Mullins's hideouts. Redford is selling up – for real this time, McPherson says; he confirmed it with me himself. She wouldn't do that while the loot was still hidden on the estate somewhere.'

'You think Haydon was in on it, don't you?'

'Not the hidden cache, no; but I do believe Haydon was foolish enough to get involved with Mullins in the past and Redford held it over him. She wanted to give the impression Stonecrest had been sold to Haydon years ago and the booty transferred then, to put the moaners in Mullins's crowd off the scent. But all the time the stuff was still *here*. Is still here. They got wind of the fact that it was all a big con, that Redford still owned Stonecrest and that Haydon was merely the patsy bullied into backing up the idea that the crock of gold had been spirited away before he allegedly purchased the estate.'

'Haydon was never a country lover, you know. He said he wanted to try being the local squire without the strings, but I never thought it rang true. He could have bought himself a big place like Stonecrest if he'd wanted to; dancing to her tune had to be for a different reason. Have you mentioned any of this to the superintendent, Roddy?'

'Hell no! Anyway, it's only guesswork. Mullins's people are hard men, Zoe; we'd be safer to play the innocent bystanders and know nothing. Let the coppers work it out for themselves.'

'I think I've already spoken to Mullins,' she said thoughtfully. 'He phoned here wanting to speak to Haydon but I told him he'd already left. I think it was Mullins who called the surgery afterwards, just before Haydon flew out to that conference in Rio. Venetia knew him as Mr Benson.'

Thirty-Two

By Tuesday morning it was clear that Redford's two security men were not coming. The lady herself had also gone to ground, the police frustration at being unable to trace her causing no small obstruction in the investigation.

'She has no record, and so far there's no evidence that she was involved in the disappearance of the proceeds of the robberies, sir. Mullins lived at Stonecrest himself before the place got too hot. He got away just in time,' the superintendent complained to his superior officer. 'Until we can squeeze more information from the men we're holding, we've hit a blank wall. Let's hope the tie-in with the bloodstained evidence held at the lab since Bert Styles went up in flames will lever off the lid of this can of worms.'

Zoe kept to her room, tranquillized by happy-pills prescribed by the doctor, leaving Meriel to deal with press interviews and the not inconsiderable onus of keeping the police search party out of the house. The rumour that a huge haul of stolen goods was hidden either in the house or somewhere in the grounds was already being whispered about the village. Many remembered Mullins from the old days, when he had spent thousands converting the neglected manor house into a showplace. Fewer remembered his girlfriend, Bobby Redford, who preferred to flit from sunspot to sunspot in Mullins's helicopter, leaving the ugly little man to supervise the transformation of his dream home without benefit of her advice.

It was late on Tuesday before Freddie McPherson put in an appearance, following a summons by the superintendent to explain the exact nature of the rental of Stonecrest and its farm properties. Roddy brought him over to the house after their own meeting in his office, insisting Zoe emerged from cover and joined them in the library for a drink. Meriel had driven back to London to help Venetia close the consulting rooms, which was a relief, Zoe having no desire to relive the shooting yet again. Meriel's interrogations were even more painful than police questioning.

Agreeing to see Freddie was a good move, Zoe's misery now reduced to sad despair. Naturally, they talked of nothing but the two murders, but having Freddie's urbane slant on the tragedies seemed to blunt the sheer horror of it all.

'You'll be glad to leave,' he said.

'Understatement of the year, Freddie. But what frightens me is that I seem to be the jinx in all this. First Max, then Bert and now Haydon.'

'You'd better watch yourself then, Roddy,' he quipped. 'But I'll be off. The fellow in charge seems reasonably bright. He's not going to let those two ruffians off the hook till they've coughed the lot. I gather Redford's henchmen never arrived. Can't say I'm surprised.'

Zoe said, 'I'm hoping to move out myself as soon as I can. The odd thing is, Haydon and I were all packed up ready to leave on Monday morning; if Redford hadn't set up the new security team so quickly and Haydon hadn't felt obliged to fill the gap till they came, he wouldn't have ended up dead and the killers would have put off their raid until the house was empty.'

'Redford wasn't going to leave any secret piggy-bank unattended, though, was she? Not once Bert was out of the picture,' Roddy put in. 'And it has yet to be proved that these two roughnecks were, in fact, disgruntled former gang members.'

'Now, you're pussyfooting,' Zoe protested. 'But at least I don't have to worry about sorting Haydon's papers, whatever the outcome. They're already stacked in my car – I'd said I'd take his medical stuff back to the flat and ask the caretaker to put it in the storeroom. Actually, it's mostly old files, former case histories, I suppose, plus slides for his talks and some books.'

'Will you move back to the flat?' Freddie asked.

Zoe smiled. 'Don't look so hopeful, chum. I suppose you can smell another expensive property on your books already. You people – you're all the same!' She grew serious. 'I hadn't thought it out, but now you mention it, no, I can't see myself doing that. Anyway, I expect his sister has plans for Claydon Gardens.'

'That means you're homeless,' Freddie retorted.

'No, she's not. I've already offered Zoe a bed at my house. Or she can use my guest cottage. What do you say, sweetie?'

She looked confused, the ramifications of Haydon's death suddenly coming home to roost.

'Yes, why not? The sooner I get out of here the better.'

When Freddie had driven off, Roddy helped her pack up the few personal things remaining in her room and stowed a final overnight bag with the others already in the boot of her car, the back seat being already piled high with the boxes Haydon had not managed to fit into his own vehicle.

She said goodbye to Brenda Clack, who

became surprisingly dewy-eyed, her apparently cast-iron persona as fragile as Desiree's had turned out to be. She left a message with the constable on duty to say where she could be found and drove off in convoy behind Roddy's mud-spattered van.

She decided to take him up on the offer of the guest cottage, not at all sure that her temporary sanity would survive too much kindness, living cheek-by-jowl with Haydon's best friend.

It was only later, when Roddy's pigman burst into the kitchen as they were having pick-me-up glasses of champagne, that they learned of the breakthrough.

'They're blasting away at the helipad,' Terry announced, his eyes alight with excitement. 'I seen it meself from the five-acre field, floodlights and everythin'. Six bloody big coppers levering off the drain covers and digging up the bloody tarmac.'

Roddy stiffened. 'They must have got a tip-off,' he murmured. 'I'll drive over and see if I can find anything out.'

Zoe gripped the stem of her glass, wishing to God it would soon be over. Roddy affectionately squeezed her hand before flinging on his Barbour to follow Terry out into the dark. She put the bottle in the fridge and tipped her champagne down the sink.

For once Roddy's cure-all for sad times wasn't working.

Thirty-Three

The hoard was discovered buried deep in a tunnel under a false drain cover on the edge of the helipad. The local police were on cloud nine, unable to believe the stroke of luck that had uncovered such a huge cache previously suspected of being hidden in several different locations. Congratulations flowed, the two banged up in custody now singing like canaries, hoping to have saved themselves from permanent incarceration by pinpointing the loot.

'We'd never have found it without them, you know,' the superintendent admitted to Roddy as they stood on the edge of the helipad, watching heavy-duty machinery level the site.

'You found their shotgun?'

'No sweat. A sawn-off little beauty jammed down a rabbit hole. The case is all but sewn up.'

'And the fire?'

The older man shrugged. 'Going to take time. One of them's definitely in the frame but says the dogs got him on a previous night when they were nosing round. They're admitting nothing about any arson, a far more serious matter than this tit-for-tat shooting. But we're working on it.'

'And the poor bloody Raz family are definitely in the clear?'

'Oh yes. Mind you, I believe the girl's story up to a point. I reckon she was being pursued by the relatives, and family honour in their culture is something we probably can't appreciate. Still, our officers putting these men through an interrogation will warn them off – give the Raz girl a chance.'

'She's a good worker, you know,' Roddy insisted. 'I'd hate to see her chased away from here, she's starting to make a decent living and the boy's more secure. Any news about Mrs Redford?'

The superintendent smiled. 'Called in at the Chelsea nick last night. As cool as a cucumber. Only just heard about the shooting, if you believe it – been on a fucking safari, she says.'

'I suppose there's nothing to connect Bobby Redford with the bank robberies? Swears she knew nothing about the hidden cash, I bet.'

He nodded. 'The doctor – Masure – knew more than was healthy for him, I'd say, but had he survived the shooting I doubt whether he would have given evidence against her and incriminated himself. That woman's got more brains than Mullins, if you ask me – keeps his troops in order without so much as getting her dainty stilettos in the shit.'

Zoe spent the week lounging about in Roddy's guest cottage, glued to the television news, avoiding company. She did endure a visit from Fay Betteridge and Saba, but there wasn't much to talk about, Zoe's resolve to keep her emotions in check precluding any heart-to-heart. They gave up and went home, acknowledging that holing herself up in solitary like a cat caught up in a road accident was Zoe's way of coping.

Keeping Meriel at bay was more difficult. Her continual phone calls about Haydon – Haydon's reputation, Haydon's funeral, the elevation of Haydon in the press to the status of popular hero – merely made Zoe monosyllabic, no longer unwilling, now physically unable, to verbalize her feelings. Meriel clearly felt that her own professional counselling would be the answer and hinted as much, excusing her absence from Stonecrest as the result of the practical business of putting Haydon's place in medical history in the right context.

'But just as soon as you come back to London, my dear, we must organize a few sessions, eh?'

'On your couch?' Zoe snapped, Meriel's chirpy tone reminding her painfully of

Haydon's bedside manner.

Realizing at last that she could not hide for ever, she determined to make a final break and get back on the roundabout. It was hard. She started by putting her photographs of Haydon and all the little loving notes from him that had been lying in her lingerie drawer like scented sachets into an envelope and burying them in a box of books.

Next she would tackle the pile of boxes he had asked her to take to the storeroom. What use were they now? Old case histories, sad before-and-after photographs of burns victims, profiles of socialites with and without their Roman noses. She sifted through the files as a matter of conscience, but knew there was no point in saving them, even as medical data.

She telephoned Venetia at the surgery, speaking with her for the first time, both of them choking back tears.

'All this *stuff*, Venetia. What shall I do with it?'

'Haydon's special cases? He kept all his "secret files", as we called them, himself – said those patients' notes were particularly private. He didn't want them mixed up with the other records.'

'Why special?'

'Various reasons, mostly because the people concerned were embarrassed by the surgery – politicians, ageing film stars, that sort of thing ... He even gave them false names on the files,' she added with a chuckle. 'Not that it fooled us in the office. These people are so *vain*, Zoe, and Haydon pretending "Mrs Smith's breast implants" were nothing to do with a pop star whose bouncing boobs were publicized in every tabloid didn't wash with us for a minute. We used to type up all the notes for him and often had a giggle about it in the girls' room. Working for a plastic surgeon, confidentiality comes with the job; but it does have its funny moments, and we grabbed any light relief that came our way. Not that Haydon was a bad boss, Zoe – don't get me wrong. He was a lovely, lovely man and I'll never forget working here; but Haydon was secretive by nature – you of all people know that. Playing hide-and-seek with his VIP records was very much in character.'

'What's happening to his regular office files?'

'His sister's in charge. Making a bit of a fuss, but at the end of the day even she had to admit shredding was the best option. We didn't want nosy journalists sifting our dustbins, printing embarrassing photographs of prominent people Haydon had cosmetically enhanced, as they say.'

Zoe put down the receiver and determined to make a clean sweep, build a bonfire in

Roddy's back yard and burn the lot. Roddy popped his head round the door at lunchtime and found her absorbed in sorting out the boxes, relieved to see her facing up to the nitty-gritty of wiping the slate clean. He wanted to help, but she insisted it was something she must do herself and he backed off, indicating the old brazier set up behind the compost heap.

The work was tedious and often heartrending. Apart from lucrative face-lifts and nose jobs, Haydon treated children – children with birth defects, children injured in accidents. Tears pricked her eyelids as she consigned these sad pictures to the brazier, the disposal of files relating to Haydon's less challenging surgery tossed into the flames without a qualm.

It was after midnight before Benson's file came to light. The name was burned into her memory, the rough demand to speak to 'Donny' still clear as a bell.

Benson was no oil painting to start with: a pugilistic face, podgy and with an expression of belligerence coming over like a mug shot. Haydon prided himself on his photography, investing in the most expensive equipment and taking all the shots himself, black-and-white portraits that he developed in a dark room at the consulting rooms. Benson's physiognomy was not only scarred by years of experience, the man's age being recorded as just forty-four, but showed signs of a brutal lifestyle. Even so, the battered features did not strike Zoe as being in urgent need of repair and if, as they say, a photograph never lies, the character of the man shone through. Benson was clearly not part of the vain coterie about which Venetia was so scathing.

Zoe sat on the floor, absorbed in the sheaf of photographs, cross-checking with Haydon's handwritten notes, the typist clearly under a misapprehension if she thought she typed up all Haydon's records, even those of the sensitive cases.

She lit a cigarette, leaning against the back of the sofa, watching the smoke curl to the ceiling. After that she lit another from the stub, her mind strangely at rest. At last she knew what had driven Haydon to launch himself on such a dangerous course. She had been right: Haydon had placed himself in the cross-hairs of Mullins's sights. He had, probably for an enormous fee, agreed to operate on Mullins. Mullins, the self-styled king of the underworld, sought for bank robberies and much else had been transformed into Mr Benson. A work of genius.

She could hardly tear herself away from the monochrome shots taken over a period of months or years, the transfiguration of a burly, instantly recognizable thug into a square-chinned Mr Ordinary, the magic touch being the introduction of an ugly birthmark, a congenital flaw Mr Benson refused to hide under a beard, an eye-averting embarrassment that no man in his right mind would have chosen to burden himself with.

At last, fearful that Roddy, anxious about her lights still burning so late, might barge in to satisfy himself that all was well, Zoe went outside, bundled the last of Haydon's files into the brazier, tossed the empty boxes outside the back door and zipped Benson's file into her briefcase.

She lay in bed unable to sleep, knowing that Haydon had been a greedy man tempted to accept a fee from Mullins, to take Judas money from a criminal who indirectly had been the cause of Bert being burned alive. Mullins's stolen hoard had been the evil thing that drew the two men who had fired Bert's cottage to Stonecrest. They had eliminated the poor bastard because they knew where the money was hidden and guessed that their gang boss and Bobby Redford had no intention of sharing it. They had decided to dig it up themselves, but first they had to get rid of the security guard, a man they might even have known – a small-time gang member himself, perhaps, but even so Bert had never deserved to die in that horrific way.

Haydon had been part of it. In helping Mullins to escape the international dragnet, he had found himself open to threats of disclosure by Redford if he didn't go along with it. Haydon's greed had indirectly made him a gang member too and, however reluctantly he danced to their tune, Haydon was never going to escape. And now he was dead, his debt to Bert still unpaid.

At six o'clock she checked the bonfire, the evidence of Haydon's best work reduced to ashes. Zoe carefully damped down the embers, blackened flakes flying up into the darkness like feathers.

After packing up all her things she left a scribbled note to Roddy on the kitchen table and drove back to London, booking into a small hotel in Waterloo and filling in the last hours smoking far too many cigarettes.

At eleven, having first telephoned to insist on speaking to Kennedy in person, she arranged to meet him by the box office of the National Theatre.

'I must insist on this being off the record,' she said.

'Such cloak-and-dagger arrangements are all very intriguing, Miss Templeman. You sound like an informer,' he said in a clumsy attempt to lighten the tone.

'Got it in one, Inspector.'

Thirty-Four

I knew what I was doing. It wasn't spite and it wasn't civic duty; it was just the right thing to do. If I could have got an answer from Pa, it would have been the same. I still loved Haydon, but even Haydon had to pay in the end.

I could have destroyed the Benson file and left Haydon's reputation intact. Why couldn't I just do the sensible thing and let sleeping dogs lie?

Perhaps that had been my trouble all along: taking the high ground, giving no quarter even to save a man applauded for his courage, his apparent one-man stand against crime.

Kennedy spotted her straight away: thin and pale, her eyes downcast, standing with her back to a pillar while the queue at the box office shuffled past the girl in the black duffle coat without a glance.

He touched her arm and she turned, saying nothing, allowing herself to be led to a corner table in the café, the place all but empty in the lull before midday.

He took off his raincoat and left her while he fetched some coffee. Zoe watched him waiting at the counter with his tray, his tweed suit so out of place in that setting, as if he were a man up from the country for a day out, filling in time before the matinee performance. She looked out at the sky where rainclouds blew like galleons whipped by a blustery wind, the surface of the river teased into wavelets as the dirty tide sloshed back and forth against the bank.

Kennedy passed her cup and they both topped up with liberal additions of sugar.

'Nice to see you again, Miss Templeman. I was sorry to hear about the incident at the doctor's country place. Terrible. Terrible for you. You've moved back to London?'

Zoe shook her head. 'Just passing through. I'm on my way to Paris.'

'Good idea. No point in brooding, if I may say so. The change will do you good; you look a bit peaky, and I'm not surprised. The Kent police treating you right?'

'They leave me alone.'

He frowned. 'There's nothing I can help you with then?'

She stirred her coffee, eyeing him as if assessing his ability to play her game. The silence grew and Kennedy began to fidget, hoping this silly young girl wasn't trying to drag him into a case that was well off his beat. She reached down to open a briefcase and brought up a bundle of papers, fanning pages of handwritten notes and eight or ten glossy photographs across the table. She took a sip of her coffee.

'I brought these for you, Inspector,' she said. 'You are the only policeman I know and I have to trust you. These papers constitute a confidential medical record: Doctor Masure's notes regarding a long-standing patient of his, a Mr Benson.'

She pushed the file towards him, her eyes narrowing. 'They are before-and-after shots showing the cosmetic surgery Haydon performed on this man. The pictures are dated on the back and the doctor's written notes provide details. It's a wonderful transformation, wouldn't you say?'

Kennedy put on his spectacles and examined the photographs with careful deliberation.

'What has this to do with me, Miss Templeman?' he said at last.

'They are pictures that will, I'm sure, make identifying the bank robber Mullins as easy as picking an apple off a tree.'

He jerked up, his expression lighting up with excitement. 'Benson *is* Mullins?'

She nodded. 'I came across this file by accident when I was disposing of Haydon's special papers. He transformed a wanted man into an unrecognizable stranger, don't you see? Mullins chose the best surgeon he could find and bribed him to make any police search well-nigh impossible. I presume the operations were carried out abroad over a period of time. Tracing Mullins even with up-to-date photographs won't be easy, I realize that. He could be anywhere. But no one but you, Inspector, has the key, and if the trap closes on him before he's had a chance to re-invent himself again, a very dangerous criminal will be out of circulation till hell freezes over.'

'And you want your part in this to remain secret?'

'It must. No one else knows I came across this file; everything Haydon left at Stonecrest has been burnt and, if questioned, I shall say I destroyed all his medical records on the advice of the people at the surgery. Papers were being shredded there under the supervision of Haydon's sister, so it will be generally assumed that the Benson file was destroyed somewhere along the line together with everything else. No one but me connected Mullins to the Benson file, I'm perfectly certain. Only Haydon knew about it and he's dead. Obviously Mullins has several aliases – Benson was Haydon's invention – but at least the police will know what they're looking for once they have these photographs.'

Kennedy shuffled the photographs, placing the earliest on the top of the pile before turning back to her.

'You want me to keep this a secret,' he

said. 'Your part in it, that is?'

'That's the deal.'

'Then perhaps I might ask you to respect my confidence too? Something that came to my notice four years ago that jumped into focus only when, through you, a name that had an interest for me came up. Your Doctor Masure was brought to my notice then in connection with another case very similar to this,' he said, tapping the photograph. 'Nothing as concrete as the evidence we have here, but a tip-off I was reluctant to believe. My informant suggested that the doctor had done this sort of thing before, on another wanted man, a fraudster still at large, as it happens.'

Zoe gasped. 'Haydon's name was known to the police?'

'Only to me. Informants being a spiteful breed, it was hardly worth further investigation, a piece of information entirely without proof. But it stayed lodged in the back of my mind, as these things do...'

'I remember now. You mentioned right at the beginning that Haydon's reputation as a surgeon was known to you. I thought at the time that your range of interest was extensive for ... for...' She stuttered, lost for words.

He smiled. 'Beyond the range of a flat-footed detective inspector, you are trying not to say.' He removed his glasses and slowly replaced them in their case, his mind churning with the possibilities this staggering breakthrough presented.

She said, 'You could say the file was left on the desk at the station for you by a person refusing to leave his name; an anonymous tip-off. Or even put it in an envelope and post it to yourself,' she added brightly. 'That would answer any questions about how it came to be in your hands.'

He smiled. 'You're wasted mending old textiles, Miss Templeman.'

'I've got to go,' she said, gathering up her things. 'I can trust you, can't I?'

He raised a hand. 'You have considered the consequences of this, haven't you, lassie?' he said kindly. 'Your young man's reputation will be in shreds once this gets out.'

'Haydon was a brilliant surgeon and his good work will stand. But he was tempted, as the Good Book says, and against his better judgement or professional morals he used his skill to save a bad man from justice. As an indirect result of Haydon's expert meddling a man died a terrible death.'

'Bert Styles? This the security man you're talking about?'

Zoe rose and stepped back. 'I don't want to go into my motives, Inspector. Some people would say I've done wrong destroying a good man's reputation, especially now he's dead, but I've done what I think is right and I leave you to do the same.'

He tried to stop her, but she sidestepped and quickly walked away, weaving between the incoming lunch crowd and disappearing into the foyer.

Kennedy hurriedly gathered up the Benson dossier and, clutching it to his chest, tried to follow her out. But Zoe had gone – gone for good, he shouldn't wonder, questions still buzzing in his head, questions he wished she had given him a chance to formulate.

By the time he was driving back to the station a plan was already forming in his head. Putting the finger on Jimmy Mullins would be something he deserved a police medal for, the only price being his promise to that little girl that no one would ever find out how the Benson file had come to light.

Thirty-Five

Zoe arrived in Paris with the tapestry and booked into a seedy hotel she remembered from years before, cheaper than the places she had become used to with Haydon but anonymous, a bolt-hole to suit her mood.

The crossing had been rough and she had spent the time on deck clinging to the rail, content to feel the salt spray in her face, as if the whipping power of the wind might tear away her guilt.

Turning over the Benson file had not been as easy as she had forced herself to expect; but it was done now, and Kennedy must deal with it. She knew she could never face Meriel again, commiserate with her over Haydon's ruin, keep up the pretence that his work on a runaway criminal was all a terrible shock to her, a complete surprise.

After all, she was a runaway herself now. Wouldn't Saba scoff if she knew? – after all the bullying tactics she and Fay Betteridge had brought into play to force the girl to face up to trouble, to meet it honestly, head-on.

She locked the door of her hotel room and slept all afternoon and most of the evening, the tapestry on its trolley propped up in the corner like a sentinel. She had at least another week before de Vries returned from holiday, a week in which to pull herself together.

The room was small, dark and extremely cold. It was the second of two attic rooms in the old building, the ground floor being taken up with a bar plus a small dining area tucked away behind looped-up velvet drapes. Across the top landing the other attic room stood empty, a narrow space under the eaves converted to slot in a cast-iron bath and a hand basin. The lavatory, blissfully, she had all to herself, December being a low point for tourists, even poor ones such as herself.

In fact the hotel was favoured mainly by commercial travellers, as she became all too aware when she went down for coffee and rolls next morning. Zoe found herself the only woman in the tiny dining area, the butt of good-humoured jokes from the other residents, the object of the middle-aged waitress's concern as she nervously took her place at a plastic-topped table.

'*Bonjour, mademoiselle. Avez vous bien dormi?*'

'*Oui merci. Très bien.*'

It had been ages since she had had whole

long days to herself, time to mooch about, to sleep in the afternoons if she felt like it, eat or not eat – hours in which to sit outside pavement cafés watching immaculately shod Parisiennes step neatly between the dog shit. How had she never noticed the *crottins de chien* before? She remembered what Pa had impressed upon her before her first student forays in Paris: 'Only drunks order white wine in a bar when not eating, girly.' She stuck to red, her thoughts washing backwards and forwards like dirty flotsam on an oily sea.

She gave de Vries a couple of days to get his bearings back after his holiday before she presented herself at the gallery. The new man, Xavier, hurried forward, unimpressed by the gamine creature in the muddy boots. She explained her presence but '*le patron* is discussing a sale with a client', he said dismissively. 'At the client's home,' he added, as if she must be unfamiliar with the personal attention that important clients deserved. Zoe left her card, the telephone number of her hotel scribbled on the back, but decided nevertheless to ring the boss herself, reminded of Anne de Vries's doubts about Xavier's efficiency.

As it happened, de Vries pounced on Zoe's message with enthusiasm, calling her that evening and inviting her to bring the tapestry to his flat at twelve o'clock the following day.

'We shall have lunch, *ma chère*,' he said. She had not forgotten what a keen mind the man had, his reputation as a dealer in only the finest art objects placing him beyond a glass wall for many of his colleagues, especially the London ones, Max having been particularly wary of de Vries's expertise. Zoe was unfazed, entirely confident in the authenticity of the de Maurnay tapestry and her own delicate repairs to it.

De Vries's apartment occupied the top two floors of a building on the Avenue Montaigne, a home chosen, she suspected, by his wife, situated as it was in an area thick with haute couture shops and jewellers – a little flash, she would have thought, for a discerning antiques dealer of formidable international repute. Zoe had dressed carefully in a black designer suit chosen for her by Haydon that spring, a severe ensemble that complemented her elfin looks.

Ascending in the elevator with the tapestry firmly strapped to its trolley, she wondered if Max had ever been here or whether de Vries only entertained at home when a pretty woman caught his eye. Madame was out. 'At the hairdresser's,' he explained, waving the maid aside to greet her himself, ushering her into the grand salon and insisting she trundle the trolley along with her. Zoe hoped she hadn't picked up any dog mess on its wheels on the way over. Acres of marble floor stretched as far as one could see, the apartment laid out in an open plan culminating in high windows with heart-stopping views of the Eiffel Tower.

He led her to the dining area off the drawing room and they seated themselves at the table, the trolley joining the party as if making up a jolly ménage à trois.

De Vries was in his sixties, at a guess, elegantly dressed in an Armani suit and cream silk shirt, his black moccasins gleaming as if lacquered. He opened a bottle of champagne, handing her a crystal flute with a flourish, his eyes eagerly glancing at the trolley and its passenger swathed like an Egyptian mummy.

He cut the bindings and unwrapped the tapestry himself, allowing Zoe to help only when the moment came to heave it on to the table. It slid across the polished surface like a red carpet and Zoe felt a fanfare of trumpets would not have been inappropriate.

De Vries was enchanted, his admiration followed by a detailed examination under a magnifying glass. Zoe said nothing, letting the tapestry speak for itself, seeing its beauty bathed in the soft December sunlight filtering through the uncurtained windows.

'C'est magnifique,' he murmured, turning to beam at Zoe before cross-examining her on the work that had been done since he had first set eyes on the tapestry in Max's studio. At last he was satisfied and they returned to the salon for a second glass of bubbly before he phoned for his driver and they sped across Paris to his favourite bistro. Zoe was glad he had chosen an apparently modest restaurant, champagne always having a contrary effect on her as an aperitif, damping down, rather than sharpening, her appetite.

De Vries was in good form, loquacious and funny, his English nigh perfect, his pleasure at lunching a pretty young woman all too evident. The place was no bigger than a squash court, the tables intimately close, the murmur of conversation as soothing as a lullaby. De Vries insisted on choosing from the menu for her, promising that his familiarity with the chef's specials was her best recommendation. He chose foie gras fried with tiny slices of pear followed by a salt cod dish that made her eyes sparkle with delight.

'Did you know that our famous Molière's father was an official *tapissier*?' he said. 'His appointment to the king's court included services less artistic than tapestry-making, for example helping to supply the army with linen and even, on occasions, being called upon to make the royal bed. The appointment as *tapissier du roi* was hereditary and much sought after, clearly lucrative, and in Molière *père's* case allowed him direct access to Louis XIV.'

'The de Maurnay tapestry began life in a cardinal's private rooms,' she said with a smile, 'but who knows what things it was a party to in later centuries? The provenance is not altogether clear in the eighteenth century, is it?'

De Vries waved this quibble aside and paused to allow the waiter to refill their glasses. He withdrew an envelope from his pocket and for an anxious moment Zoe wondered if she would have to explain the details of her financial arrangements with Max, and later Desiree, about her expenses. She had already been generously paid for her work, including the delivery to Paris. He passed the envelope to her, his expression contrite.

'My sincere apologies, dear Zoe, for this dreadful oversight. I must lay the blame at the feet of the wretched Xavier. This letter addressed to you care of the gallery arrived some weeks ago, and my useless assistant, not recognizing your name, pushed it into my desk without a word. It became over-sighted – is that the right word? He only reminded me of it on my return from holiday and I am desolate with apologies. Please forgive me?'

'But why should anyone write to me at the

gallery?' she replied with astonishment.

He shrugged with that Gallic gesture unique to elegant Frenchmen. 'Perhaps a billet doux? A secret lover thinking you were due here at the end of October?'

She tore open the envelope, scanning the closely written pages. She paled, looking up at him with enormous brown eyes before pulling herself together and thrusting the letter into her bag. 'It's nothing,' she said. 'Entirely my fault for taking so many weeks to deliver the tapestry.'

'It is not important?'

'Not at all,' she lied, attacking her ice cream as if it were the north face of the Eiger. He relaxed.

'Did anyone ever tell you how much you are like that wonderful actress we have,' he whispered, 'Juliette Binoche? Such an expressive face, so tender, that smile and the lovely short black coiffure – so French!' He touched his lips with his napkin, his eyes dreamy. Zoe decided it was time to break up this little tête-à-tête and steered the conversation back to her work, telling de Vries about the flood at the workshop, carefully omitting any mention of the real tragedies, the fire and the fatal shooting at Stonecrest. Fortunately, mayhem in English country houses belonged, in the view of civilized Parisians, safely tucked between the covers of those detective novels they did so well, and rarely got reported in the French press. She did not trust herself to speak coherently about Haydon's death. It was too soon. Too soon and much, much too raw.

They parted on excellent terms, Zoe assuring de Vries that she would call at the gallery to admire his latest acquisitions before she returned to London. She caught a taxi and waited until she was safely locked in her hotel room before reading Max's letter.

After that she knew she would never go home. She must stay here in Paris for ever if need be; there would be no place for her on the old art circuit.

Thirty-Six

Christmas came and went, then New Year. Zoe had come to a special arrangement with Madame regarding her room, promising to move out just as soon as she had made up her mind about work.

In truth Zoe's mind was still in turmoil and renting a flat seemed a decision too far. Christmas cards had arrived from Fay Betteridge and Saba, including photographs of Ali in the nativity play. Roddy sent brief messages, urging her to come home, telephoning her at least once a week, arguing that her flight at a time when she needed her friends as never before was psychological suicide.

She put him off with lies about work, mythical contracts she was bound to fulfil, the pressure of demands from French dealers who found a freelance textile conservator too good an opportunity to let go. In fact, de Vries had persuaded the man who undertook fabric repairs at the Louvre to employ her from time to time, which had two advantages: (i) of allowing her access to his specialist workroom and (ii) in forcing her to improve her French.

Her social life was nil, which, in her present state of mind, was welcome. She wrote letters to Pa enclosing picture postcards of Paris, hoping that the message would get through his foggy brain that she *would* visit just as soon as work allowed.

Zoe spent most of each day just walking, pounding the streets in unplanned routes, criss-crossing the city, her mind dwelling constantly on the trap in which she was caught.

The windy stretch outside Notre Dame featured in her wanderings to a worrying degree, the attraction of this space as hard to fathom as the beggars silently confronting those passing through the great doors, who seemed to accuse her personally as she hurried past.

She never went inside, walking quickly as if on a genuine errand, but the force of the gaze of one particular down-and-out burned into her retreating back. Perhaps that was the skill of it? – reminding the passer-by of ungenerosities, sins best hidden even from themselves.

It was towards the end of February, the snow falling in great flakes on to the piazza. Reluctantly, she decided she must return to the hotel at least until the blizzard abated. Madame came out of her office to insist Zoe must share one of her special tisanes before the girl climbed back to the former servants' room, which Madame guiltily admitted to herself was really only fit for summer visitors. Zoe collapsed on to the bed, dragging the duvet over her head, trembling with the cold.

She awoke with a start to loud rapping on the door and scrambled to unlock it. It was Marie, Madame's skivvy, a half-witted teenager up from the country who rarely emerged from the kitchens. Behind her on the dark landing loomed a man's figure and Zoe stood blinking, trying to make sense of Marie's garbled message – something about a farmer, it sounded like, but then she must have got that wrong, Marie's accent reducing the simplest phrase to gibberish.

She gently pushed the girl aside and the man spoke.

'Zoe, for God's sake let me in; I'm freezing my balls off out here.' It was Roddy.

She laughed, pushing her thick fringe out of her eyes and grabbing the sleeves of his overcoat as if to substantiate a dream.

'Roddy! Roddy, you fool; why didn't you warn me you were coming?'

They stumbled into the room, closing the door on Marie's round-eyed stare. At midday the room was still dark, the snow clouds hanging heavy above the view of chimney pots from the window of her garret.

'Blimey, girl; it's no warmer in here! What possessed you, holing up in a ratty place like this? Do you need money?'

She shook her head, grinning like a fool, still entranced by the surprise.

'Here, sit on the bed, Roddy; I'll drag up a chair. What *are* you doing in Paris? Who's babysitting the pigs?'

'Terry. Listen, sweetheart, we can't sit here. It's like the set of *La Bohème*: any minute now I expect you to start coughing your lungs out. Lunch?'

She stroked his lapel and laughed, a full-throated chortle, a golden moment of pleasure coming, it seemed, right out of the blue; and, pulling on her duffle coat, she pushed her feet into boots that it suddenly occurred to her were so badly down at heel as to be

311

all but crippling.

They ran downstairs, Zoe shouting 'au revoir' to Madame, who stood like a concierge in the doorway of her office, assessing the romantic potential of this transformed hotel guest of hers.

Zoe steered him to a bistro nearby, a place mostly frequented by students, where the menu was robust and the clientele lively. On this bitter winter day the early customers were few. They shook out the snow from their hair and rubbed their freezing hands before the continental stove in the corner. Roddy wore a Shetland sweater and heavy boots, his eyes lighting up as the aroma of garlic and pot-au-feu hit him.

She pushed him to a table and rattled off an order for wine, her cheeks flushed with pleasure as she stared at this ghost from the past. Stonecrest seemed so long ago, the intervening months in Paris an unending sojourn in the nether regions.

They ordered bouillabaisse and dipped chunks of bread in a saucer of olive oil as they sipped their wine and caught up with the news.

'Stonecrest's been sold – went almost before Freddie McPherson had perfected his sales pitch.'

'It was in perfect condition, of course – no worry about refurbishment, if that sort of house appeals.'

'Have you heard from Haydon's sister?'

'I didn't leave my address. Meriel and I were never close; I'm sure she prefers things as they are. I suppose there's been a terrible scandal about Haydon's illicit surgery?'

'The press made a meal of it, but they would, wouldn't they? There was a letter in *The Times* from one of Haydon's eminent colleagues pointing out the excellent work he did for burns victims, an effort to salvage some justice from the police disclosures; but people can be pretty bloody if they feel they've been bamboozled. First the hero, then the villain – too much for the average punter to swallow. You saw none of this garbage printed in the papers?'

She shook her head.

'Mullins is still at large, of course. Sod's Law – Haydon getting all the flak while the real bad guy just moves out of the searchlight and sets himself up in a new bolt-hole.'

'Lost the money, though, didn't he? And if Mullins is not so flush these days, I bet the Redford woman won't hang about.'

They scoffed their fish stew like starving peasants, Roddy encouraged by Zoe's animation, his initial shock at discovering her shacked up in such a miserable hotel room abating. She was still the same goofy girl he had fallen in love with the first moment Haydon had brought her down to Stonecrest.

She talked about her freelance work and he talked about the pigs. Finally, over brandies, they talked about what really mattered.

'You can't hide yourself away like this, Zoe. It's time to pick up the pieces.'

'I can't come back,' she said defiantly. 'Don't ask me again, Roddy. I just can't.'

'You're punishing yourself because of Haydon, aren't you? Why? Haydon ruined his reputation by greed. He's dead. Time to move on, Zoe darling. Come home.'

Her expression changed to anger. 'Is that what you all think? You think I'm so ashamed of the showdown about Haydon's association with Mullins and his bloody girlfriend that I can't face it? That I'm living some sort of act of retribution for Haydon's stupidity? You don't know me, Roddy; you don't know me at all. Listen! I can't go back to England. If I go home I have to blow the whistle on something far worse than Haydon's unethical nonsense, and I just can't do it. Living here in Paris I can pretend it's not my problem. But it is. I have been lumbered with a secret, and if I return to London it will all be real and I won't be able to ignore it.'

'I haven't a clue what you're on about, girl. You've clearly been alone too long. Come back with me and put all this behind you. I've been thinking. Why don't I convert one of my barns into a workshop for you? You can have the guest cottage all to yourself – no strings, I promise you.'

'But I thought you said the estate was being sold.'

'Redford put Stonecrest on the market in six lots. The house is sold and two of the farms are under offer. She's accepted my bid for my pig fields, the shop and the two cottages. It's all settled. You are talking to a man of property here, Popsie,' he said, grasping her hand across the table, his false jocularity barely masking the sheer anxiety eating his heart out.

She pulled her hand away. 'I can't, Roddy. I've made up my mind. If you really want to know why, you'll have to come back to my room and then you'll understand.'

Thirty-Seven

Madame accosted them as they passed through the crowded bar, her sentimental heart vanquishing natural parsimony.

'I 'ave sent Marie to your room to make the fire, Zoe,' she said with a sly smile, darting a knowing look at the fine upstanding English gentleman who was clearly the girl's beau.

Zoe's eyes widened in surprise, but Roddy smoothly covered her astonishment with a barrage of grovelling French, causing Madame's cheeks to wobble in a smile wide as an advertisement for denture adhesive. Zoe pushed him ahead of her up the stairs, laughing, ribbing him about his appalling accent.

'Did the business, though, didn't it? Pity you never appreciated my charm, you ugly little poodle.'

The door stood open, the wide backside of Marie masking her efforts to get the fire going in the tiny grate. She fed the flames with dry sticks and small pieces of coal, her concentration almost palpable. Swivelling on her haunches to face the two blocking the daylight she grinned, breaking into a flurry of rough phrases that slid past Zoe without touching a single point of comprehension. The fire was already taking hold, wood ash glowing in the heart of the blaze, reflections flickering in the boudoir mirror standing next to Zoe's bed. Roddy helped Marie to her feet and pushed a crisp euro note into her grubby hand, his fractured phrases clearly hitting the button with Madame's maid-of-all-work. She pointed to a bucket of coal before scuttling out, and Zoe gazed round, dismayed at the difference the fire made to the wretched room. She followed Marie on to the landing and went into the other attic room to acquire another chair, a basket seat that let out a fusillade of splitting canework as Roddy dropped into it.

'It's not warmer,' he complained, 'but pretends to be homey. Now, stop fussing round, girl, and tell me: what's the problem with coming home?'

She perched on the upright chair Roddy had shoved up close to the hearth and stared into the flames. After a moment she got up, crossed the room and pulled an envelope from a drawer in the table set under the window, closing the curtains on the darkening afternoon before returning to her seat. She turned the envelope over and over in her hands, staring at the bold handwriting as if it signified some sort of judicial sentence, then started to speak, very quietly, Roddy craning to catch her words.

'Before the shooting I spent the weekend away visiting my father and, if I'm honest, taking some time out to think over my relationship with Haydon, which was difficult at that time. While I was in the area I indulged my curiosity by visiting a place where an acquaintance had been brutally killed. Call it intuition if you like, but it was my bad luck to stumble into something that has haunted me ever since. From sheer nosiness I made other enquiries before I drove back, which tied up with suspicions I

317

had every reason to harbour. Then Haydon was killed, the police moved in and I found myself in possession of damning information about a man the press had hailed as a modern hero.'

She paused, gathering her thoughts. 'Apart from the police, no one else knows this, Roddy, so everything I tell you this afternoon is in the strictest confidence. You see, it was me who informed against Haydon. I gave Inspector Kennedy – the policeman who investigated Max's suicide and the only officer I trusted – proof that Haydon had operated on Mullins, restructured his features in such a way that no "Wanted" poster would be of the slightest use. Kennedy then admitted that police suspicions about Haydon's surgery on missing criminals was already on file, but no evidence was available. I was the one to hand over that proof. I was the person, Roddy, who nailed Haydon down and ruined his reputation.'

Roddy frowned. 'Haydon ruined his own reputation, Zoe. Making yourself a recluse is to punish yourself for nothing.'

'I didn't intend to leave England permanently after the disclosures to Kennedy. No way. You've missed the point, Roddy. I left because I had to deliver a tapestry long overdue to an important dealer who has been patience itself. I'm not stuck here because I'm ashamed of blowing the whistle

318

on Haydon. It was a terrible decision to make, but because Haydon was indirectly involved in Bert's death I knew it was the right thing to do, the only chance the police would have to catch Mullins, who was the snake in the garden, the instrument of evil that tempted Haydon and ultimately led to the killing of poor bloody Bert.'

'Snake in the garden? You're over my head with this, Zoe. If shopping Haydon isn't what's keeping you here in France, why can't you come home with me now?'

'I did it once. I shopped Haydon, as you so inelegantly put it, Roddy, but I can't do it again. Next time it would be worse; next time I couldn't hide as a police informer; next time I would have to go the whole hog and appear in court. Haydon's death was brought about by his choice to involve himself with Mullins. This other business involves Max – you remember my old friend Max? I pulled the plug on Haydon, but I can't do it again. Frankly, I don't blame Max for what he did. In the eyes of the law it was terribly, terribly wrong; but I haven't the strength to run back to Kennedy and ruin the reputation of a *second* man. Max's standing in the art world meant everything to him, more than life itself. But he was being viciously manipulated and could see no end to it except the death of his tormentor or himself. It may sound extreme to us, but the poor old man had nothing else, don't you see? He was a gentleman of the old school, the sort who traded on his word being his bond, and all that had been thrown away in an effort to escape from shameful gambling debts. If I go back to England, I might end up seeing things differently, betray someone whom I admired. I can't admire Haydon for what he did. He didn't need Mullins's money. Haydon misused his genius probably as a challenge, knowing he was the best in his field and knowing he could get away with it.'

She paced the room, the silence only broken by her footsteps on the bare boards. After a moment she continued.

'Max was different. Since he chose to share his secret with me I've been on the rack. He *wanted* the truth to come out, if only after his suicide, whereas Haydon believed he was invulnerable. The odd thing is, it's me, poor stupid Zoe, who links them, and I've been burdened with *their* guilt, been called out to set the record straight yet again. And I can't bring myself to do it. For weeks I've been wondering how four people died violently and the only connection was me. Why me? Why them?'

'Four people?'

'First a man called Chris Mayhew, a dealer I barely knew; then Max; afterwards Bert Styles and, lastly, Haydon. I feel as if vengeful gods have chosen me as their instrument of retribution and their malicious joke is that the deaths were *not* all connected: Max and Chris Mayhew were amateur partners in crime, as it were, but Haydon and Bert were both victims of a professional criminal element. Funny that. The murder of Bert Styles drove me to disclose Haydon's liaison with Mullins and his hoodlums, although Haydon, with all his faults, had no direct hand in the poor man's killing. And yet Max, who really was guilty and deserved all the fires of hell, according to the laws of justice, is the one I cannot bring myself to blame.' She sat down, covering her face with her hands.

Roddy wondered if the girl's self-imposed seclusion had damaged her fragile balance of mind, tipped her over the edge. He leaned across and touched her arm, but she pushed him away and passed him the envelope.

'Read this. I received it when I was on the point of coming home. Kennedy had promised never to reveal the source of the evidence against Haydon, so I was in the clear. No one in a million years would have guessed it was the stupid art restorer who had put Mullins's new face in the hands of the Interpol search unit and, believe it or not, my conscience is clear on the Haydon front. I was all ready to take up my life in

London again, and then this bombshell arrived in my lap, and now I know I can never go back without betraying my friend. Poor old Max suffered enough – if the police had worked it out for themselves, fair enough; but I can't bring myself to point the finger a second time.'

Roddy pulled the pages from the envelope and began to understand at last.

Thirty-Eight

My dear Zoe,

By the time this letter reaches you I shall be dead. I have made up my mind to kill myself for reasons I shall explain to you. I realize that I am placing a heavy burden on you, my dear girl, but there is no one else I can trust to carry out my wishes. My wife, Desiree, would flinch at the responsibility of ruining my professional reputation because, you see, the dear lady is overly concerned with my status in the art community regardless of the greater sin I committed without regret or compassion.

I am writing this letter tonight in order to catch the first post in the morning before you arrive, as arranged, to collect the tapestry. I shall be here to see you for the last time before I carry out my plan tomorrow night. This letter will await you in Paris on your arrival; my good friend de Vries will ensure its prompt delivery. I am addressing this letter care of his gallery, as I wish you to be out of range of any friends who might persuade you not to accept my final instruction. You must deliver this letter to the police in London together with the keys I will leave in the drawer for you here.

As the recipient of my confession and my appointed delegate, you, Zoe, must be in command of the full facts.

More than two years ago I faced financial ruin occasioned by an unfortunate juxtaposition of debts. A colleague, a man called Christopher Mayhew, invited me to share an investment in pre-Colombian artefacts that had come on the market. I declined, explaining my temporary cash-flow problem, but he scoffed at such minor difficulties, insisting that my part in the transaction would be on a commission basis – as a salesman, one might say. Mayhew knew I had, over the years, traded with his potential buyer and other foreign institutions and enjoyed an international reputation as an honest broker. I pointed out, rather tersely I'm afraid, that my expertise fell well short of Colombian art, but his offer was beguiling: no financial input, all expenses paid, and the prospect of further excursions of this kind, which would swiftly cancel my current embarrassment.

Dear Zoe, I was tempted. I undertook several forays for this vile serpent Mayhew and only suspected the truth when an item I had sold in good faith to a prestigious private collector came under severe scrutiny. The matter was hushed up, the owner of the fake statuette accepting a private settlement backed up, no doubt, by a sincere desire to hide the inevitable conclusion that he had been duped by a rogue trader and was therefore a target for other con men, among whom I now regretfully counted myself.

I tried to break off my association with Mayhew, but he refused, claiming that correspondence that had passed between us would put me in the dock. I was forced to continue, this man having placed all the risk on my head, having ensured that his own part in the deception had remained hidden. He admitted that I had unwittingly off-loaded several fake items that had never been unmasked but gossip is rife in this line of work and, having settled privately in respect of that other matter, my name would inevitably be drawn into the spotlight if real experts entered the picture.

We used to meet at an appointed rendezvous away from the auction rooms, Mayhew insisting on keeping any closer liaison secret from the other dealers. I, too, was anxious to distance myself from this man, but as his demands became unedurable, I found myself seeking a final escape. I began to have pains in my chest.

It occurred to me that killing Mayhew would be the only way of preserving the secrecy of our criminal pact, and if I was suffering from a terminal illness of some sort, even official retribution would arrive too late if I had only months to live. A very neat idea, wasn't it? I wonder that more patients under a medical sentence of death do not take the opportunity to settle scores without fear of punishment – a race against time if one could estimate one's forecast lifespan with any degree of accuracy. But, forgive me: I digress.

I called on my doctor and spent ludicrous sums on private consultations, the only patient to long for a poor prognosis. But my chest pains augured no such escape. 'Stress,' I was assured; 'time to retire from the anxieties of the art trade.'

But the notion of killing Mayhew had taken root. If I could not escape a prison sentence by terminal disease, it occurred to me there was another way out. If the police got on my trail, I could always kill myself. I hated the man, you see, hated the way I had allowed myself to ruin a lifetime's work for short-term profit. My friends in the trade swore by my honesty, the people I had sold to over the years trusted my judgment and it was this, my repututation built up over decades, that enabled Mayhew to cheat my clients, using me as a tool in his filthy business.

The murder was no impromptu act, dear girl. Your old friend Max planned it most meticulously, booking into a small bed-and-breakfast establishment overnight and agreeing to a meeting with Mayhew early in the morning at a regular haunt of his near his home. He always settled with me in cash passing over my pay-off as if I was nothing but a common runner.

For a newcomer to homicide I was surprised how easy it was. I had used a bayonet in the course of my army service in Korea, I'm ashamed to say, and perhaps this nefarious experience stiffened my resolve when I plunged my knife into Mayhew's ribs. I wish I could say I felt remorse, Zoe, but I did not. The man was the sort who rots the core of the antiques trade. He had ruined me and probably destroyed the professional morals of others, for all I knew, other fools like myself who through greed had allowed themselves be drawn into his circle.

As Mayhew lay bleeding, I took his money and his keys and such valuable items as would indicate a mugging, and all this time I was fending off his dog, which ran in circles around us, barking frenziedly and likely at any moment to attract attention even at that early hour, when our remote meeting place was normally deserted. I ran back to my car pursued by the dog, slammed the door on it and reversed out of the lay-by. Up until then everything had gone according to plan, but Fate intervened. In my haste I accidentally ran over the poor animal. It screamed in pain and I stumbled out of the car to see it bleeding in the muddy lane just like its master. But this creature was innocent, a victim of my carelessness not of my intent. I felt a terrible guilt such as I had not felt for Mayhew. The dog was in agony, its pelvis clearly broken under my wheels. I decided the kindest thing was to put it out of its misery and I killed it with a hammer I keep in the car for emergencies.

Killing the dog upset me most awfully, a ludicrous guilt in a comparison with the murder I had just committed, and the eyes of that poor beast haunt me still. But I had work to do. I drove away and let myself into his house. I knew he lived alone but had never been there before, and I began to shake from the aftershock, you might say. However, I stole what papers incriminated me, together with some items I suspected were 'wrong' and might be linked with the transactions in which I had been involved.

Then I attended an auction in Chester and played out my role as a genuine dealer before driving home. I disposed of his watch and the suspect antiques in a flooded quarry I knew of on the outskirts of Bath when I attended a second auction this week.

But I have been having bad dreams, Zoe. Not on account of Mayhew and not on account of any police investigation. For a novice in assassination I had performed exceptionally well, leaving no clues, erasing any blot on my reputation, the incriminating correspondence Mayhew had held over me burnt in the studio grate. No, my bad dreams featured the unfortunate dog. His eyes follow me, as accusing as any tormentor. I had killed a man and I had escaped justice; I had not even suffered a loss of reputation, that badge of honour we stupid old men cling to long after everything else has been destroyed. Why was I holding on to life? What was left to live for? Having achieved my purpose, I had lost all hope of peace and all because of a dog accidentally run over, a mischance no one could blame me for.

And so, my dear child, I have decided to take leave of this life and pass to you the unenviable burden of returning to England to pass this document to the right authorities. To back up this account I have left Mayhew's keys at Bisley road for you. I discovered them in my car only yesterday, having planned to throw them away with the other things; but since my anxieties have formed into resolve, I decided the keys – as the only remaining proof of my guilt – must be preserved after all. Too bulky to enclose with this letter, Zoe, but the police will locate them for you when they investigate my suicide.

I do not assume that this belated confession will allay any justifiable hatred for a murderer, but I do so hope you will find it in your heart to forgive an old man his wickedness.

With all my blessings,
Max

Thirty-Nine

Roddy finished reading and folded the letter back into its envelope. They looked across at each other as if across an abyss, the fire leaping in the grate causing shadows to stain the walls of the unlit room.

'You see now?' she said. 'You see why I can't go back? Max trusted me to turn him in. But because I hadn't left for Paris when he thought I would, his plans went right off course. He had to go through with it; he'd already posted the letter. He killed himself that night.'

'He must have realized you hadn't collected the tapestry when he hanged himself.'

'Maybe. Maybe not. I could have nipped in through the garden door at any time without him hearing me if he was in another part of the house. The tapestry was stacked up in a corner out of casual view, but if he did see I hadn't taken it, then he knew I would deliver it eventually and so get his letter in the end. It was too late for him to change his mind about suicide and he must have though Saba would be the first one down in the morning, the one to find his body.'

'Why not just do as he asks? It's never too late.'

Zoe shuddered. 'I can't. I betrayed Haydon to the police. He deserved it. Max was blackmailed, a victim – I just can't do it, Roddy, even though I suspected the truth about Mayhew's death months ago. If Haydon hadn't been shot, I might have stumbled on to Max's crime all on my own without his confession.'

'How come?'

She told him about visiting Mayhew's house and talking to his sister. 'Penny told me about the killer's tyre tracks at the scene of the crime and also in the muddy lane outside Mayhew's cottage. I had already worked out from his auction catalogues that Max had attended a sale in the vicinity on the day Mayhew was apparently mugged, which led me to ring Jason on his mobile as soon as I left Penny to check up on Max's car. Desiree had disposed of Max's car through her security man, so I asked Jason about it, pretended I was interested in buying an old banger for my assistant. Jason warned me off, said Max had never maintained his wretched vehicle and doubted whether it would pass its MOT test. Even the tyres were bald, he said, only one of them brand new. This tied up with what Penny had confided in me, the only real lead the police had, she said.'

Roddy sighed, closing his eyes in an effort to keep the sequence of events in order.

'And then there were Mayhew's keys. Desiree had given them to me in an envelope addressed in Max's hand, thinking they were mine, of course. I hadn't a clue where they had come from, but there was so much else going on at the time, the keys got shoved to the back of my mind. They're still under the dashboard in my car; they've been there all this time. The bloody keys didn't feature in my suspicions at all; it was the dead dog. Too much of a coincidence, I thought when Penny told me about it being run over during her brother's attack. It was a Spinone, Roddy, just like yours. Funny, wasn't it, that it was the dog that made poor old Max give up in the end?'

'Would you have reported your suspicions?'

'I honestly don't know. As it happened, as soon as I got back to Stonecrest after that weekend away, we were thrown into packing up. Redford had given Haydon the boot. Then Haydon was shot and playing detective over Max's involvement with Mayhew slid right off the agenda. I chose to turn in evidence against Haydon; I haven't the stomach to do it against Max. Not a second time, Roddy. Why me, for God's sake? Why couldn't Max put the finger on someone else?'

'Desiree would have destroyed the letter – you know she would. Who else was there?'

'He could have left it for Saba, couldn't he?'

'Saba was scared stiff of the police and Max barely knew the woman. He could hardly trust a girl he'd picked off the streets to involve herself with a murder inquiry, could he? Saba was terrified of getting her picture in the paper, which could only lead to her family tracking her down, and Max must have known that. No, Saba wasn't his ideal confidante. He needed someone not directly involved, someone sensible, strong enough to see it through.'

'Well, he picked the wrong partner in his

game, didn't he? Now I'm stuck here, too traumatized to drag Max out of his nice quiet grave and put myself at Kennedy's mercy over this. First thing he'll ask is: why didn't I hand in Max's letter weeks ago?'

'You tell him they mislaid it at the gallery. De Vries will back you up.'

'But that was before Christmas! I've been sitting on this time bomb ever since I got here, Roddy. I can't go back unless I turn him in as he trusted me to, and I can't seem to face settling down in Paris to work. Between them, Haydon and Max have fucked up my entire life – can't you see that?'

'No I can't. There is a simple solution.'

Roddy leaned forward and before she could blink had thrust the letter into the flames. He held her fast as she struggled to retrieve the smouldering pages, sobbing like a child, watching the paper finally disintegrate.

He cradled her in his arms until the storm of weeping blew itself out, then purposefully moved around the room, flinging her clothes into a suitcase, even emptying the ashtrays. They were still wearing their coats, the temperature in the room refusing to budge much above zero.

'You're coming to my hotel,' he said, pulling her to her feet. 'And after that we're driving back to England in your car and I'm not letting you out of my sight again. Forget Max. He got away with it; let the poor sod rest in peace.'

'Do I have no say in this?'

'You've had your own way long enough. Put a brave face on it, sweetheart: smile now, die later.'